# The Yellow Barn

REUBEN ANDERSON & SONS

A TRILOGY
Written by Gary Solomonson
Edited by Julie Solomonson

BOOK ONE
REUBEN'S JOURNEY BEGINS

**Outskirts Press, Inc.
Denver, Colorado**

This is a work of fiction. The events and characters described herein are imaginary and are not intended to refer to specific places or living persons. The opinions expressed in this manuscript are solely the opinions of the author and do not represent the opinions or thoughts of the publisher. The author has represented and warranted full ownership and/or legal right to publish all the materials in this book.

The Yellow Barn
Reuben's Journey Begins
All Rights Reserved.
Copyright © 2013 Gary Solomonson
V5.0

Cover Photo © 2013 Frances E. Clanton. All rights reserved - used with permission.

This book may not be reproduced, transmitted, or stored in whole or in part by any means, including graphic, electronic, or mechanical without the express written consent of the publisher except in the case of brief quotations embodied in critical articles and reviews.

Outskirts Press, Inc.
http://www.outskirtspress.com

PB ISBN: 978-1-4327-9468-2
HB ISBN: 978-1-4327-9480-4

Library of Congress Control Number: 2012914632

Outskirts Press and the "OP" logo are trademarks belonging to Outskirts Press, Inc.

PRINTED IN THE UNITED STATES OF AMERICA

*Cover Art by Frances E. Clanton*

*Chapter Illustrations by Burt J. Elmer*

Trent & Shauna,
It is always great to have you went us. We enjoy your positive spirits and friendship. I hope you enjoy the book. When you find an opportunity to volunteer with seniors in their eighties and nineties, your time with them will be a forever gift.
Blessings to both of you,
Gary

# Table of Contents

Dedication ...................................................... vii
   To John Goodman

Foreword .......................................................... x
   Remember the Bendy Straw
   ~ Robin Katchuk

Chapter One ..................................................... 1
   Labor Day Weekend: Friday & Saturday

Chapter Two ................................................... 43
   Labor Day Weekend: Sunday

Chapter Three ................................................ 65
   Labor Day Weekend: Monday

Chapter Four .................................................. 89
   The Prairie Receives a Daughter

Chapter Five ................................................. 156
   The Thanksgiving Club

Chapter Six .................................................. 193
   The Cribbage Game

Chapter Seven .............................................. 226
   A Christmas Day Promise

Chapter Eight ............................................... 251
   Veterans' Courage

# Table of Contents

Epilogue ................................................................ 303
   Of Barns, Shamans and Storytellers

Tribute To ............................................................. 306
   Our Mothers and Fathers Who Led the Way

Acknowledgements ............................................. 308

Notes ................................................................... 312

# Dedication

## To John B. Goodman

This book is dedicated to John B. Goodman, to whom I am deeply indebted for giving me the opportunity to spread my wings and grow in the wonderful service industry of senior living and health care, working to provide exceptional living environments, services and life enrichment programs, primarily for individuals in their 80s and 90s.

Over a period of thirty-four years, John gave me the opportunity to participate in the design, construction, marketing, managing and programming of a new generation of senior living and health care communities that raised the bar in terms of living environments, services and programs. He was committed to the development of several innovative intergenerational programs for children and seniors. His passion for excellence, his desire to create new and better models, his generosity of spirit, and his devotion to customer service and the enrichment of the lives of children, seniors and staff were an inspiration to those of us had the privilege of working alongside him.

The mission John created for his company is "to create and manage living environments that emphasize quality of life and enable residents and staff to achieve an optimum level of well-being.™" It was an empowering culture where I practiced my craft and philosophy of 'marketers as creative healers.' As individuals in their 80s and 90s become residents in senior living communities, there are often psychological, spiritual and physical challenges in their lives that need attention and/or support from others. The stress and sadness of leaving a home of many years and moving into a new environment; the frustration of not being able to return to home because of an episodic health event or memory loss; the challenge of needing assistance in daily living activities; the grief from the passing of a spouse; or having lived alone for years and desiring to live in a social environment close to old and new friends -- these are just a few of the circumstances in which a senior living community can offer support and services. Simply put, the role of the marketer as a creative healer is to discover the needs, wants, wishes and interests of the prospective resident through careful listening, and then offer a path to healing and an opportunity to live life to the fullest, wherein they can experience an optimum level of well-being.

John Goodman gave me a wonderful canvas on which to 'paint' my dreams into reality, practice my craft of 'marketers as healers,' and work to make a positive difference in the lives of others, especially those wonderful individuals in their 80s and 90s. For that, I will be forever grateful.

*Gary M. Solomonson*

# Foreword

## By Robin Katchuk

There is a saying that goes something like, "everyone has one great novel inside of them waiting to be written," and so when Gary Solomonson told me that he was writing a book, I thought, "Okay, Gary is finally writing his great novel!" The privilege became mine, to read and review proofs of this wonderful series of books. This first book took me back to a wonderful time in my life.

When I was in 5$^{th}$ grade, we divided up the fifty states and were given a task of creating a report on one state to share with the class. Minnesota was my assignment. I still remember the front with blue construction paper for lakes, and uncooked rice glued to the cover to represent wild rice and a silhouette of a Native American in a wooden boat floating among the rice hulls. After all, Minnesota is the Land of 10,000 Lakes. I think the report still exists in a drawer somewhere. To read Gary's trilogy is to discover another Minnesota and the great southwestern prairie it shelters, which was partly settled and farmed by Nordic peoples. They were and are hard-working, honest, and generous, and you will find yourself longing to belong to their community of culture and caring.

It is speculated that the great farmlands of Minnesota greeted and were settled many more years ago by ancestors of these Norsemen. The Kensington Runestone was discovered in the late 1800s by an industrious farmer, Olof Ohman, while clearing a field for planting. A large rock with engraved writing, it was not translated until nine years later, and carries a fascinating story of "8 Goths and 22 Norwegians on an exploration journey from Vinland over to the west" one hundred and thirty years before Columbus started out on his adventure. So it seems that Minnesota has long been the land of the Vikings.

Gary Solomonson and I have been friends and colleagues for many years, and as I delved into this wonderful tale of a significant life, I realized that the central figure, a generous and gentle man, is much like the author, with a passion for varied interests and a true love for people and their stories. And here it is – the stories are Gary's gift to us. We have the guide. Now it is up to us to stop making excuses to volunteer and find the one way we can; to make that difference. How many times have you longed for a life of value, to know your purpose in life and to live it often? Follow the pages and the answers will be there.

You will come to know and feel great warmth and caring for the central couple, Reuben and Ruth Anderson, and the life that they have built together. I did not want to read Ruth's "final" chapter and experience the loss of this lovely woman. Continuing on, I was uplifted again by her legacy and memories, and isn't that the greatest thing that we can achieve. We didn't lose Ruth after all. We gained so much more, including courage and hope, as Ruth goes with us on this journey during all three books.

The Yellow Barn is for anyone who has volunteered to read the daily news to someone who can no longer see. These books are for the docent, whose free time is spent sharing the art and history of museum collections, so that we can all enjoy the creativity and beauty on display. The Yellow Barn series is for those who have driven a neighbor to the doctor, and waited to drive them home. The books celebrate you when you picked up your elderly neighbor's daily newspaper and placed in on the front step. The books are for the volunteer that was a foster mother through the animal shelter to the abandoned kittens, that helped a student learn to read, that spent time working to raise money so a foundation could continue to fund its programs, that assisted someone to write a check to pay their bill, that cut coupons to send to military families, or that proffered to sort book returns at the local library. Your life is valuable when you phone someone who lives alone to make their day with conversation, when you pick up groceries for someone who can't drive, when you offer to spend time with a patient in a nursing home or pediatric hospital. Big gestures or small endeavors, your actions have infinite value to the lives you touch, and become pearls without price.

So settle in and enjoy. Let the stories inspire your own ventures. One word of warning, however: you will eventually be desperately craving a root beer float, so put your favorite vanilla ice cream in the freezer and root beer in the fridge. Oh, and don't forget the bendy straw.

*Robin Katchuk, Executive Director*
*Royal Palms*
*At The Palms of Largo*
*Largo, Fl*

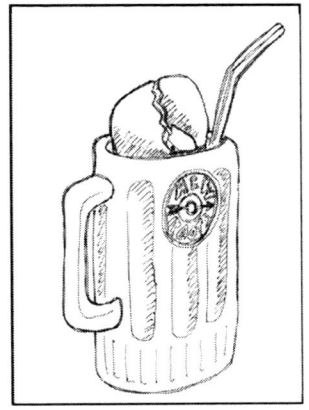

# Chapter One

## Labor Day Weekend 1990

## Friday Evening, August 31$^{st}$

It was late when he got in from doing chores. One of the milk cows had an infected scratch on a teat and needed his attention. Another had injured her shoulder while rubbing on an old wooden fence post in the east pasture and had a nasty cut from an exposed nail. He patiently cleaned both wounds first with warm soapy water, then a cleansing wash with a disinfectant, and finally applied a generous amount of McNess's Krestol Salve – known by its famous red, black, white and gold tin container – which you

# Reuben's Journey Begins

could find on almost every farm in southwestern Minnesota's prairie from the early 1900s on. While it had a slightly medicine-like petroleum odor, it was used to treat everything from cuts to scrapes of all kinds known to beast and man; at least, that was his father's practice which he continued religiously. For Reuben Anderson, the healing salve was a godsend for the animals and, occasionally, his own scratches and cuts.

His youngest son, Willard, and Willard's wife Louise, son Christopher and daughter Catherine, who all lived on the homestead in a second house, had gone away for the Labor Day weekend to visit Reuben's oldest son, David, who lived in Stillwater, Minnesota, and so all the daily farm chores and tasks fell to him alone. From feeding the horses, chickens, ducks and calves; picking, washing and crating eggs; cutting, raking and baling the final crop of alfalfa hay for the season; and, finally, feeding and milking the cows, this Labor Day would be a full weekend's work.

As Friday, the last day of August, drew to a close, his shoulders ached from lifting and setting the last hay bales in the barn that needed to be restacked before putting up the last cutting. And after milking, there were always the clean-up chores. First, there was cleaning the manure out of the barn alleys, pens and gutters and piling it in the barnyard; next, sweeping out the feeding mangers, quickly cleaning the watering cups and then putting down fresh straw in the alleys, pens

## Reuben's Journey Begins

and gutters for the next milking. In the milk house attached to the barn and milking parlor, he always broke a sweat washing out the milking equipment. Hot water, strong disinfectant soap and vigorous brushing made for a strenuous workout if you did it right. It seemed to take forever on this evening and, finally done cleaning the barn and the milk house and putting the milking equipment in order for morning, he buttoned up the barn, an extraordinary two-story structure, saying goodnight to Barney, a two-year-old barn owl perched on a beam above the barnyard door, to the cats cuddling into an old woven reed basket full of old work shirts, and to his two patients who had to stay in for the night, limiting further chances of irritating their injuries. He was so tired that he hadn't noticed the absence of his dog. But then, that wasn't unusual this time of day.

Next, he walked over to secure the door of the chicken house about thirty yards away and shut off the outside light that hung over the entry door. Finally, he walked over to the horse barn to check on Dolly, Duke, Duchess, Dancer and the two-year-old, Boots. They were the Belgians, the offspring of many generations of hearty and sturdy draft horses which had come from Europe with his grandfather, Rudolf, and other European immigrants.

Reuben's father, Caleb, had built an enormous horse barn north of the milking barn that housed some two dozen horses in its heyday. Reuben

# Reuben's Journey Begins

had converted four stalls into an office and 'personal den,' another three stalls into a gardening shop, and four stalls into a grand playhouse for the grandchildren. Around three sides of the horse barn was a beautiful corral and pasture where the horses could graze at will, and run and play to their heart's content. His mother, Amanda, who had passed away fifteen years earlier, always felt that whatever the horses wanted and/or really didn't need, they got from his father, Caleb! Reuben, too, treated them like royalty and his wife, Ruth, carried on the tradition of reminding him that they were spoiled rotten. In days past, the Belgians' ancestors had worked the Anderson's prairie farm fields, pulling plows, planters and cultivators; and for transportation, pulling coaches, carriages, wagons and the school buses before the first motorized buses came to be in the late 1920s.

These days, the offspring of these earlier Belgians had privileged responsibilities, year-round, of pulling carriages in summer and fall parades, wagons for hayrides in the fall and winter, sleigh rides on winter weekends, and carriages for special events like weddings, anniversaries and funerals. Every school and church group for miles around had been on some type of ride through the Anderson's woods and along the Red Rock Creek that meandered through their farm, as well as the Taggert's, Peterson's and Johnson's farms. While each of Reuben's wagons, hayracks, carriages

## Reuben's Journey Begins

and sleighs was awesome in its own right, an amazing collection, his pride and joy were his old funeral hearse and the wedding carriages. They were the pristine jewels of his collection.

The Belgians often seemed 'larger than life' to most people, and were always smartly groomed and beautifully rigged for their public appearances. And Reuben was always proud and honored when driving the team, feeling a deep sense of pride in preserving this important part of the southwestern Minnesota prairie's history. Bidding the horses goodnight, he closed the oversized double Dutch doors in the front of the horse barn and locked the latch.

As he started toward the house, now wondering where his dog had disappeared to, he realized that one last job loomed eighteen feet above him. He had forgotten to change the burnt out bulb in the yard light midway between the large stone-based and yellow-painted lap siding dairy barn and the yellow brick house. He walked over to the machine shed and garage, where he had a rustic shop and supply room, to get a new bulb. He carefully placed it in a canvas shoulder bag and set off for the yard light pole. Reuben wasn't one to put off until tomorrow what could be done today, or tonight. He didn't feel much like climbing the eighteen-foot pole this night, but thought it would be cooler than doing it during the day tomorrow. The end of August often brought hot, muggy weather to the prairie and some jobs were better

## Reuben's Journey Begins

done late in the day or early evening. The evening sky had grown darker because of a cloud cover, yet the light from the front porch of the house threw just enough light across the yard so he could see what he was doing. He used to climb the light pole in seconds; tonight it seemed like a mountain as he paused partway up, thinking maybe he was getting a little too old for this type of work at the ripe age of seventy-two. But a quiet smile and remembering that his dad was still climbing this pole in his eighties – a memory that brought a chuckle – helped lift his energy and legs. As he reached the light fixture and carefully switched bulbs, he felt a sense of accomplishment and turned his mind to the treat that awaited him in the kitchen. Climbing back down, he was sure glad he had installed the iron stepping stakes on each side of the pole in his younger days. It was a whole lot easier climbing that pole on those, compared to the old strap-on tree-leg spikes. Finished with that last task, it was time to call it a day and he set out for the house some fifty yards away. As he walked to the house, he once again wondered where his dog had gone; calling for him had produced nothing.

Pausing for a moment on the bottom step of the five stairs that led up to the great porch which surrounded the entire yellow brick yellow brick prairie farmhouse, he scraped the manure and dirt carefully off his shoes while holding onto the dinner bell post next to the porch. He smiled as he noted

## Reuben's Journey Begins

the shape of the shoe scraper, a buffalo, which his friend Ted Parker had sent him from Montana. With his shoes scraped clean, he walked up the steps, across the great porch and into the house. Inside, he dropped down into the wooden captain's chair in the mudroom, a modest-sized bathroom and changing room just off the entry hall, to remove his shoes. He was so tired and his shoulder muscles ached from all the lifting the day had bestowed on him. Slowly taking off his bib overalls, blue chambray shirt, t-shirt, boxers and white athletic stockings, he stood before the sink and looked in the mirror. He saw 'tired and achy.' Yet he smiled and felt satisfied about having once again completed a good day's work. He reached into the small corner shower in the mudroom and turned it on. While the water warmed up, he quickly cleaned his round-shaped wire rim glasses and set them on the side of the sink.

The short shower felt great. The warm water massaged his achy muscles and washed away the sweat of the day. Quickly toweling off, he put on his traditional pajamas and robe, abandoning his father's tradition of a sitz bath and sleeping in his underwear, which Reuben always thought was sort of tacky. Ready to settle in for the evening, Reuben made his way through the spacious country kitchen to the refrigerator.

Inside the refrigerator was his treat for the night: vanilla ice cream and root beer. Removing the soda and ice cream from the fridge, he set them on

## Reuben's Journey Begins

the kitchen counter next to a wonderful antique, thick-glass root beer mug that someone had taken home as a souvenir from the Prairieville Drive-in. He started making the float with three scoops of ice cream and then continued with the ritual of pouring just a little root beer in the mug at a time as it fizzed and foamed up. Occasionally, he would poke his long-handled spoon into the ice cream, breaking it up a little, mixing it with the root beer, creating sort of a slushy float which he liked best. The final touch was adding just a little more ice cream to firm up the slushy mixture and inserting the 'bendy' straw. The making of root beer floats had become both a science and an art for Reuben; one of many skills and traditions he had inherited from his father, Caleb. The trick was to eventually succeed in creating a balance of solids and liquids in the mug without having it spill out over the edge and drip onto the counter or table. As he made his regular evening root beer float, or an occasional other-flavored soda float, he silently reminisced about his dad, who had done likewise ever since he could remember.

    Their talks after chores while drinking floats in the kitchen had been special times. Even though his father had passed away some ten years earlier, there was sort of a spiritual connection with him each evening as Reuben made and enjoyed his float. He smiled quietly as he remembered how his mother, Amanda, would always confine them to the kitchen. Reuben's mother had forbidden the

## Reuben's Journey Begins

men – and occasionally his sisters who weren't that big on floats – from ever taking them into the living room as it was always a sticky mess to clean up when tipped over by one of the cats or the dog. However, when she was at work as a nurse at River's Edge, the Prairieville nursing home, they would sneak into the living room to listen to the radio and, in later years, to watch television. There was something special about being 'bad' with Dad! The floats even seemed to taste better in the living room on those occasions.

Generally, one of his five sisters told on them and then his dad would get the standard lecture, "Caleb, how do you expect the boy to ever learn right from wrong if you're always breaking the rules when I'm at work?" Amanda would scold in a soft manner.

And his dad would always say, "Depends on the rule and the person making it! Sometimes I should be able to make one or two, don't you think?" smiling at Amanda with affection.

The conversation would end with her saying, "Oh, you're just impossible sometimes;" all this said in the context of smiles and caring glances thrown at each other above the conversation.

Fondly remembering his parents this Friday evening, Reuben sat quietly at the kitchen table drinking his float and working on a puzzle of the Split Rock Lighthouse that he and his wife Ruth had visited while on vacation along Lake Superior's North Shore. Satisfied and finishing his

## Reuben's Journey Begins

evening treat, he poured the last little bit into the cat dish by the sink and rinsed out the tall glass mug. Before he had dried the mug, Mitsy, the black and white royal female cat of the farm, had lapped the treat up quickly before Cougar, the giant yellow and white tabby prince of the farm felines, even knew what had happened.

Reuben laughed, "Cougar, the ladies are always faster than we men!"

Exhausted, yet feeling the rewards of a productive day, he walked into the living room and sat down in his recliner and turned on the television, thinking he could catch the last couple innings of the Minnesota Twins baseball game, but it was over. It was 9:45! They were still in the seventh inning when he left the barn. Where had the time gone? Then he remembered that it had taken him twice as long for follow-up chores with Willard gone, such as closing up the barns and changing the bulb in the yard light.

As he flipped through the channels, he landed on The Jerry Lewis Labor Day Telethon. It was Labor Day Weekend! A rush of excitement came over Reuben. He loved Jerry Lewis's annual program and was a devout follower of his cause. But just as Jerry was talking to a young boy and announcing the next entertainment act, he fell fast asleep.

And somewhere in the late evening, a helping hand guided him to his bedroom. Unknowingly, he was tucked in by the hands of a caring angel. He

## Reuben's Journey Begins

drifted off into a deep sleep as the telethon continued throughout the evening. He had forgotten all about his sister, Marie Synnova Thomas, who had come to stay with him for the weekend while his son and daughter-in-law were away. Since her husband, Glenn Orville Thomas, who volunteered for the Salvation Army, was busy with a project for the weekend, Synnova thought it best to spend some time with her brother. That night in his dreams, Reuben and his dad went fishing at Lake Augusta, just south of Prairieville.

**Saturday, September 1st**

Reuben always seemed to wake up just a few minutes before the wind-up alarm clock rang out. It was an old, black, square-shaped Westclock alarm clock with green phosphorescent numbers that glowed in the dark. It had been a gift from his grandparents, Rudolf and Marie Anderson, when he graduated from high school in 1934. The ring of the wind-up clock always reminded him of the 'bell tone' of the alarm clock on the teacher's desk at his one-room country schoolhouse. Reuben transferred from the country school in 1931 when he started going to the town school in the 9th grade. The bell was different at the town school.

The town school bell that rang between classes was more like a loud rapid-clanging ring, almost like the bell on his old Schwinn bicycle which he used to feverishly ring with fast repetitive thumb

# Reuben's Journey Begins

pushes when peddling his way to school during good weather. Many times, he would see the classroom clock nearing the time town school would be let out for the day, close his eyes and guess when it would ring, counting down 'ten, nine, eight .... one.' He got very close or 'right on' most of the time. When the final bell of the day rang, he would bound out of his desk, down the stairs and through the hallway to band practice or, on other nights, to the boy's locker room to dress for the seasonal sport.

During his high school years, he had loved sports, and it didn't matter what season. The hour after school was a passionate time for him but also presented some minor obstacles. Living three and a quarter miles out of town in those days, it was a challenge sometimes getting home after practice. There were many times he had to ride his bike, walk, hitchhike, run or arrange a ride with friends. His mother, Amanda, generally worked until 5:00 at the Prairieville Nursing Home, now part of The Cottonwoods, and known as River's Edge, however, his dad liked him home to help with chores as soon as possible. By 4:30 or 5:00, his dad was already starting evening chores and his sisters were preparing supper for the family, so he was left to fend for himself many times. However, his love for band, chorus and sports overrode all challenges. In the spring, it was track and baseball. In the fall, it was football. And winter brought basketball. His favorite sport, though, was

## Reuben's Journey Begins

baseball.

Not only did he love playing the game, he loved reading about his baseball heroes of the '30s like Babe Herman, Al Schacht, Lefty Grove, Bing Miller, Luke Sewell and others. Reuben was also enamored with the idea of the Negro Leagues that flourished in the '20s, '30s and '40s. The players he read about like Willie Wells and Ted Radcliffe and others who performed great baseball feats but weren't allowed to play with the white players, both intrigued and bothered him. He had only met one African American during his high school career, and that was a speaker who had come to his church, Bethany Lutheran, at the beginning of his junior year to talk about having become a missionary after his baseball career ended abruptly from an injury. Reuben was captivated by the man's baseball history, his speaking voice, his singing and preaching. He wondered if the young minister they had now in the 1990s would still introduce him as a Negro, as the older minister did in 1933! Very few African Americans lived in southwestern Minnesota during most of Reuben's life so his interaction with them had been very limited. Other than occasional stories on television or in *Life*, *Look* and some of his sports magazines, his exposure to their world was almost nonexistent.

As he lay in bed still waiting for the sound of the alarm on this Saturday morning, he mused again about that final bell of the day those many years ago in town school. Was it more than a notice to

## Reuben's Journey Begins

the students and teachers that school was out for the day? 'Why this type of bell?' he wondered. 'Why not a horn, or maybe a dinner bell like they had on the farm?' He smiled and chuckled, as he loved to play with ideas in his mind as he reminisced. 'Why didn't they just rely on the classroom clock and when it landed on 3:30, everyone could just leave?' And as quickly as he posed that question, he remembered why: students were always moving the classroom clock ahead to get out early, or behind to have more time for a test. The main bell was controlled in the office where Mrs. Thompson dutifully rang it at the exact moment the official school clock moved its hands to the appointed time. Maybe the real purpose of that last bell, which could be heard a country mile away, was that it served as a warning to the town grocers and general store merchants – Witt's General Store, Miller's Grocery and Bakke's Fairway Foods – that they were about to be invaded by the students. Or was it a notice for the bus drivers to step out their cigarettes and get into their buses, ready to await the waves of energized and extremely loud-talking, giggling, occasionally fighting and screaming kids? Perhaps it was all of the above.

He thought about the many times he had taken the school bus, even though he only lived three miles north and a quarter mile east. Those buses were nothing like the modern day buses. Reuben started his school career in 1922, riding in horse-

## Reuben's Journey Begins

drawn wagons as buses, and it wasn't until his 8th grade year that the motorized buses, which were simply trucks with wooden boxes and benches, became standard transportation for the schools on the prairies. But he didn't ride buses for long in high school.

   A bit of serendipity came into his life at the beginning of his sophomore year when he got to drive his first car. It wasn't much by today's standards, but the two year old 1930 Chevrolet Sports Coupe was a beauty. Well, not exactly a beauty at first. Hans Jensen, a local county assessor and farmer who bought it new, had wrecked it running into an old sow on the Taggert farm two days after he bought it. A team of horses had to drag it on skids over to the Jensen farm a mile away, and there it sat in the grove for two years with a smashed-up front end and a crushed-in top, as he had rolled into a telephone pole after hitting the pig. Hans gave the car to Reuben to fix up for helping him the summer and fall just before his sophomore year. He had helped Hans with baling hay and putting it up in the barn, picking corn, auguring oats into the oats bin and putting up silage in the twin brown and white concrete block silos. The car became his 'industrial arts' or 'shop' class project at school during 1932 and became the center of much disruptive attention. He remembered with great fondness the nights that his father, Caleb, and his shop teacher, Mr. Knutsen, worked on repairing the damaged roof,

## Reuben's Journey Begins

front bumper and grill.

    Suddenly, the alarm rang and formally ushered in Saturday, September 1, 1990. He reached over to shut off the 4:30 a.m. call-to-the-day. Stretching and rubbing his eyes, 72-year-old Reuben Anderson sat up on the edge of his bed to ready himself for another day on his farm. He still lived on the home place just north of Prairieville in southwestern Minnesota's rolling prairie. Even though Minnesotan's often boast about their 10,000 lakes, southwestern Minnesota is cradled on the south by Iowa and the west by South Dakota and features a wonderful rolling prairie with grove-sized woodlands, streams, marshlands, lakes and some of the richest farmland in America. A gentle breeze drifted through the partially-opened bedroom window, softly moving the curtains and sheers. It sort of reminded him of the Russian ballet dancer he had once seen in high school during a lyceum program. Although she wore a flesh-colored body stocking, he remembered thinking, perhaps imagining, that she was completely naked under the 'sheer-like' dress she wore and how she moved like a soft, late summer's wind. Along with the breeze that morning came the aroma of yesterday's fresh cut hay from the alfalfa field near the west side of the house, reminding him that he had fieldwork to do after milking today. The sparrows, cardinals, house finches, chickadees, blue jays, wrens and mourning doves would soon begin their morning

## Reuben's Journey Begins

chorus of songs, and within the next couple of hours, morning light would create soft shadows in the room. The cry of a Killdeer began the chorus and Stanley, a Rhode Island Red rooster, would soon be out in the yard crowing, assuring the farm that dawn was once again at hand.

He rubbed his right hand over the bumpy texture of the chenille bedspread and started to reach over to give his wife, Ruth, a 'pat,' a habit of 52 years, before heading out to the barn, but just as quickly realized that his wife was gone and still in the hospital. Ruth's muscular dystrophy had taken a turn for the worse again last week, with the heart problems and the breathing difficulty, and it was uncertain if she would ever return home. She had been at the Prairieville nursing home, River's Edge, part of The Cottonwoods senior living campus, off and on for the past three years.

He once again felt the pang of loneliness, a hurt in his throat as he swallowed, and wished she could be home just one more time for a little while. His eyes welled up with tears for a moment and the hurt in the back of his throat intensified. Waking up was so different with her gone. Starting the day without her touch and a gentle kiss left an empty feeling in his heart. This business of growing old was becoming a real pest for him. He mused on a saying posted on his bulletin board in his horse barn office/den, "Growing old isn't for the faint hearted." And even as he wished for her return home just one more time, he knew in his

## Reuben's Journey Begins

heart that she was nearing the end of her life. Trying to put that thought out of his mind, he took a deep, soulful breath and wished for school days again.

'Growing old. There isn't much golden about it,' he thought whimsically. He wondered silently about all the ads on television and in the magazines touting The Golden Years. He asked himself silently with an indignant tone, 'Who in the world writes these ads? Golden years? Who are these people in the ads with perfect hair, perfect teeth, smiling as if they had no problems in life? And the wine glasses, white linen restaurants and golf courses, oceans and mountains behind them? Golf? Sailing?' Although Reuben still golfed a little, his experience didn't seem to match the ads. He thought about his friends living at The Cottonwoods senior living community in Prairieville. None of the pictures in the ads matched their lives very closely, either! If these people are young writers, they simply don't get it. If they are older writers, they seem to be in denial or creating a fantasy for a very elite few. Did they have even a little clue about the vagaries of growing old? Certainly, not someone in their seventies or eighties created them. For Reuben, aging, at best, was a growing pest and he held the belief that one has to manage it the best one can in spite of the cocoon that grows old, wrinkled and gray, thinning and blotchy skin, weakening muscles and aches in places never thought about

## Reuben's Journey Begins

in earlier years. And the butterfly inside – one's mind, spirit and soul – well, as positive as some writers would describe it, it has its good days and bad days, too. Even though he accepted it as part of life's journey, he didn't have to like it.

His momentary reflection on aging was suddenly interrupted by a loud yawn from a sleepy dog who had just sat up below the window across from the foot of his bed and, stretching, looked at Reuben as if to say, 'Do we have to go get those darn cows already?'

Reuben looked down at his constant companion around the farm for the past seven years. "Where were you last night, boy, when I was finishing chores and making our root beer float?" Reuben queried.

Socrates, a very large and regal German Shepherd, son of Gidget and Blitz, both who had been by Reuben's side for eleven and twelve years respectively, barked with an answer not quite registering with Reuben and then stared toward the kitchen. Socrates was slowing down a little, too, and aging was also becoming a growing pest for him.

Reuben smiled and said, as Socrates headed toward the kitchen, "Socrates, time to do it all over again, ol' friend."

Reuben's gentle spirit and unfailing work ethic that prompted him to rise every morning at this time embodied the very best of Midwestern farming behavior and values. His work ethic was

## Reuben's Journey Begins

impeccable. Life on the prairie farms that dotted the landscape in southwestern Minnesota was demanding and the daily schedules rarely changed. Only the seasons brought about a change of wardrobe and slightly different routines. Other than that, every day of each season was almost exactly the same on his medium-sized dairy and grain farm; filled with rewarding, soulful work. His wide, friendly smile came from the depths of his soul. Slightly balding and featuring a roundish Nordic face and muscular build, he sported a medium length, handsomely-trimmed white beard. This six-foot three-inch, 230-pound strong Norwegian farmer made the very best of each day. The rolling prairie had given birth to many Renaissance men, and he was certainly a prince among them.

Reuben was a very bright and well-educated man, mostly self-educated. Although his only diploma was from Prairieville High School, Class of 1934, at age 16 he was constantly reading a new book or rereading one from years past. He did complete two years of Ag School at the Farm Campus in St. Paul at the University of Minnesota, and then returned home to farm with his father, Caleb. His wide variety of interests gave him great joy and intrigued everyone around him. From religion to history, archaeology to science, genealogy to astrology, biology to agriculture, astronomy to oceanography, fishing and hunting ... he loved learning about people, their customs, the

## Reuben's Journey Begins

world and the universe. More recently, the launching in April of the Hubble Space Telescope was one of his favorite things to follow in the news. His favorite reading included all the new things in *Popular Mechanics* and *Science* magazines; the stories of King Arthur; and for many years, he had lost himself in the world of Westerns by Zane Grey and Louis L'Amour. At other times in earlier days, he had traveled the world by reading *National Geographic*, *Life*, *Look* and *Reader's Digest* magazines. Today, he subscribed to *Time*, *Newsweek*, the *Farm Journal* and *Progressive Farmer*. He had a way of always imagining himself in the middle of the article or story, whether print or pictorial. In more recent times during the past three years, with Ruth nearing the end of her life, he had returned to reading the Bible more often, and other books that explored topics such as faith, spiritual growth, caregiving, gerontology, volunteering and holistic healing which were ever-present in his mind as Ruth journeyed through her health challenges. His reading habits were picked up from his father, Caleb, who held that books were the door to knowledge, the future and peace – the keys to understanding the world – and that reading books was the best food to feed the brain and embolden one's spirit. And now, in 1990, his 15-year-old grandson, Christopher, and son, Willard, gave him his first computer along with several travelogue disks. With a couple keystrokes and mouse clicks, he could travel the

## Reuben's Journey Begins

world and find even more great information about all of his favorite interests! Although he had many VHS tapes on some of these things, the computer fascinated him. It also gave him a special connection with his grandson.

In the house, the walls of the living room, his study and bedroom were lined with bookshelves, as well as one-half of the kitchen, where magazines and papers dominated the reading habits at the table before and after meals, along with an ever-present jigsaw puzzle during the past year. He and Ruth used to keep a card table set up in the living room with a puzzle on it, but since she had been living at The Cottonwoods most of the past three years, he had moved the puzzle into the kitchen. There, he and the cats would move pieces around each day before and after meals. Ruth would simply scream if she knew Mitsy and Cougar were allowed to get up on the table sometimes. Out in the machine shed where he had his shop and workbench and his 'office/den' in the horse barn, and even in the dairy barn milk house, there were books and magazines piled everywhere.

On his nightstand, below a beautiful Tiffany lamp he and Ruth bought on their honeymoon in St. Paul, was his Bible with the Apocrypha, Webster's dictionary and thesaurus, and several books on ancient and modern shamanism. On a single shelf above the bed, adorned with several photographs of their grandchildren who were

## Reuben's Journey Begins

slowly getting squeezed to the edge, were some recent books about caregiving, aging, retirement and volunteering. Above and to one side of this shelf hung large, oval-framed photographs of his Norwegian grandfather and grandmother, Rudolf and Marie. On the other side was a beautifully framed photograph of Jesus of Nazareth praying in the Garden of Gethsemane. These had been his mother's photographs and prints. Surrounding these were his and Ruth's wedding pictures and those of their three children and grandchildren. On another wall were many photos of years past featuring the Belgians plowing, threshing and pulling a variety of sleighs and carriages. And one of his favorite photographs depicted him winning both the 4H and FFA blue ribbons at the State Fair his sophomore year for his prize Holstein bull calf; a two-year project. Behind him were his dad, grandfather and the judges who presented the ribbons to him.

Equally important were the pictures of their children who were now all married and raising their own families. David, his oldest son, had moved to Stillwater, Minnesota, not far from St. Paul and Minneapolis, where he was a United States Marshall. He began his law enforcement career as a deputy police officer in Prairieville after attending a police academy in Wisconsin. Since that time, he had advanced quickly through the ranks to his present position. He was the eldest of the three, married to Kathy and father to Tammy from a

## Reuben's Journey Begins

previous marriage. Next was Janice, a beautiful and talented lady, now a social worker who married Terry Ryan, the administrator of The Cottonwoods senior living community in Prairieville. Terry and Janice's two children, twin daughters Mary and Megan, were twin apples in grandpa's eyes. Still living on the farm and working with Reuben was his youngest son, Willard, who married Louise, and they were the proud parents of a son and a daughter, Christopher and Catherine. Surrounded by family and his most precious books, his bedroom was a sanctuary for Ruth and him.

Reuben got up and put on his morning robe. Walking through the living room, he turned on the television to catch the early farm news. Suddenly, he was startled when he heard noises in the kitchen, smelled coffee already being brewed and then, a voice.

"Welcome to the world, brother!" said Synnova.

Embarrassed that he had completely forgotten his sister was spending the weekend with him, he walked into the kitchen.

Laughing with surprise, he said, "So that's how I got from my chair to the bed! Good thing I had my pajamas on, or you would have had to help dress me for bed."

"I doubt it," Synnova laughed, "I would have just left you in the chair, had that been the case."

They hugged and Reuben sighed, "It's good to have you here, little sister. With Willard away and

## Reuben's Journey Begins

Ruth in the hospital, your company means a lot to us. Right, Socrates?"

A loud, approving bark followed and they both laughed. Synnova had just finished preparing a tray with his favorite breakfast of toast, strawberry jam, eggs, bacon and oatmeal.

"When did you get here and where's your car?" asked Reuben.

"I got here when you were milking, parked my car behind the machine shed in case you needed to get something out, came in and went to bed. I was exhausted from the day. I helped Glenn Orville distribute food and clothes over at Comfortville for the Salvation Army. That tornado they had this summer sure made a mess of things. When I drove up, Socrates greeted me and came upstairs with me, lay down on the braided rug I made David years ago, and stayed with me until I came downstairs to shut off the television and walk you to bed," said Synnova.

"So that's where he was last night," exclaimed Reuben.

"Now I've set up a TV tray by your chair so you can catch a few minutes of the telethon before you go out to milk. And don't forget to make your call on Sunday. Mr. Lewis is counting on you. You can catch the news on WCCO radio in the barn. I think I just heard Maynard Speese starting to do the farm report. Boone and Erickson will be on the radio at eight o'clock with the Good Neighbor Show while you're finishing up milking. You know

## Reuben's Journey Begins

they have been out at the State Fair doing their broadcasts this past week. They have the best time talking with fairgoers, and they do tell the funniest stories."

Reuben loved listening to the news, be it local, regional, national or international. However, today was a special day for him with the Labor Day Weekend Jerry Lewis MDA Telethon, and interrupting his ritual of starting with the early farm reports and news during breakfast was perfectly okay. Breakfast before milking was a custom for him. He never liked doing early chores on an empty stomach like his father, who generally ate breakfast after milking.

From the other room came the loud, shrill voice of Jerry Lewis doing one of his crazy antics. Now in the twelfth hour of the annual telethon, Reuben remembered that he had watched a couple of minutes last night before falling asleep in his chair. Over the years, he had become a great fan of Jerry's. And even at 72 years of age, he fancied himself to be one of Jerry's Kids. Then when Ruth was stricken with Limb Girdle Muscular Dystrophy fifteen years ago, his devotion to the MDA took on a new dimension. He planned to call in to the telethon again this year as he had done for the past twenty years, and then send his check, which was the 'extra money' that he always set aside from selling eggs and hay to other farms, like Donny Johnson who lived on the place next to him, as well as the money from his hayrides and other

## Reuben's Journey Begins

carriage rides.

Donny, in his late forties, had been injured in a racecar accident years earlier and leased his land to Reuben and Willard. Donny loved a good ol' farm breakfast with ham, eggs, toast and cottage fried potatoes every morning. So, Reuben sold him a dozen eggs each week, as he did for others from Prairieville who loved farm fresh eggs. Whenever he had some extra eggs for sale, or not quite enough to fill an egg crate to take into Grahams Produce, he would hang a black sign on the bottom of his mail box out by the highway with yellow letters, "Fresh Farm Eggs for Sale Today." Reuben also provided him with hay, as Donny raised a couple of horses and a half dozen feeder cattle to busy himself in spite of his limited ability to work. Donny had been a close friend of David's, Willard's and Janice's ever since kindergarten.

Reuben finished his breakfast, drank the last of the coffee, thanked Synnova, filled his favorite morning pipe with tobacco and walked to the barn. Over the years, Reuben had accumulated an extraordinary collection of tobacco pipes from all over the world. He kept the collection in his office/den in the horse barn as Ruth didn't like them in the house, although she loved the smell of pipe smoke when they sat together on the great porch. The grand dairy barn was about the length of a football field away, and the large open yard in between the house and barn was a great manicured lawn where many picnics had taken

## Reuben's Journey Begins

place and many baseball, softball, football and soccer games had been played over the years. At other times, it featured large tents for community and church celebrations. And in recent years, the grandkids were beginning to use it more often again. That meant a lot to Reuben, who was a consummate caretaker of his lawns and gardens and loved when they were viewed and used. With this new generation came large plastic swimming pools in the summer and an ice rink in the winter with hockey nets at each end. Broomball games were occasionally played when church and school groups came out for winter sleigh rides. In place of horseshoe were the more popular yard darts in the summer, yet Reuben kept the four clay horseshoe courts in top condition on the chance that someone would stop by to pitch a few shoes. His pals Hans Shandler, Fritz Hinkle, Hans Bill, Clair Peterson, Henry Peterson and others were Southwestern Minnesota Champions several years in a row. And while their main courts were in the Prairieville Community Park, the group liked coming out to Reuben's farm occasionally, to practice their trick throws or just kick back with some fun workouts without the 'townspeople' watching them. A tethered volleyball hung lifeless on the south side of the lawn and a badminton set next to it. As he walked to the barn, occasionally puffing on his pipe, he noticed the dew sprinkling his leather steel-toe work boots, and how the walking path was a bed of low ground-hugging pigweed that ran

## Reuben's Journey Begins

from the house to the barn through a lawn of beautifully groomed Kentucky bluegrass.

Walking into the barn through the west Dutch entry door and setting down his pipe in a large marble ashtray, he walked over to the east Dutch door and sent Socrates out to the nearby pasture where the cows were already beginning to make their way to the barn. Then he began carrying baskets of ground feed and dispensing it in front of each of the stanchions. As he worked, he noticed that Barney, the two-year-old barn owl, was snuggled in the corner of the rafters, watching him; Barney would soon move up to another space where he would spend most of the day sleeping.

Reuben knew it was a rare treat to have a barn owl in Minnesota, but there were a few throughout the southern part of the state. Soon the Holstein cows began to make their way into the barn. It was almost more than one person could handle efficiently, but Reuben had done it many times before, when the boys or his dad weren't around to help. It was somewhat of a gymnastic challenge to feed hay to those who had finished their ground feed and at the same time, check the drinking cups to make sure they were all getting their complete 'breakfast' as he began milking. In the background, the morning news and other WCCO radio programs filled the air, along with all the rich and satisfying aromas of the barn. Reuben had always thought it would be fun to be named 'WCCO's Good Neighbor' of the day, but couldn't

## Reuben's Journey Begins

imagine what it would be for. Barney now moved and huddled in the corner of an exposed rafter, seemingly musing on the theater of activity below him. In the evenings, Barney always watched the cats as they continually begged for 'just one more squirt' as Reuben stripped the last of the milk from each cow's teat before moving on to the next cow.

Chores over and the milk house once again put in order, Reuben walked to the house. Socrates sat next to the rocking chair on the great porch where his sister, Synnova, was busy crocheting an afghan.

"I think I've lost my buddy to you, Sis," said Reuben, taking a last puff on his pipe that he had re-lit on his walk back to the house from the barn.

"Oh, he came up to the house while you were milking to get a treat and decided to hang around for more, I think," replied Synnova with a smile in her voice. "He always seems to like hanging around me when I'm here. Or it may be that I'm a sure bet for a piece of leftover chicken or steak!"

"Well, I've got to rake hay this morning and then we can go to town and see Ruth. I called Doctor Carlson while I was milking and he said that Ruth is resting reasonably well and breathing better. Her heart is not looking good, though. He is going to transfer her to River's Edge mid-morning. Socrates, you take care of Synnova while I rake hay," said Reuben with a kind and concerned voice.

Socrates barked approvingly, thinking that

staying near Synnova might bring some more leftover chicken which seemed more appealing than chasing rabbits, pheasants and stripped gophers around the hot and dusty alfalfa field today.

As Reuben pulled into the alfalfa field close to the house, he stopped to greet Helen Stendahl, who had just driven up the driveway, and her daughter, Sarah.

"Hi, Helen," boomed Reuben in a voice to be heard above the restored John Deere B with its putt-putt engine sound.

"Hi, Reuben," yelled Helen back. "Do you mind if Sarah and I go down to the marsh where I want to paint her picking cattails?"

"Of course that's okay," yelled Reuben. "You two are always welcome, and someday I want to see all the paintings you are creating. You know my sister, Synnova – she's crocheting on the porch. Stop and say hi and maybe after you are done painting, she can find some coffee and lemonade. Have fun and be sure to close the gate to the pasture on your way to the marsh. I've got Herman, our young bull, in that field. He got out last week and it took us three hours to get him back."

"Thank you so much, Reuben, and we'll say hi to Synnova and be sure to close the gate," echoed Helen. She and Sarah stopped to greet Synnova and Socrates, who ran out to greet the car and get some big hugs from Sarah.

# Reuben's Journey Begins

Helen Stendahl had met her husband, Reverend Jonathan Stendahl, while she was an art student at the University of Minnesota and he was in the seminary at Luther Theological Seminary in St. Paul. She loved the prairie, and especially the marshlands, and capturing them on canvas with watercolors was her passion. Her daughter, Sarah, just eleven years old, had become a constant subject in her prairie paintings.

It was almost noon by the time Reuben finished mending one fence and the second raking of the hay so it would dry out properly and be ready for baling on Monday, provided it didn't rain. By rights, he should probably bale on Sunday but with Synnova here and Willard gone, he thought Monday would work just as well. Then on Tuesday, Willard could help put the bales in the barn. Reuben was hay dust from head to toe and as he undressed in the mudroom to take a quick shower, he heard the phone ring. It was Donny Johnson calling about eggs and wondering if Reuben could drop them off on his way into town. Reuben said he would, showered and got dressed to go to the hospital.

As he started out to the machine shed to get his 1932 Ford pickup roadster, Helen Stendahl and Sarah pulled up in their car. Getting out, Helen opened the hatchback to show Reuben two paintings, almost exactly alike. "Here, Reuben," said Helen, "this one is for you."

It was a beautiful watercolor of the marsh with

## Reuben's Journey Begins

the Campsite Grove in the background and Sarah picking cattails in the foreground. "Oh, Helen," exclaimed Reuben, "it's beautiful! How about a quick cup of coffee and a nice tall glass of lemonade for Sarah?"

"Oh, I would love that, Reuben, but we are already late to make lunch for Jonathan and he tends to get cranky when it isn't ready," said Helen, with a little angst in her voice. "Maybe next time." They hugged and Reuben graciously accepted the gift. Waving goodbye, Helen and Sarah went on their way.

Summoning Synnova and Socrates and picking up a dozen fresh farm eggs, they made their way to the machine shed garage where Reuben also kept his cars and trucks. Synnova smiled as Socrates jumped in the front seat of the brightly painted, antique 1932 red Ford roadster truck with its natural-stained wooden, oak-rail box that his good friend, Leroy Paulson, had helped him restore. Socrates snuggled up next to Reuben, and the three of them were off to Prairieville.

On their way, they briefly stopped at the Johnson farm where Synnova brought the eggs up to the house and delivered them, along with a big hug, to Donny. Back in the pickup, they continued their drive to town.

"You're awful quiet, brother," said Synnova.

"I'm sorry, Sis," Reuben said apologetically. "It's just that this drive gets to me some days. It's been three years of back and forth, never knowing

## Reuben's Journey Begins

what tomorrow will bring. Sometimes I'm resentful of having to be a caregiver for Ruth and every time I think that way, I feel guilty as heck," anguished Reuben. "Then I think, 'What if it were me lying in the hospital or the nursing home? What then? I would certainly hope and/or expect Ruth to visit me every day.' And when I think that way, I feel even worse. Some days my mind becomes such a swirl of thoughts, kind and unkind ... and while I know that isn't really me, it is really me! It is confusing and frustrating. So I've started reading books on related topics and everyone seems to see it differently, but there have been some good points, too. Maybe I'll glean something of substance soon that will make sense to me. This business of getting old is really a pest. I look at Ruth and many of our friends at The Cottonwoods. Whoever coined the phrase, 'The Golden Years' should have their head examined! I was thinking of that this morning and it seems these are the most painful times for us, both spiritually and physically. In a way, it just doesn't make sense to me sometimes. Shucks...when corn, oats, wheat or soybeans get golden, we harvest them. So does that mean the vagaries of growing old and death is our harvest in the Golden Years? Crops that are golden are pretty and regal; they're valued for what they've produced ... do we really view our seniors in that way? Seems to me that there should be some type of 'comfort reward' for us for having lived good lives, cared for our family, tended the earth, gone to church and contributed to the community. I would rather see that than waiting until the hereafter. I'm hoping to find some explanations in the books."

"Oh, brother, the things you come up with," laughed Synnova as she reached over Socrates and put her hand on Reuben's shoulder. She knew exactly what he was experiencing as she had just been through similar times two years earlier with their sister, Carol, for whom she had been a caregiver for several years. Socrates, too, put his head on Reuben's shoulder as if to add to the consoling touch offered by Synnova. She knew these visits were getting tougher for him as Ruth's health declined.

"You know, Sis, it's a strange disease, this Limb Girdle Muscular Dystrophy that Ruth has. Those first ten years after she was diagnosed, our lives didn't change much at all. Oh, she had some trouble getting out of chairs and getting up from the toilet, and sometimes it was hard for her to climb the stairs but she could still work and do everything she wanted to do. Her shoulders would get a little tired doing hand work, but that didn't stop her. And then, all of a sudden five years ago, her shoulders became really weak and she started to have trouble combing her hair or arranging things on a high shelf or carrying anything heavy … and it was around the same time that her hips worsened and she was pretty unsteady sometimes, and even fell once or twice before she started using her cane

## Reuben's Journey Begins

regularly."

"I know, Reuben," Synnova confirmed. "Since it doesn't have to be a fatal disease, we all hoped that she would live a long life ... perhaps the last part of it in doesn't have to be a fatal disease, we all hoped a wheelchair, but still among us."

"I believed that would be true," echoed Reuben. "There was some worry when her heart muscle showed signs of weakening three years ago and she had episodes where she had no energy. But it was just a year ago that she developed any breathing problems. It has been a tough three years, with her in and out of River's Edge, but we have cherished this time, too ... and when she could come home for a while, that was truly grand."

As they drove into the parking lot of The Cottonwoods, Synnova said, "Reuben, perhaps you should take off your husband hat today and put on your good neighbor volunteer hat. Think of yourself as volunteering some time for a friend who doesn't have time to come and see his wife. You've done this so often for others here at The Cottonwoods and you always talk about fun things going on around town and even sort through the gossip. During lunch, don't focus on the kids and what they're doing, or how much you miss her around the house ... that always seems to make her seem worse, like she's responsible for your sadness. Instead, talk about Ruth's friends and have some fun asking her about the gossip she heard around the hospital last week before coming

## Reuben's Journey Begins

back here. I would do this often when our sister, Carol, was ill and although it is a little bit of a mind game, it got me out of the 'sorrowful place' you sometimes get into with family members, trying to let them know you care for them. Sometimes it helps to focus on other people, places and things. It's a nice change of pace. Remember, too, such conversations help them stay mentally connected to the community that they were an important part of during their active years. In their minds, they still want that. When we focus too much on immediate family and health, we create a bit of a prison that locks us in too tight; sometimes into a limited world of self and immediate family. "

Reuben smiled and, silently nodding his head affirmatively, he acknowledged her thoughts as a good plan for today. As they walked across the parking lot, Reuben put his arm around his sister's shoulder and they entered the gracious lobby of The Cottonwoods' River's Edge Nursing Home that had recently been renovated and redecorated by his friend, Danny Curtis, from Prairieville Interiors. Walking down the hall, they were greeted by staff and friends, eventually walking into Ruth's room where she was lying on her side, reading the newspaper. She smiled and received warm hugs from Reuben and Synnova, as well as a 'wet-nose nuzzle' from Socrates.

"Hi, Honey," said Reuben with a glint in his eye. "Any good gossip going around the hospital yesterday?"

# Reuben's Journey Begins

Synnova smiled at Reuben with an approving look, thankful that he had taken her advice to heart.

Ruth smiled, somewhat surprised at his opening comment, and replied, "Well, yes, as a matter of fact. I heard from Bill Flowers, one of the Certified Nursing Assistants, that Doctor Carlson told him that Martha Jensen and Ole Peterson were seen at the movies in Jefferson last night! Now, what do you suppose is going on there? Ole's wife's body isn't even cold yet and he's out at the movies with Martha? Why, for the love of Pete, what are people going to think?"

They all laughed and got lost in fifty minutes of stories about people around town as they ate lunch together. Finally, Ruth acknowledged that she was getting tired and thanked Synnova ten times for spending the weekend with Reuben while Willard and his family were away visiting David in Stillwater.

As they prepared to leave, Reuben put his hand on the side of her face, bent over and kissed her gently on the lips, telling her that he loved her and would be back tomorrow.

Ruth replied with a thought, "Perhaps we could work on our special project tomorrow? Maybe Synnova could help you bring in the Christmas Box."

Reuben acknowledged her suggestion with a smile and a 'thumbs up' gesture.

Back home after a quiet ride from The

## Reuben's Journey Begins

Cottonwoods, Reuben excused himself and took an hour nap before going out to fix some wooden fence posts that the cattle had broken when rubbing on them. The naptime passed quickly and, rising from his short rest, he quietly stepped past his sister who had fallen fast asleep while crocheting and watching the telethon in the living room. Socrates followed quietly and they both snuck out through the kitchen and past the mudroom onto the great porch. At the machine shed, Reuben loaded up hammer, nails and staples, four new wooden fence posts, some extra barbed wire and a posthole digger and off they went to the south pasture to mend the broken fence.

The afternoon and early evening passed quickly as Reuben and Socrates mended the fence, then later at home made calls to David, Willard and Janice to report on Ruth's condition, did the evening chores in record time and finally settled into the root beer float tradition with Synnova, Socrates, Mitsy and Cougar. With their floats in hand, they retired to the living room to watch the telethon where Waylon Jennings was singing one of Reuben's favorite Country Western songs. Synnova had started a fire in the fireplace as the temperature had dropped unusually fast for an early September evening. Sitting down and listening to the music, Reuben thought about how he often loved to sing and play his guitar in the evening after a day of fieldwork and attending to

## Reuben's Journey Begins

his chores. Although his fingers were thick from working with his hands every day and this made it hard to fret very well, muting many of his chords, he wasn't worried about what Socrates, Ruth, his kids or the grandkids would say; he just loved to sing and amuse himself. He loved the Hank Williams, Willie Nelson and Waylon Jennings Country songs, and the Gospel songs were his favorite. From Elvis Presley to Aretha Franklin, he loved to belt out a good old Gospel song as they took the lead on radio, record player or television. His favorite time to sing along with the radio was in his tractor cab when picking corn. There, no one would judge his vocal skills as he imagined being a virtuoso entertaining a large crowd.

As the fire began to dwindle in the huge living room fireplace, which was built with fieldstone by his grandfather and father, shadows moved silently across the room. He watched the shadows dance around the room and march across the Christmas Box in the corner by the staircase leading upstairs, reminding him that tomorrow he needed to bring it to The Cottonwoods. In the box were the contents of their Christmas gift project for this year. He and Ruth had begun working on the project in January with hopes of finishing before Thanksgiving, in order to avoid a last minute rush before Christmas Eve. He made himself a note to remember to take the box along in the morning.

As was always his evening routine before bed, Reuben turned to reading for a while, provided he

## Reuben's Journey Begins

didn't fall asleep too long in his recliner. On this particular evening, with all the kids away, Synnova sleeping on the sofa with her crochet needles still in her hands, and choosing to leave on softer music and to wait to check up on the progress of the telethon in the morning, he went in the bedroom and got Kahlil's Gibran's book, *The Prophet*, and returned to his chair in the living room. He opened to page seventeen and reread one of his favorite passages.

*"And a woman who held a babe against her bosom said, speak to us of Children.*
*And he said: Your children are the sons and daughters of Life's longing for itself.*
*They come through you but not from you,*
*And though they are with you yet they belong not to you.*
*You may give them your love but not your thoughts,*
*For they have their own thoughts.*
*You may house their bodies but not their souls,*
*For their souls dwell in the house of tomorrow,*
*Which you cannot visit, not even in your dreams.*
*You may strive to be like them,*
*But seek not to make them like you.*
*For life goes not backward nor tarries with yesterday.*
*You are the bows from which your children*
*As living arrows are sent forth.*

# Reuben's Journey Begins

*The archer sees the mark upon the path of the infinite,*
*And He bends you with His might*
*That His arrows may go swift and far.*
*Let our bending in the archer's hand be for gladness;*
*For even as He loves the arrow that flies,*
*So He loves also the bow that is stable."* [1]

Reuben loved this piece and always thought of David, Willard and Janice as the greatest gifts in his life with Ruth, along with the grandchildren. He was glad for his gifts from God and his parents, hoping that he would always be a strong and stable bow.

He slipped into a warm rest and an hour later, a gentle hand touched his shoulder and a soft voice suggested they all go to bed.

That night, comfortably in bed and fast asleep, Reuben played baseball with his old high school buddies. It was a great game and he played both with old friends living and those on the other side.

# Chapter Two

## Labor Day Weekend 1990

## Sunday, September 2nd

The 4:30 alarm seemed to ring early on Sunday morning. Socrates was already up, standing on his hind legs looking out the partially opened bedroom window, whining and growling at two squirrels running around on the great porch. The smell of freshly raked hay wafted through the open window once again. Reuben lie squeezing Ruth's pillow this morning. As he awoke, he prayed softly for her, his children, his sisters and friends as he once again recalled the words of *The Prophet* read just hours ago. He so wanted to be

## Reuben's Journey Begins

the strong and stable bow, but what did that mean when your wife of 52 years lie dying at River's Edge?

Getting up, Reuben pulled on his robe and walked into the living room where Synnova had already set a fresh cup of hot black coffee on the TV tray next to his chair. He sat down in his chair and looked up at a photograph of his family on the fireplace mantle. It wasn't often that one of the kids or grandkids weren't around. Was this, too, part of becoming older... more lonely times? How should he start managing these moments? He thought again about aging and what a pest it was becoming. Was it like this for his dad after he moved off the farm and into his little house in Prairieville, before moving to the retirement home? Had his dad felt this way when he and the family weren't around every day? Should he have had some insight into this in earlier life? He felt sad and wished for his dad to be alive again, just for a day.

"Thank you for the coffee, Little Sister," he said in a loud voice as he turned on the television. "What are you doing up so early?"

"I couldn't really get back to sleep after waking up at three o'clock," replied Synnova from the kitchen. "I got thinking about Ruth and you, here on the farm, wondering if you would be happier moving into town. I worry about you, Brother. You're not a spring chicken anymore. And I'd hate for something to happen to you when no one was around."

"Oh, for Pete's sake, Synnova. I have Willard and his family, the horses, cattle, cats, Socrates and all sorts of critters to keep me company," responded Reuben. "Besides, there are a million books I want to read, re-read and things to do before they bury this old body!" Laughing, he said, "I couldn't imagine living in town ... why, I would go stark raving mad sitting around a little house with a postage stamp for a yard like Dad had during his last couple of years. There wouldn't be room for a dozen tomato plants, let alone the sixty plants I just harvested, and that was just fifteen percent of my vegetable garden! "

"Easy for you to say, Brother, when you are a young 72-year-old," quipped Synnova. "Dad was 96 years old when he moved into town. I suspect you'll change your tune when you hit that age in another 24 years."

As he sipped his coffee, he returned to his musings about his father, wondering if it had made him crazy when he moved off the farm. Was he revisiting an unresolved guilt issue he had buried some years ago? He noted that he should ponder this a little more throughout the day. Pondering was the thing he loved most about his days as he settled into the routine of milking, doing field work, mending fences, gardening, feeding the livestock and all sorts of other daily chores.

Thinking about his gardening comment, Synnova replied, "Oh, I know, but you'll find it isn't

## Reuben's Journey Begins

the same when Ruth is gone. Remember how Dad was after Mom died? The farm was different, wasn't it, even with you here? He seemed lost without Mom and would just sort of putter around, sometimes creating more work for you than help. You're lucky Willard is here on the farm with you, and that Terry and Janice are in town helping you look after Ruth. Over the years, I have observed that for many people who lose a spouse, the community overwhelms them with attention after the death for a few weeks and then it is like someone flips a switch and the living spouse is alone, save a few words of sympathy at the store or church, on occasion. It was like that for our brother-in-law, Leon, after Carol died and after everyone got used to her being gone and when people saw he wasn't very sad anymore ... people just sort of stopped talking about her, and their friends who were couples didn't come around as much anymore. Why, he hardly had time to cry during the funeral week, and there were so many people around the first couple of weeks after the funeral that he literally had no time to himself. Then it was like someone flipped that light switch. Suddenly, very few people came around and he was very alone and the world went on almost as if she had never been there," Synnova concluded with a lamenting voice.

Slightly taken aback by her words, Reuben turned the channels to the telethon. There he was, still going. Reuben marveled at Jerry Lewis. He

## Reuben's Journey Begins

had always enjoyed the Dean Martin and Jerry Lewis movies in the '50s and '60s and their television shows. He was sad when they appeared to go their separate ways. Jerry didn't seem as funny without Dean and Dean didn't seem quite as energetic without Jerry. It just seemed they should always be together. But Jerry was doing something now with the telethon that touched the lives of thousands of people, young and old, throughout the country. While he felt most of the television fundraisers and preachers were not much more than hucksters who talked about 'healing,' this man walked his talk and served those who were healers.

It was time, as Sunday morning had always been during Labor Day weekend for the past twenty years, that Reuben would write his check out to Jerry's MDA foundation. There would be their personal check and then a check from his "Special Projects Fund." This year, Jerry & His Kids would get five thousand dollars from him. He wished there could have been a cure for Ruth, and yet felt that somehow these checks might help another Ruth somewhere else and sometime in the future. Reuben had a very strong sense of altruism. And in some strange way, there was a healing feeling that took place in his heart when writing the checks. Sending on the contributions from groups for whom Reuben, along with his five Belgian draft horses, gave hayrides, sleigh rides and other carriage rides during the year, as well as

## Reuben's Journey Begins

some money from selling extra eggs and hay, was a gift of joy for him. Each year, as he would again this year in 1990, Reuben called his pledge in to the Telethon Center in St. Paul and he always felt a deep sense of pride in this annual contribution.

    Reuben finished his coffee, went to the bathroom and, once in the mudroom, laced up his boots. The mudroom featured a large pedestal sink, a mirror mounted in an antique leather horse collar, an antique water box toilet and a curved glass corner shower. It was just one of the many unique features of this home built by his father and grandfather in the early '30s. When they finally installed running water in the early '50s, the shower was added. Before that time, it was a task to always pump the sink pump to fill kettles on the stove for hot water and then carry to the bathtub, and to fill the toilet tank by hand for flushing. He loved all the unique features of his wonderful home.

    It was a large, yellow 'prairie brick' home, not commonplace on the prairie but found in small numbers in some communities. It was a two-and-one-half story house with a generous attic and a turret type lounge atop the attic, making it appear as almost a three-and-one-half story home. There were about eighteen hundred square feet on each floor and a full basement, complete with an underground root and wine cellar that served as an underground connecting link to the washhouse and woodshed. This was an innovation his father had

## Reuben's Journey Begins

developed, having grown up without such a luxury on his boyhood farm. It made the winter weather much more tolerable when stoking the wood furnace at night, in carrying the wood over from the woodshed and in carrying the wash back and forth to and from the washhouse.

The turret above the attic had windows on all sides and in the roof. Reuben, his grandfather, Rudolf, and his father, Caleb, all had a keen interest in astronomy. It was here that they had spent hours some nights, looking at the sky through a newer telescope his dad had bought during a trip to Europe in the '50s. Oh, how he wished his dad and grandfather could see the photos taken with the Hubble telescope. In addition to astronomy, his father, Caleb, was also a passionate inventor who developed several patents for early generators for tractors, trucks and cars for a company that were later bought by General Motors. And around their farm were all sorts of unique innovations related to buildings, fences, pulley systems, doors, livestock pens and machinery. For Reuben, both men were intriguing individuals and had simply been fun to be around. He missed them both dearly.

On the main level of the house was a living room with a grand stone fireplace, a dining room, Reuben's magnificent study with a grand old desk and piles of books and magazines everywhere, the mudroom with its bathroom, another bathroom, the master bedroom and a large farm kitchen with lots of counter space, full ceiling-height cabinets on three walls, two stoves – one gas and one wood burning – and on the fourth wall was another fireplace and in front of it, a big, round oak table that would expand to comfortably hold up to twelve people.  Above the table, there hung a beautiful brass and stained glass chandelier from Norway.

On the second floor were four bedrooms, one for each of the kids and a guest bedroom as there was always company, a large playroom and a bathroom.  The hallway walls were covered with art and photographs, and there was a porch overlooking the backyard, wooded grove and fields just off the playroom.  And perhaps one of the most unique features of the house began on the second floor with a circular staircase leading up to a third floor tucked into a unique roofline.

On the third level, which was regarded as a half story, there was attic space, their nighttime observatory in the turret housing a beautifully crafted telescope, an off-season clothing storage for each bedroom and another playroom area where children could get lost in a paradise of toys and books.

There was rich oak woodwork throughout the house, in a mission style design, along with hardwood floors. All the lumber for the house had been harvested from the farm, logs stacked and dried, cut at their small sawmill – another of his father's creations – boards stacked and air cured and then planed.  It was truly a rare house in that

## Reuben's Journey Begins

almost every stick of wood in the house had come from the woods that were scattered throughout the farm and which grew so densely along Red Rock Creek on the north side of the farm.

Walking out onto the great porch this Sunday morning, which was one of the most spectacular features of the house as it wrapped all the way around it, Reuben paused as he lit his pipe. He looked around at the empty rocking chairs and benches where he and Ruth had spent many, many hours talking, reading, slapping mosquitoes in the summer, drinking hot coffee and chocolate in the cooler seasons, playing with their children and later their grandchildren, watching the dogs and kids race around and around the house on the porch ... he could almost hear the laughter and screams of excitement as they played in those days past. He wished for Willard and his family to be home. He wished Ruth was here sitting in her rocking chair, knitting as she often did after a long day as an RN at The Prairieville Hospital and later at The Cottonwoods. Just as Reuben's mother had done for years, both women had been wonderful nurses and active farm wives, and both had loved to do needlepoint and to knit and crochet.

The front of the house faced the east, and directly across the big open yard was the large limestone-based, yellow painted lap sided barn with its two silos and milk house. The pastel wooden lap siding was painted to match the

## Reuben's Journey Begins

yellowish Kasota limestone. On the south end of the barn's upper haymow door, facing the highway, were large brown letters reading, "Reuben Anderson & Sons," which could be read from the road some two hundred yards away. As he faced the milking barn, about fifty yards away to his left was the machine shed that housed two tractors, four additional vehicles and his machine shop. Behind it was the chicken house, the carriage barn and an old hog barn that now collected all sorts of junk.

Reuben had a passionate dislike for pigs and after his father passed away, he sold the hogs immediately and turned the hog barn into a storage shed. No more slopping the hogs! Oh, how he hated that job, and other than the putrid smell of chicken manure that sat all winter in a pile before loading it in the 'honey wagon' to spread in the field, hog manure was the worst smell for him. It just sort of hung on you all day, he felt, whereas cow manure had a sweet aroma and dissipated quickly after you left the barn.

Across from the old hog barn to the east and north of the milking barn was the horse barn. And beyond them all, toward the woods forested by walnut trees, oaks, cottonwoods and blue spruce, were four large corncribs awaiting the fall harvest. To the east of the old hog barn was another machine shed housing a bailer, an antique pickup truck, an older John Deere C for the sawmill and a few other implements.

## Reuben's Journey Begins

To the northwest side of Reuben's house was Willard's house, which was a more modern manufactured home they brought in by truck and put together in one day! Next to it was a guest house that Reuben and Ruth lived in for several years before moving into the big house to raise their family, when his mom and dad moved into the smaller house. The smaller house was still used as a guest house for company. It was ideal for relatives who would come from the city for a long weekend or a week's vacation.

The morning chores this day seemed to take forever, and Reuben was pondering the trip to church and then going to see Ruth. They recorded the church services on Sunday and Reuben always brought a tape to Ruth when she couldn't attend in person. In some ways, he dreaded talking to people after church these days. While he always appreciated everyone's concern about Ruth, it did become a little too much at times. He didn't much like repeating the story ten times as he walked between the church and his parked Ford pickup truck roadster. He thought it would be easier just to skip church, however, that never sat well with him either. By 10:00 all the chores were done and Synnova had fixed him a mid-morning brunch. She was all ready for church and prompted Reuben to hurry up, shower and dress so they wouldn't be late. By 10:40, they were on their way to the 11:00 worship service.

Arriving at Bethany Lutheran Church,

## Reuben's Journey Begins

Prairieville's largest church, there were the typical groups of folks gathered around the front and sides of the church. The smokers' group was off to one side while a group of farmers had gathered near the front steps, discussing expected crop yields. The kids from Mrs. Ingvalson's Sunday School Class, all dressed in their new school clothes, were racing around the building, as she had let them out early so she could prepare the bread and wine for the Communion service which was the first Sunday of each month. Three teachers from the high school were talking about the summer conference they had just attended, and starting school on the coming Tuesday. And in front of the Fire Hall next to the church was a group of Main Street businessmen talking about the fall city elections. The Baptists, at the church directly across Main Street, were already well into their Sunday School program and one of the ladies was asking the Lutherans to quiet down a little as they had all their windows open, given the warm temperature of the day.

Reuben was warmly greeted by everyone standing outside the church as he and Synnova made their way to the sanctuary. As expected, everyone assured him they had been praying for Ruth. And then, as he had been doing for years, Bunny Ford, one of the town's few mechanics, rang the church bell at five minutes before the hour to let everyone know it was time to get into their pews and to get their hymnals open to the opening

## Reuben's Journey Begins

song. With that summons, Socrates lay down on the steps outside along with a couple of other dogs from town. Reuben and Synnova entered the sanctuary quietly and sat down in the seventh pew from the front, on the pulpit side, right where his father and grandfather had sat for well over eighty years.

Then, the three gongs of the bell to signal the beginning of the service and the opening hymn. The service seemed to go on forever. Today, the young Pastor Jonathan Stendahl was upset that more people hadn't been in church during the recent summer months. Offering dollars were down and this being his first year, he was worried the church would not be able to pay their bills, much less his meager salary which he had come to complain about often. Pastor Stendahl had obviously thought a 'Welcome Back to the Fall Schedule' sermon would be too lukewarm and instead, chose this day to lecture a full church in a disapproving tone that God doesn't go on vacation or forget to tithe during the summer, and that everyone should be more thoughtful about not taking the summer off from attending services on a regular basis. In his youthfulness, and being a city boy somewhat ignorant of the prairie farming culture, he suggested that they should probably continue Sunday School during the summer, and that would maybe help attendance and the treasury. And while no one in the congregation groaned out loud, Reuben could see that no one was buying the idea either, and most appeared to be disapproving of the young pastor's arrogant tone of voice. The good reverend was obviously not yet tuned in to the culture of the community where the harvest dollars would eventually fill the treasury to overflowing.

He didn't much care for this new minister, who was the fourth minister to occupy the pulpit during his lifetime. Reverend Stendahl was always down on the Catholics, constantly picked theological arguments with the Baptists, and couldn't imagine why the world hadn't embraced Lutheranism as a world religion. After all, it was a state religion in Norway and certainly that had worked well there. Why not in Prairieville, too?! Such remarks always made Reuben absolutely crazy. Reuben had come to develop a deep appreciation for all world religions during his lifetime, nurtured by his enthusiastic reading habits. During the past decade, he had become very interested in the Native American religious and spiritual traditions. He even taught the adult Sunday School class for five years, and one year they had spent an entire year comparing similar aspects of Native American religions and Christianity. But far be it from him to even open up that discussion with this minister, or volunteer to teach the same course again. The poor guy would probably 'stroke out' listening to Reuben's thoughts on the subject; especially his interest in shamanism, which he knew wasn't a religion, but played a role in spiritual traditions and

## Reuben's Journey Begins

was a special aspect of the spiritual and healing nature of some individuals.

And then there was the pastor's wife, Helen, a beautiful person who was much more liberal and open about her views of Lutheranism. 'How in the world did she ever hook up with this guy?' thought Reuben with a perplexed expression on his face. 'Why, it actually gives some credibility to the idea that opposites attract.'

Finally, the last hymn and benediction! As they were systematically ushered out, an old custom that dismissed people from the front of the church to the back, Synnova and Reuben were once again the recipients of many well wishes for Ruth. They finally made it to the pickup where Socrates was patiently waiting for them both. Soon out of earshot of Reverend Stendahl, Reuben had to vent.

"That man drives me crazy, Sis. I'd like to …," sniped Reuben as Synnova interrupted.

"Now, Brother, he's a man of God and I don't want you belittling him!" she began. "He means well, even if he is a little young and off the mark sometimes. He'll learn our ways, and the Lord's, soon enough."

"Off the mark! Learn our ways! And the Lord's ways!" bellowed Reuben. "He's a narrow-minded religious bigot! Why, I have half a notion to give him a piece of my mind someday. If it weren't for Ruth's situation right now, I'd give him a piece of my mind today. Sis, that man hasn't opened up

# Reuben's Journey Begins

*his* mind since the third grade, and one thing I can't stand is a preacher who is not well read and more knowledgeable and tolerant of other religions. Why, his comments about the Jews today almost made me jump out of my pew and debate him right there. Pa always said that what made Pastor Sundae a great theologian was his knowledge and appreciation for the greater world and diversity of religions. He always said that God sent his Son to the world, not to the Lutheran church! While Pastor Sundae was a passionate Christian, he was equally passionate about others being able to worship as they chose! This clown needs to get a clue and open up his mind."

"Reuben David Anderson," said Synnova in a disapproving voice, "enough now. You can tar and feather the preacher later. Let's turn our thoughts to Ruth. You don't need to walk into her room all riled up and get her started. My goodness, I haven't seen you this worked up since Tovar Knudson lost the election to the school board!"

"Oh, you're right, Synnova," Reuben replied, disgust in his voice. "I shouldn't let him get me so worked up about things. And I won't excuse him just because he is young. Heck, he's never milked a cow, rode a horse or shoveled manure. What does he know about us farm folks? Lecturing us about slow attendance in the summer! It just makes me mad. Or, better yet, I wonder how the businessmen and women around town feel about his ranting about profit as an evil motivator taking advantage of the poor. I thought William Eckerson, Sr. was going to throw a hymnal at him. Gosh, he just gets my goat. I had wished for a minister who has some intellectual depth, an appreciation for farming and business, and who would be more patient and compassionate with folks in our rural community. I'm not sure our search committee really interviewed him very carefully. The Altar Guild ladies had too much influence in this decision to call him, probably because he is so into his vestments and the altar finery. I almost threw up when he was patronizing them at his installation service."

"Maybe you should introduce him to the farm, Brother." said Synnova with a gentle challenge, hoping to change the direction of the conversation. "Might be a good way to settle your nerves and teach the lad a thing or two. Who knows, maybe you could get him to open up his mind. Remember, you've been exploring the world, its people and cultures for well over sixty years, ever since you wandered into seventh grade. Why, you have two legs, or should I say 45 years, up on the young man!"

Reuben took a deep breath, shrugged with a 'maybe' movement of his shoulders and a tipping of his head as they walked toward the truck. Suddenly, Bunny Ford summoned Reuben to 'wait up' as he brought the tape of the service to Reuben for Ruth.

"Don't know that this sermon today will be all

## Reuben's Journey Begins

that uplifting to Ruth, but here it is," said Bunny with a laugh. "Give my love to Ruth and tell her 'thank you' for the two blankets she donated to our orphans' blanket drive. We're celebrating the history of the Orphan Train again next week and sending things to an orphanage overseas."

"I'll do that, Bunny," said Reuben appreciatively as he and Synnova, along with Socrates, got into the pickup and off they drove to The Cottonwoods.

It was almost 12:30 when they arrived. Reuben reached into the back of the roadster pickup to retrieve the Christmas Box he had loaded earlier that morning, remembering Ruth's wish to work on the gifts for the kids. As they entered her room, they saw that Ruth had fallen asleep waiting for them. As of late, she dozed off often during the day. The dining services staff had left three covered hot plates with turkey dinners complete with mashed potatoes, gravy, fresh cooked carrots, fresh cranberries, buttered rolls and coffee. And for dessert, there was fresh apple pie. Setting the Christmas Box down next to the bed, Reuben bent over and gently kissed Ruth's forehead.

"It's nice to see you back here, Honey, and out of the hospital," he said softly.

She looked up with a lazy look in her eyes, then smiled and invited them to sit down and join her for dinner.

As they all began to eat their lunch, they resumed Saturday's conversation about 'happenings and gossip' around town for about an hour and Ruth seemed to perk up as Reuben set the Christmas Box next to her bed.

Finishing their lunch, Reuben said, "Maybe we should spend some time on the Christmas gifts."

Ruth nodded approvingly and began to proudly tell Synnova about their plan.

"We started this project just after New Year's Day, Synnova. We've been collecting special things for each of the kid's hobbies for years and we thought it was time to put them together in a creative way so they could be displayed in their homes. Our hope is to complete the project before Thanksgiving so there won't be a last minute rush to finish them. We've gotten a little behind because I've been up and down lately, but we're close to finishing now. It has been great fun."

Ruth continued in an upbeat voice, "For David, who has always loved the cowboy sheriffs of the past and his sheriff colleagues of the present, we have been collecting sheriff badges for years and Reuben is helping me mount them in several shadow boxes with a backdrop of red velveteen material. We've collected over eighty badges going back as far as the late 1800s to the present. Here, this one is from Stillwater and where David now works. He'll really love it. We know David will like the collection and that gives me a very warm feeling. And every time I imagine what his expression will be when he opens his present, I get goose bumps." With that, Ruth smiled and set down the badges she was holding in her hand.

# Reuben's Journey Begins

Picking up a bag of antique bullets, shells with slugs in them, she continued. "For Willard, who has been an avid hunter and collector of hunting ammunition ever since anyone can remember, we've been collecting rifle bullets and shotgun shells for decades. Reuben is building additional shadow boxes for Willard's collection. He's helping me mount them in the boxes as soon as I label each one. I have to look through several books to identify them and, having collected over two hundred of these, it has taken a little longer than expected. Here is a ceramic slug from the Civil War and it was also used years ago for hunting deer."

Setting the ceramic slug aside, she reached for a doll lying in a small box. "For Janice," she continued, "we have found some great porcelain dolls. If you remember, Synnova, my mother, Grace, gave Janice her first porcelain-faced doll when she was born, and she continued to give her dolls through her high school years. Since that time, Janice has collected others. I've always wanted to make a special contribution to her collection so I started collecting them, too. I've given her one now and then, but she doesn't know about these. It has become a special connecting point for us over the years ... you know, those times when you need to escape from the daily routines and just enjoy a hobby. And you should see the antique baby buggy Reuben has restored that we bought at an auction two years ago, in

## Reuben's Journey Begins

which we want to place special pillows and blankets, and these seven dolls."

As Reuben and Synnova worked with Ruth for another hour on the project, Ruth dozed off. Reuben told the nurse who was walking past the room that they would probably go home shortly, and to call her if Ruth's condition changed of if she wanted to see him again this evening.

Reuben and Synnova quietly left the room and were joined by Socrates, who had been down the hall visiting other residents.

Back home, Reuben turned on the old Philco radio in the living room and tuned in the Twins game on WCCO. Even though they were on television, he loved listening to the game over the radio, as he and his dad had done for years. The Twins were playing the Detroit Tigers and already in the 5$^{th}$ inning of the game. Synnova also loved baseball and joined him in the living room, sitting on the sofa and resuming her work on the afghan she was making for the Jensen's new granddaughter. Constantly crocheting afghans, she was always working on one for somebody. Soon both had dozed off on this warm September Sunday afternoon.

About 4:45, Socrates awoke and went over to Reuben, nudging his arm as if to say, 'Time to do it again, Master.' Reuben woke up realizing that he had missed the end of the game but he would catch the score on the 6:00 news out in the barn. As he left the room, he draped one of Synnova's

## Reuben's Journey Begins

afghans over her; one she had made for Ruth years ago for their 40$^{th}$ wedding anniversary.

One last night to do chores alone and 'thank goodness Willard, Louise and the kids come home tonight,' he thought. Socrates even seemed to have a little notion about it. Together, they raced through evening chores and before they knew it, they were back in the kitchen making their root beer floats. Synnova had also made up some ham sandwiches, thinking a bedtime snack would be appropriate since both had skipped supper. Once again, they retired to the living room with TV trays to enjoy the telethon. And once again, they both dozed off within the hour.

Socrates awoke to quiet footsteps moving about the house. It was Louise and Willard. Willard gently woke his dad and walked with him to his bedroom, giving him a short summary of their trip to the Twin Cities and Stillwater. Louise walked Synnova up the stairs and to her bedroom, as she was complaining about a slight dizzy spell. Socrates had raced over to Willard's house to see the kids and would return later through his special door cut through the wall in the mudroom, to take his place below the window in Reuben's bedroom.

This night, Reuben and his dad visited the stars and fixed their telescope on old friends in the sky.

## Chapter Three

### Labor Day Weekend 1990

### Monday, September 3rd

Reuben awoke just two minutes before the 4:30 alarm rang. He was glad that Willard and his family were back from their trip. Today, things would return to a more normal schedule, even though it was still a holiday. It was nice to have Synnova visit and keep him company, and he had appreciated her thoughts about dealing with Ruth's situation. Anticipating that she would return to Windy Marsh this afternoon, where she and her husband, Glenn Orville, lived, he thought it would be nice to have a big lunch together. As he pulled on his robe and walked into the living room, his coffee was once again waiting for him and the television was once again turned on to the telethon, now in its final hours. Synnova had

## Reuben's Journey Begins

already packed her overnight bag and it was sitting by the front door.

"Leaving so early, Sis?" queried Reuben.

"Oh, no, just thought I would bring my bag down now and probably leave sometime this afternoon," said Synnova. "I'd like to stop by and see Ruth for a little while before driving home."

"Great," exclaimed Reuben. "Let's go see her together. I thought we could have a nice big lunch together first. I'll barbecue some steaks and chicken on the grill and we can boil the last of the sweet corn. The raccoons have finished off most of the late ears but I was able to find a couple of dozen good ones yesterday. How those crazy critters love their sweet corn, too! We'll eat a few ears for lunch and you can bring some others home to Glenn Orville."

Walking down the stairs to the basement, he grabbed a few things and quickly returned to the kitchen. "Here are two fresh pumpkins, an acorn squash and potatoes from the garden that we can cook up, too. Your pumpkin pies are as good as anything our mother ever made for us. What do you say?"

Synnova smiled as Reuben continued, "The flour and crust makings are in the cupboard to the left of the stove. And there is plenty of fresh butter for the squash and fresh cream in the refrigerator for some good old-fashioned whipped cream for the pie."

"My only secret for the pumpkin pie is Mom's

## Reuben's Journey Begins

old recipe she got from her mother, and I would be glad to make the pies if you will clean out the pumpkins before you go to the barn," replied Synnova.

Reuben quickly halved the pumpkins and cleaned them, leaving quartered pieces of the pumpkin meat on the prep counter next to the sink. He also halved the acorn squash and cleaned out the seeds and middle, leaving it ready for the brown sugar and butter, and the oven. With the clock nearing 5:15 a.m., he finished dressing, lit his pipe and hurried to the barn.

As Reuben and Socrates walked into the barn, Willard was already putting ground feed into the manger in front of each stanchion where each cow was fed and quickly checked before going through the milking parlor. Although not everyone continued to use their stanchions after converting to milking parlors, Reuben did, so that he would have a chance to look over each cow, maybe do a little grooming and check for cuts, infections, etc. Willard had been working in the barn since 4:30, cleaning two calf pens which housed his daughter's 4H calves.

On the radio was the news from WCCO radio in Minneapolis, and later they would listen to his favorite morning show, The Boone and Erickson Show, in its last day at the fair. Reuben had stopped by to say hi to Boone and Erickson at the Minnesota State Fair on Wednesday last week, during his annual visit to Machinery Hill. Reuben

# Reuben's Journey Begins

often recalled a trip to the fair in the late '50s with his dad, sister Synnova and brother-in-law, Glenn Orville, when they met Cedric Adams, a WCCO personality who had a fabulous voice and had become a major radio celebrity in Minnesota. Cedric had autographed a black and white photo that was still in a frame in his den in the horse barn. Labor Day was always the last day of the Minnesota State Fair and today on WCCO, they were talking about the Magellan space probe sending back its first high resolution photographs of the planet Venus. For the first time, there were detailed photos of the planet's craters, hills, and ridges!

"Morning, Dad. And Socrates, are you ready to get the cows?!" Willard asked laughingly, rubbing Socrates' head and scratching his ears.

The German shepherd rubbed up against him, almost knocking him down, barked and jumped over the half opened Dutch barn door and headed for the east pasture. Soon the herd of Holsteins would contribute their milk for the morning.

Reuben checked the water in the individual stanchion cups to see if they were all full and working properly while he continued to put fresh straw in the gutters before letting the cows into the barn.

Finished with that task, Reuben walked over to the barn door, called Socrates and said, "Let's get them in the barn, pal."

And with that, he opened up the door to the

## Reuben's Journey Begins

east barnyard. The cattle were mostly up and waiting, and Socrates raced among them as they filed into the barn and went to their stalls to eat and drink.

"Well, Dad, how were things Friday, Saturday and Sunday?" asked Willard as he began securing each of the stanchions. "I stopped at Donny's last night to drop off some supplies we picked up in St. Paul and he said you and Aunt Synnova had stopped by the other day with eggs."

"Things went pretty well, Son," replied Reuben. "Chores took longer without you and my old bones and muscles aren't used to that amount of work now. I love working around the farm, but I could never do it alone anymore. Glad you're home. It was nice to have Synnova here and I guess the only tragedy of the weekend was Stendahl's sermon on Sunday. He was all upset about the summer attendance and the church treasury is empty. Don't get me started on that citified preacher. How were David and his family?"

"I fear one day you and the young preacher will tangle," replied Willard, laughing. "As for David and family, things are pretty good. You know how he loves his sheriff work. He was telling me about a prisoner he had to pick up in Arizona and fly back to Stillwater Prison. Guess the guy stole a dozen fancy sports cars in Minnesota, repainted them and then sold them through a used car lot in Phoenix. The way they caught him was one of the previous car owners had lost his billfold in the seat

# Reuben's Journey Begins

and when the new owner found it, he called the guy thinking he was being a Good Samaritan. Turns out the previous owner got the new owner's phone number, called the police and they arrested the poor soul thinking he had stolen the car. They finally got it all straightened out and arrested the fellow from Minneapolis who was staying with his girlfriend in Phoenix. He told the whole story to David on the way home and David was handcuffed to him the entire time on the plane. As for Reverend Stendahl, Dad, I agree he is pretty green, but you have been unusually intolerant of him, which isn't quite like your nature. Has he done something to upset you?"

"Yes and no," replied Reuben. "If he weren't so arrogant, I could deal with his youth, weak theological ideas and the just plain stupid things he says. I don't know, Willie, he just gets under my skin."

Willard and Reuben continued to talk about the weekend as they worked their way through the milk cows. Willard had become a disenchanted fan of milking cows. For the past eight years, he had wanted to convert to a more modern milking parlor as compared with their current small one, but Reuben felt it was just as easy to continue with the system they had created some years ago. Willard also felt that there just wasn't any money in selling milk anymore. With some occasional low crop yields in past years, and rising feed and fuel cost, selling the milk wasn't really a great business

## Reuben's Journey Begins

anymore given the investment and time, and fluctuating milk prices were now at about $13.73 CWT, or per hundred pounds. Times had changed and the cost of veterinary bills and repairing milking equipment was bringing the age of the average dairy farm to a close, at least for them, Willard thought.

Willard had developed an interest in buying and/or renting additional acreage to farm for raising corn, small grain and alfalfa. The demand for those crops was increasing. However, he joined Reuben every morning and evening in the barn to milk the cows as he knew it was something his dad wanted to do to feel a sense of value and, more recently, to distract and cope with Ruth's absence. Besides, Reuben had been milking cows for 68 years, ever since he could carry a milk pail at the age of four. For him, milking cows was not only a ritual that was a major piece of the fabric of farming on the rolling prairie, but it also represented the care and feeding of the life that made the farm an enterprise for family and community.

Reuben and Willard had talked often about selling the milk cows and just having feeder cattle, especially when the sub-zero winter days or steaming hot days in July and August diminished the joy of doing the milking and related chores. Reuben loved his farm and selling the milk cows just didn't seem right; he felt it would be less of a farm without them. It wasn't a big farm, however,

## Reuben's Journey Begins

their 240 acres plus another eighty they rented kept him and Willard plenty busy – along with the milk cows, a few feeder cattle for butchering, some young calves, five horses, a few cats, ducks and geese, and a chicken house full of Ruth's best laying hens.  They also had a dozen sheep that were Christopher's 4H project, and Reuben always enjoyed sheering them in the spring and watching Louise and Christopher clean some of the wool and spin it into yarn.  The rest they sold to a company in Kansas City who came through every spring, buying the small amounts of wool from area farmers.

And we can't forget Alice and her offspring, rogue Rhode Island Red laying hens that he was scheming to eat for dinner one night after being pecked by one of them to the point of a bleeding hand while attempting to pick eggs from underneath them.  Boy, he disliked those hens! However, Ruth always asked about them, her favorite laying hens for the past few years, and if he was being patient with them.  He would say 'yes' and show her the battle wounds on the back of his hand and they would laugh.  They loved to laugh together.  It was a rich laughter shared from the depths of their souls.  And although the volume and pitch of her laughter had now become much weaker, they still celebrated this simple joy during their daily visits.

Chores done, it was time to bale hay for a couple of hours before lunch.  Reuben was grateful

## Reuben's Journey Begins

that it hadn't rained. He used the restored John Deere B tractor for baling, pulling their New Holland baler, and Willard hooked the bales as they came out of the baler and stacked them on the hayrack. They had thought about going to the larger round bales in recent years but decided to forego it; at his age, it was easier to work with the smaller bales and allowed for putting them easily into the two barns. They both loved the field work and always felt a great sense of accomplishment as they finished a field of hay. They had four hayracks and the field just west of the house would fill them. With all four racks full and the clock pushing 1:00, they headed for the house where Synnova and Louise had prepared a feast!

"Wow, what a spread, Synnova, and you've already barbequed the steak and chicken, too. My goodness, I don't know what to say," said Reuben with deep appreciation.

"Well, the best thing you can say is 'grace,' and then we can enjoy our meal together," replied Synnova as she made sure that Willard, Louise, Christopher, Catherine and Reuben were all ready to sit up to the table and enjoy their meal.

Socrates had already begun chewing on one of the T-bone steak bones Synnova had put in his dish.

"Dear Heavenly Father," prayed Reuben. "We thank thee, Lord, for this sunny and dry day to put up hay and for this time to be together as family. Please bless Ruth and give her strength and

## Reuben's Journey Begins

comfort; be with David's and Willard's and Janice's families; all of the grandkids; and now bless this food to our bodies so that we may serve you in right and truthful ways. In thy holy name we pray, Amen." All joined in a group "Amen."

As they began to eat, Synnova said to Reuben, "I forgot to ask you about Terry and Janice's trip."

"Well, as you know, they went to Tennessee to spend Labor Day Weekend with his folks and two brothers," replied Reuben. "The staff at The Cottonwoods almost had to force them to go. They never take any time off work and I worry sometimes that they'll burn out. Of course, my mother and Ruth have both worked there just as many hours, and getting them to take off for a weekend or a special holiday was almost never heard of unless they were sick. They always felt they should let others be with family. Go figure."

"It's quite a place, isn't it? The Cottonwoods senior living community, that is," said Synnova. "I remember when it used to be just a small country rest home with six rooms and about ten people, when mom ran the home for the Schultz family. Then the bakery burned down on Main Street and they rebuilt it near The Cottonwoods. Later, as I recall, Doctor Henry Schultz decided to tear down the old homestead and build 24 small apartments and a twelve bed nursing home so he didn't have to add more beds onto the hospital. People thought he was nuts, but it wasn't many years later when they added 36 larger retirement apartments

## Reuben's Journey Begins

and then five years ago, they did a total update. What all did they end up with? I missed their grand opening because I was sitting with our sister, Carol, that weekend."

"Well," began Reuben, "The Cottonwoods now has 72 apartments they call The Manor and they are for retired persons who are independent, or at least mostly independent. They get two meals a day, housekeeping once a week, transportation around town and things like that. They have a lot of activities, too. The older, smaller 24 apartments, built years earlier that you mentioned, have been converted to assisted living and they call them The Annex. Of course, you know about the eight-unit memory care center they named after mom, Amanda's Garden, which is attached to The Annex. They did add more beds to River's Edge Nursing Home and now have 32 beds in that skilled nursing facility, along with rehabilitation services. Terry and Janice have done a great job developing the project. The Prairieville Bakery and The Red Rock Creek Arts & Crafts Store, as well as the new laundromat and dry cleaners, make up the rest of the campus. It has really become a neat little area on the east side of Prairieville, and nestled in the midst of those beautiful cottonwood trees by Red Rock Creek makes it a very pretty place."

"You know," added Willard, "I think Terry and Jan have really put together a great staff, too. Terry's assistant administrator, Angie Perkins, has to be one of the most hardworking people I know. I was talking with Nancy Bauer, his Director of Nursing, the other day and she said Angie went in and sat with Mom all night at the hospital the day she had her breathing episode. Mom was the one who initially hired Angie at The Cottonwoods as an Assistant Director of Nurses before she became Terry's assistant some years later, and she feels so close to Mom. She'd do anything for her."

"She is an angel," continued Reuben. "Angie is always spending extra time with residents, whether they are in assisted living or the nursing home. Terry told me last week that Angie's husband, Kevin, just finished repainting eight rooms at River's Edge and wouldn't take any payment for it because everyone had been so kind and supportive of his mother when she was alive and lived there for nine months. They're good folks."

Suddenly there was a knock at the door and Socrates ran to greet the visitors. It was Helen and Sarah Stendahl, wondering if they could return to the marsh to do another afternoon painting. Reuben stepped out to visit with them, assuring them it was okay, and returned to the kitchen table.

They continued their conversation for another forty minutes and then Reuben, looking at his watch, suggested that he and Synnova go in to see Ruth as it was getting toward mid-afternoon and, winking at her, said, "We need to put the finishing touches on the project."

Synnova smiled and acknowledged his words

## Reuben's Journey Begins

with a wink to Louise, who knew about the project. Christopher and Catherine offered to help with dishes if they could ride along in the back of the Ford roadster and get dropped off at the Dairy Queen. The Prairieville Dairy Queen had become the new hot spot for teenagers to meet and hang out if they didn't drive yet.

Reuben smiled as he reminded them, "That's fine with me if your dad foots the bill for malts and floats for all of us. I'll buy the gas; he can buy the treats!"

Everyone laughed and it was agreed that as soon as the dishes were done and put away, they would venture into Prairieville.

As they drove into town, Reuben told Synnova about the possibility of him and Willard renting more farm land in West Creek, seven miles to the west of Prairieville; a smaller community of twelve hundred persons. His alfalfa sales had been steadily increasing and two area corporate farms that raised feeder cattle wanted to contract with him for silage and hay. In addition, a new ethanol plant was being planned south of Windy Marsh and was also looking for contracts with those who could supply large quantities of corn. They had looked at land nine miles to the north of Prairieville in Lumber Mill, a community of eight hundred persons built around a saw mill and old railroad shipping yard for farm machinery. However, the distance and small acreage just didn't make sense. Six miles to the east, in Jefferson, a smaller

## Reuben's Journey Begins

community of six hundred persons and primarily a farming community with a large grain elevator complex serving a larger agricultural area, they planned to rent an eighty-acre farm for small grain planting and alfalfa. Twenty miles to the south of Prairieville in Windy Marsh, a community of five thousand persons and the county seat, were two of the family farms and also where Synnova and Glenn Orville lived. They rented their eighty acres of farmland to a neighbor, Oscar Smith.

Arriving in town, they dropped the kids off at the Dairy Queen and cautioned them about being nice and to stay there and not ride around town in cars. As they drove through town, both Reuben and Synnova talked about some of their friends as they passed by businesses and through the eastside neighborhood. Of special note was Rusty Olson's Town Café. As kids, they had all grown up together and Rusty, who lived in town, had loved spending occasional weekends on the farm with Reuben, Synnova, Carol, Harriet, Doris and Iris.

"Dad always considered Rusty an adopted son," said Synnova. Reuben acknowledged with an affirmative nod of his head.

"Terry and Jan should be back from Tennessee," said Reuben as they approached the entry to The Cottonwoods. "They were flying back to Minneapolis this morning and thought they would be in their offices this afternoon if they were able to catch the earlier flight."

Walking into the lobby of River's Edge, they

## Reuben's Journey Begins

saw Terry and Janice coming out of Ruth's room. Janice walked over quickly to Reuben and hugged her dad. Terry followed suit as they both hugged Reuben and Synnova. And, of course, Socrates barked approvingly as he, too, wanted some attention from them.

"Hello, Socrates," said Terry in his Tennessee drawl, "Ruth is waiting to see you, buddy, and Mrs. Schultz is also waiting for you to stop by and see her. I swear that we have more requests for you to stop by and visit residents than those for Doctor Carlson." Everyone laughed.

As they entered the room, they found Ruth reading *Life* magazine. She looked up, asking, "Did you see Terry and Jan?"

"Sure did," Reuben replied as he leaned over and gave her a kiss. "We thought we should come in for a couple of hours and finish up the Christmas gifts and Synnova has offered to store them away in her guest bedroom when we get home so the kids don't discover them before Christmas."

"Honey, can you mount the Stillwater Sheriff's badge on a raised piece of wood or something to make it stand out more in the center cabinet?" asked Ruth.

"Sure, no problem, and I'll have Synnova wrap the wood with the red velvet." replied Reuben. "And I think that will finish David's present. Three beautiful cabinets."

"Oh, he is just going to love this gift!" smiled Ruth with great satisfaction.

## Reuben's Journey Begins

"Ruth, do you mind if I add these doll-sized afghans and blankets to the doll carriage?" asked Synnova. "I made them during the weekend while Socrates and I were keeping an eye on the house and refrigerator." They all laughed.

"Synnova," exclaimed Ruth, "they are beautiful. Jan will love them and, someday, what a perfect gift – the dolls, the clothes, the blankets and baby carriage – for her to pass on to Mary and Megan. That will complete Jan's gift."

"I'm done making all the labels for Willard's bullets and slugs now," Ruth continued, "and Synnova, if you wouldn't mind taking the shadow boxes home and coming up with an idea for mounting the labels for me, I would really appreciate it."

"I would be glad to," responded Synnova. "I'll do it this evening and stop by to show you an example tomorrow morning when Glenn Orville and I go to Comfortville where, lately, we have been helping the Salvation Army distribute clothes, food and toiletries to those who lost their homes."

Ruth's eyelids were closing frequently, and both Reuben and Synnova knew it was time to let her rest. They hugged and kissed her goodbye and walked down to talk with Terry, Janice and Nancy who had gathered in the coffee shop to visit.

"She's slipping away from us, isn't she, kids?" asked Reuben, tears now running down his cheeks.

Janice reached over and hugged him as her

eyes filled with tears, too.

"Dad, her body is tired and not functioning well," she said. "I don't want her to leave us, either, but we have to accept the fact that it may be her time to go to a better place."

"Reuben, Ruth has dealt with her condition better than most of us," offered Nancy. "I've appreciated everything she has done for me during the past years and value her more than I can ever really describe to anyone. Yesterday, she had me help her into a wheelchair to go down to see Walter Olson who was in his last hours, to give him comfort. She is simply a saint."

"Dad," began Janice, "Mom's body may be tired but her spirit hasn't changed. She will always think of others before herself, even in her last days. For now, you need to go pick up those teenagers and get Aunt Synnova back to the farm so she can go home."

Standing up, Janice gave her aunt a big hug as she said, "Love you, Synnova, and thank you for caring so much for Mom and Dad."

Finished visiting with Terry, Janice and Nancy, they left The Cottonwoods to go get the kids. As they got into the roadster, Reuben sighed and a single tear found its way through his beard and hung there like morning dew on a leaf.

"I know how you feel, Brother," said Synnova in a quiet voice. "I remember when Doctor Stoneberg told me that Carol would only be with us for a few more days, all sorts of thoughts ran

## Reuben's Journey Begins

through my mind. Funny how I knew he was right, but part of me wanted to imagine him wrong. Maybe it would be months and not days? Maybe there would be a miracle and she would regain enough strength to be around another year? And then I finally allowed myself to let go and accept his words that she was to soon complete her life. When that happened, I found myself accepting her passing less reluctantly and for the first time, I began to imagine my life without her. Who would I drink coffee with most mornings? Who would now sit and crochet afghans with me for the Salvation Army? Who would go with me to visit sick friends in the hospital? Glenn Orville would go with me in the evenings and weekends, but Carol always went with me during the weekdays. We always went together. Of all our sisters, I was closest to her and I wondered what or who would fill that void in my life. We saw each other almost every day since we were kids. My Lord, that was seventy years of being together."

    Reuben sat listening intently to his sister as he, too, had pondered, without resolution, who or what would fill the void he had been experiencing the past few years. Up until now, he had continued to imagine Ruth coming home and filling the empty space in bed next to him; being there when he would reach over and touch her; returning to eat suppers together again and work on their jigsaw puzzles; watching the evening news together on television and enjoying the good times on the great

## Reuben's Journey Begins

porch together. Now, for the first time, he began to see the bed, the chairs and rockers empty, with no hope of them being filled with Ruth again. Tears rolled down his face and onto his beard and dripped on the steering wheel and Socrates. The morning dew had turned to rain.

They sat there for a while longer as Reuben quietly processed the events and words of the last hour. Synnova dried his eyes and beard with her hanky and asked, "Would you like me to drive home, Brother?"

"No, I'm okay, it's just that this whole thing has been building up in me so much lately and I keep fighting the idea that Ruth is going to pass away soon," said Reuben with deep resignation. "When you were talking about Carol not being with you anymore, my mind raced around the house and farm, imagining the places where she has always been for the past 52 years, imagining them being empty ... and it just kills me. I guess I need to let go, too, and prepare for this change in my life."

After a pause, Reuben said with a deep sigh, "Well, I suppose we should go get the kids. They've probably spent every dime they have on treats and borrowed more from friends. That Christopher could sit there eating hamburgers and french fries all day long. During the 4$^{th}$ of July celebration this past summer, he ran up a sixteen dollar bill hanging out with friends. Willard made him work off every penny when we did the second cutting of hay. Maybe he will have changed his

## Reuben's Journey Begins

ways a little. Of course, who cares, they're just kids and they've been here almost three hours."

There were no additional charges and the kids had lived within their means. They were still sitting around the tables outside, talking with friends. Catherine had made a new friend, Diane Kenneth, who had just moved to Prairieville and she was impressed with the jewelry Diane had made during summer vacation. She promised to teach Catherine how to make jewelry.

After chatting with the Ladermans, who had come over to Reuben's roadster to see how Ruth was doing, the kids were now in the little oak box that adorned the brightly-painted, red 1949 Ford pickup roadster, and ready to go home.

When they arrived at the farm, two of Willard's friends, Chuck Wendford and Craig Edson, were just leaving. They had been out to the farm to talk about pheasant hunting plans to go to South Dakota and northeast Nebraska on opening day in October. After greeting Willard's friends, Reuben walked Synnova to the house where they hugged and said their goodbyes.

Reuben carried her bag as they walked to her car and said, "Thanks, Synnova. I'm not sure I could have gotten through this weekend as well as I did, had you not been here. Oh, I know that Terry, Jan, Willard and Louise are here for me to lean on but it's different with you. Your experience with Carol helped me see some things I hadn't really looked at very clearly and accepted yet, and

## Reuben's Journey Begins

while it is all still very painful for me, you were good medicine today. You have the spirit and energy of a shaman, Little Sister. Besides, you saved the preacher's life Sunday. That alone was a healing act! I was ready to kill that little brat. You know, I just think the world of his wife and daughter, Helen and Sarah. I wonder sometimes How two people so seemingly opposite ever get together! Anyway, thank you for coming."

"You're quite welcome, Brother," she said, hugging him. "We'll get through this together and life will go on. And don't be so hard on the preacher. Remember, you were young once. As for you and Ruth, there are many wonderful memories of Ruth to cherish and you need to simply be near her whenever possible over the next few weeks. I learned from the last days with Mom, Dad and Carol that one doesn't really need to say much during these days, but just be there. After all, as you once told me after reading one of your shaman books, spiritual presence and nonverbal communication can offer the strongest comfort of all. We sometimes underestimate the value of simply being present, letting our spiritual energy work its healing magic."

With those words, Synnova smiled, they hugged again and she got in her car and began her drive back to Windy Marsh.

As Reuben walked to the barn to help Willard finish up with chores that evening, he thought to himself, 'Synnova is like a shaman, or better yet,

## Reuben's Journey Begins

she is an angel.  Maybe that is what some sisters are meant to be.  My older sisters have always come to family gatherings and helped out around the home place from time to time, but Synnova is different in that she always seems to appear when someone needs that extra strength to deal with a challenge.  She was always like an old soul, a shaman who was wise beyond her years, and her words and actions have always been comforting.  Hmmm, some sisters as angels and shamans … I like that idea.'

Walking into the barn, Reuben was greeted by Socrates and Willard.

"Synnova leave, Dad?" asked Willard.

"Yes, she wanted to get going before it got too late and I suppose Glenn Orville will be expecting her to make dinner for him yet tonight.  It was really nice to have her here over the weekend and spend some time with me and Ruth," replied Reuben with a quiet sense of appreciation.

Willard nodded in agreement as he moved another cow into the milking queue.  "She has always been a favorite aunt of mine and always seems to know what to say at the right time.  I remember once when David and I got into a fight over who was going to drive the new tractor years ago and she suggested that we let Grandpa Caleb be first.  It caught us both off guard.  We knew she was right, and we raced to the horse barn to get him and ask him if we could ride with him while he went out to pick up a load of hay.  From that day

## Reuben's Journey Begins

on, we used to stop and think about alternatives to fighting over silly things. It was a good life lesson."

Chores done, barns closed up for the evening, Reuben and Willard bade each other goodnight and walked to their houses. As he made his root beer float that evening, his mind trailed off to years earlier, remembering the days that preceded his mother's sister's death ... and he remembered a beautiful quote she often read to the family at devotions after the Sunday evening meal, a tradition for many years: *"Courage is what it takes to stand up and speak; courage is also what it takes to sit down and listen ..." ~ Winston Churchill*

He had appreciated the words of his sister, and listening ... they had brought him comfort.

Suddenly, his silent reflections were interrupted by the phone.

"Hi, Reuben, it's Doc," said the voice on the other end of the line. It was Doctor Carlson. "I just came from visiting Ruth. Vi and I stopped over for a social visit and I noticed that her breathing was getting difficult again, and I think it would be good for you and the family to spend some time with her tomorrow. I called Janice a few minutes ago and suggested she call David and Willard. There is no need to come in tonight, as I gave her some medication that will help her rest through the night. I would suggest that you all come in tomorrow morning after you are done with chores.

"Are you sure that I shouldn't come in this

## Reuben's Journey Begins

evening?" asked Reuben in a worried voice.

"You certainly can, and perhaps for a short while sitting in the chair next to her for a few hours tonight might give you a sense of being with her during this time," replied Doc. "But don't stay all night; you need to take care of yourself, too." And Synnova's words about spiritual presence echoed in his mind as he hung up the phone and headed for his bedroom.

Reuben quickly dressed and he continued to think about the power of being present that he and Synnova had talked about earlier in the day. He drove in to The Cottonwoods where he spent a few hours holding Ruth's hand, sitting in the chair next to her bed. Ruth occasionally opened her eyes and smiled, but said nothing. Medication had made her sleepy but they would occasionally lightly squeeze each other's hand. As the clock rounded to 11:00 p.m., Reuben stood up and kissed Ruth gently on the forehead and returned to the farm.

Back at home, Reuben finished the root beer float that he had put in the freezer and watched an old Western movie for a while and fell asleep.

That night for a short while, he and Synnova went swimming at Campsite Grove with friends from their seventh grade class on a hot 4th of July day.

## Chapter Four

### The Prairie Receives a Daughter

### September, 1990

    As Reuben lie in bed, slowly waking up, Tuesday morning ushered in a sense of knowingness for him, a sense that he had not experienced before, almost as if time was standing still and he was frozen in it. He was sort of dazed, yet realizing events were progressing. He had known this day would come sometime soon, given the events of the past year. The news that Ruth's heart and kidneys were now growing steadily weaker and her breathing problems becoming more acute, according to Doc Carlson, was hard to accept, yet he needed to own up to the time at

## Reuben's Journey Begins

hand. The call made things seem more imminent now. Yet in the midst of a failing body, her spirit remained positive and appreciative of everyone caring for her. Reuben was having a hard time putting the two things together ... her declining health, coming death and steady, positive spirit. While she thought people were doting too much over her, several people, including Reuben, would remind her how she doted over every one of her patients through the years, first working at the Prairieville Hospital for twenty years and then, semi-retired, working at River's Edge Nursing Home for ten years until she had become too ill five years ago to work anymore.

As the shadows in his bedroom began to disappear, he thought about his impending visit. What should he say? What should he do? And then he remembered his conversation again with Synnova, about the power of spiritual presence, and thought he would simply start there.

As the rising sun began to paint the eastern sky with its brilliant yellows, pinks, oranges and lavenders on a partially cloudy canvas, Reuben arose from his mostly sleepless night, made a cup of coffee, filled one of his favorite pipes with fresh tobacco and went out onto the great porch to watch the morning sun paint the farm.

Socrates lay by Reuben's rocking chair on the great porch and knew something was different. On this day, Reuben had not uttered a single word to him or anyone else since he got up.

## Reuben's Journey Begins

Socrates usually awoke to an enthusiastic master who was always greeting him with an energetic, "Hello," scratching his head, rubbing his ears and saying something like, "Come on boy, let's go get those cows or feed those hungry horses."

But today, Reuben was silent, almost as if he was lost in another place. Socrates rested his head on the scratched and scarred tongue-and-groove maple flooring that had been painted grey many times over the years, his eyes open, watching Reuben rock anxiously and puff on his pipe. And yet, there were no words. No stroking of his head or rubbing of his ears. It was so different.

Reuben sat on the porch, smoking his pipe, and worried about how the day would go for him at River's Edge. He thought about the stops in town he normally made along the way before going to see Ruth. Should he change his routine this morning? Would that change the outcome of the day? He drifted for a moment, thinking about the stops generally made at the post office, the bank, the grocery store and the farm store for supplies. When he arrived at Ruth's room at The Cottonwoods, he always had stories to tell her about the things he had done and the people he had met. She so enjoyed hearing about the happenings out at the farm and from around town. Would his changing the morning routine change their normal visit? Would it make it easier or more

## Reuben's Journey Begins

difficult? His mind was a whirl of questions.

Finished with his pipe and coffee, Reuben, still silent, returned to his bedroom where he gathered up several boxes, one large one and a smaller one full of items, and draped the shadow boxes with burlap feed bags he would bring to Ruth to finish working on the kids' other Christmas presents, as well as showing Ruth the progress and finishes on the major gifts. He wanted to put them into the roadster before doing morning chores so he wouldn't forget them later. As he carried them out to the truck, he felt sad and worried about failing in today's visit with Ruth.

Would today be the day she would now want to talk about the preparations for her funeral service again? How he disliked that conversation. She had started down that road several months ago after a mild heart attack. Reuben was surprised to see that she had written out the entire family and funeral services, naming her pallbearers, singers, piano and organ players and a menu for the lunch afterwards! He was stupefied by the vision of the service all written out. He wasn't sure he could deal with it today or, for that fact, ever. Death was something that happened to other people and animals, not to him or Ruth.

When Reuben finally went down to the barn to help with milking, Willard noted that his demeanor was different.

"Everything okay, Dad?" Willard asked. And for the first time that morning, Reuben spoke.

## Reuben's Journey Begins

"Doc Carlson called last night and said that her heart and kidneys seem to be worsening and her breathing difficult. He said her heart and kidneys will both fail her soon and we should be prepared for her passing. He was going to give her something so she would sleep comfortably last night and said that I should probably wait to come in later this morning as she would probably sleep well into the morning. But I went in anyway for a few hours last night, and sat by her side, holding her hand. Jan also called and said she and Terry would help move her and her things over to a private hospice room at River's Edge early this morning. I didn't sleep much last night ... guess I have been dreading this moment and now I'm not quite sure what to say to Mom this morning. She'll probably want to work on that darn funeral service again!"

"Well, Dad," Willard said in a soft and quiet, understanding voice, "we've all been sort of avoiding this time and now it is coming. Mom's really dealing with her declining health better than we are ..." Willard paused as if to choke up some, and then continued, "... Guess she'll be the one helping us through this, too," as he half chuckled in a sad and respectful tone.

Reuben and Willard finished milking. Willard offered to clean the barn and milking equipment so that Reuben could finish his few chores in the horse barn and henhouse before leaving for town. Socrates followed him everywhere, noting that he

## Reuben's Journey Begins

was moving faster than normal and was glad he was speaking to someone, if not to him. As the horse barn Dutch doors were opened up, there was a mood of excitement as Barney flew out over Reuben's head.

"Hmmm, wondering what he's doing over here, Socrates?" said Reuben, "He should be sleeping now." And then looking up, he saw the answer: a female barn owl and two little heads peered over a small corner nest above a corner rafter.

"Well, I'll be darned," said Reuben, "guess we've got babies in the rafters again." Reuben loved his barn owls and was always tossing corn cobs at cats who attempted to reach their perching or nesting areas.

Duke and Dolly were the first to get their feed and hay; next, Dancer and Duchess; and then, Boots, a two-year old foal from Dancer and Duchess. Reuben opened the door to the horse pasture and Boots took off like a bullet, bouncing and kicking up his heels as he raced around the yard. Reuben finished up his feeding and watering chores quickly in the horse barn and then walked quickly to the house, anxious to go see Ruth. As he walked, he thought quietly to himself, 'I need strength, dear Lord, to get through this day. Please help me say and do the right things for Ruth.' His step quickened as he changed clothes and went straightaway to his red Ford pickup roadster with Socrates in tow.

Reuben arrived at The Cottonwoods within

## Reuben's Journey Begins

minutes, deciding to forego the normal stops. His heart was racing and he dearly wanted to talk with Ruth and spend the day visiting with her, but not about her funeral. As he entered the lobby of River's Edge, Janice and Terry were just coming out of a meeting with the staff. They both greeted Reuben with hugs and Janice joined her father as they walked down to Ruth's room. Socrates went with Terry to see Mrs. Schultz who had been asking for the dog all morning, and then Terry went out to the roadster to retrieve the other boxes for Reuben.

Ruth was still sleeping and Janice went over to gently wake her.

"Mom, there's an old farmer here to see you," she said with a soft humor in her voice. "He's also got a big box with him and I'm not sure what's in it. Or perhaps he thinks he's going to sneak you out of here!"

Ruth opened her eyes and smiled.

"That's the best idea anyone has had around here in months," Ruth said while clearing her throat and reaching out to hug Janice and then Reuben. "Well, if he thinks I'm going to fit in the box, he'd better have expansion panels in it!"

They all laughed and Janice explained that she had to run to another meeting with the Schultz family, closing the door behind her as she left.

Ruth took one look at Reuben and in her upbeat 'nurse voice' she said, "Boy, you look a mess today. Did one of the horses run away or

## Reuben's Journey Begins

something? That's got to be it, because it's the only thing that would bring you to tears and I can see you've been crying, you big ol' Norwegian."

With that, Reuben sat down on the chair next to her bed, took her hand and wept. Crying wasn't something that Norwegian men of Reuben's generation did very often but he couldn't hold it back. His mother had always told his dad that Norwegian men keep most of their tears inside and eventually the buildup of pressure would cause the heart to explode! The few times in his life Reuben had cried like this, he later admitted that he felt better afterwards.

As he wiped his tears from his face and beard with his sleeves, Ruth spoke in a soft and loving voice:

"Reuben, dear, please listen to me. None of us can live forever and my body is tired and not working well anymore. You've got to accept that fact. We're no different from the cats, dogs and horses, Honey. We all have a life span and sometimes it is shorter when disease appears. In many ways, we're not different than the animals. We've had a good life together. And look at our kids and grandkids. We did good, my dear Renaissance man. You're still in good health and you need to fill in for me too, now, with the family. I'm not in any great pain and Doc Carlson is taking good care of me. I'll still be around for a while. That is, if you don't break my hand."

Reuben's grip on Ruth's hand had increased so

## Reuben's Journey Begins

much that he was starting to bend it. "Oh, my gosh, Ruth, I'm sorry. I guess I was making up for all the lost time holding hands lately," he said, looking at Ruth with the first smile of the day. "I know that I'm not handling this very well. Is there anything I can do for you today?"

"Well, as a matter of fact, there is," she said with some vigor in her voice. "Since I won't fit in that box so you can sneak me out of this place, why don't we put the finishing touches on the Christmas gifts? I can't wait to see what the two different shadow boxes look like for the boys, with the final touches you put on them yesterday, adding the glass doors and all."

Reuben went over to the boxes and undraped the shadow boxes featuring David's badges and Willard's hunting shells.

As he brought them over to Ruth's bedside, she gasped, "Oh, Reuben, they're beautiful!"

The center shadow box for David was approximately twelve inches wide and three feet long. There were twelve rows of badges with four badges in each row, all fastened to a red velveteen background and the Stillwater sheriff's badge now mounted in the center just the way Ruth had wanted. He had taken the shadow box idea one step further by adding a glass door, making it seem more like a cabinet, and a small light had been added at the top. As Reuben showed her the various aspects of the case, Ruth looked on with a great sense of pride, knowing that David would

# Reuben's Journey Begins

love his gift. The two side shadow boxes were smaller; ten inches by two feet, and allowed space for future badges to be added.

Next, Reuben brought over one of the cabinets he had made for Willard, and Ruth was equally pleased and excited about it. It was similar in size to David's large shadow box, however, Reuben had used a royal blue velveteen cloth background for the ammunition. Ruth and Louise had worked diligently and patiently in making sure the labels were all framed with little brass surrounds; Synnova had placed them in the boxes perfectly, and returned them to Reuben. It was truly a work of art.

Reuben and Ruth continued to talk about upcoming events in the fall and he expressed hopes that possibly she could come out to the farm for a visit. She acknowledged that that would be nice, however, she would like to wait until she felt a little stronger. For now, all this excitement about finishing the Christmas gifts had made her tired and she said she would like to rest for a while and maybe he could come back after chores tonight.

"Are you sure you don't want me to hang around here for a while?" he asked in a more upbeat voice.

"No, the farm needs attention and I know you need to start getting things ready for the fall harvest," she said warmly. "Willard called yesterday and said you still have four racks of hay to put up in the barns, so you better get that done

## Reuben's Journey Begins

today. I heard that it's supposed to rain tomorrow and you know how you hate wet hay!" she said, smiling and chiding him to get on his way as she began to fall asleep.

The visit had gone better than he had imagined. No mention of the funeral service. They had enjoyed looking at the finished gifts and even worked on the cards. And with Ruth now slipping into another nap, Reuben thought that maybe it was a good time to leave and return to the business of the farm and come back after the evening chores were done. As he removed his jacket from the back of the chair next to Ruth's bed, she opened her eyes and said,

"See you later, Big Guy?" with a chuckle in her voice.

"Yes Ma'am, I guess I will finish putting up some hay that is still on racks and grind some corn and oats for ground feed. I almost ran out this morning," he said with a return smile, in a kidding voice.

"Honey, would you hand my Bible to me? It's lying on the shelf next to the family picture," she asked him quietly. Reuben promptly retrieved the Bible and as he handed it to her, he noticed a pen clipped to the top of a small notebook in the middle of the Bible and his heart began to race. He felt a wave of electricity flow through his body. It was the notebook in which Ruth had been making notes for her funeral service. His mind raced in a thousand directions, wondering wildly about what

## Reuben's Journey Begins

to say and not knowing at all where to go with this observation. But as he turned to hand her the Bible, Ruth's eyes were closed again and she was drifting off into another nap. He breathed a deep sigh of relief and placed the Bible with the notebook and pen in her right hand resting comfortably at her side. Reuben quietly patted his hand on his hip to signal Socrates that it was time to go. The two slipped out of the room and walked in the direction of Janice's office.

"May I come in for a moment, Honey?" Reuben asked shyly.

"Oh, Daddy, you don't have to ask to come into my office," Janice said, chuckling. "How's Mom doing?"

"Well, that's what I came to ask you," Reuben replied with a sigh. "We had a very nice visit and worked on a little Christmas project for you kids and the grandkids today."

"I've heard rumors about the 'little' project," she said, smiling. "Mom is resting comfortably, Dad, and we can only leave this in the hands of our staff, Doctor Carlson and God. I know this is extremely hard for you and it is for us, too. But you know ..."

Reuben interrupted, saying, "... we can't all live forever. I know, your mother has repeated that quote several times and now you sound just like her."

"Daddy, for one who is as well read as you and has dealt with so many funerals with your carriage

## Reuben's Journey Begins

service, I'm surprised that you seem almost angry about this," Janice said, coming around from her desk and sitting in the chair next to him.

"Perhaps I am, Jan," said Reuben with a voice of resignation. "I've been thinking about it for weeks and I'm stuck in this place where death is something that always happens to others, or older people – not young folks like your mother."

"Daddy, I'll be here for Mom and I promise to call you if anything changes," said Janice, hugging him. "Socrates, you take good care of Daddy today and help him around the farm. Before you go, I have a list of things people wanted to have you pick up for them. Would you mind?"

"Of course not. I guess I've sort of neglected my volunteer duties here the past couple of weeks, with everything else going on and your Aunt Synnova visiting," replied Reuben. "I have to stop at the bank, anyway, to draw another check for the Muscular Dystrophy Association and send it off to Mr. Lewis."

Janice handed him a list of requests:
1. Current *Newsweek* and *Time* magazines for Ned Forden
2. Check on new stamps at the post office for Alma Klarrup
3. Pick up a prescription for Maria Knudson at Prairieville Drug
4. Cashews and peanuts for Mike Peterson
5. Deck of playing cards for Bill Hanson
6. Two skeins of black yarn for Ethel Thomas

# Reuben's Journey Begins

7. Two bags of dog food for Jack Taggert's dog
8. *The National Enquirer* for John Bloomquist
9. Four large print books at the library for John and Mary Woods

"Thanks for everything you do for Mom, Honey, and I'll be glad to take care of this list before I go home this morning," Reuben said as he reviewed the list. "Say 'hi' to Terry."

As he left Janice's office and began walking down the hallway, he said hello to Mrs. Mattson who was sitting in her wheelchair, half slumped over and drooling. There was no reaction from her and he wondered about her. She had suffered a severe stroke three years ago and didn't really have any family locally. She was somewhat of a mystery woman to almost everyone. The staff had told Reuben that she was sort of senile and that when she tries to speak, it's hard to understand her. People mostly avoided her, however, she seemed to remain calm and quiet if they let her sit in the hallway in a chair most of the day, where she could see people. Reuben had always wanted to sit and try to talk with her when visiting The Cottonwoods but the opportunity had never presented itself.

The afternoon was busy with the hot, sweaty work of putting up the hay. Reuben, Christopher and Willard labored well into late afternoon. With the hay bales put up into the haymow, the men walked over to Willard's house where Louise had prepared a snack for them before they started the evening chores.

"Jan called, Reuben, and said Ruth was resting well this afternoon and you should probably plan to go in and visit her around seven o'clock tonight," said Louise.

"Thanks Louise, I was thinking about going in after feeding the horses and maybe Willard and Christopher can finish up milking tonight," replied Reuben with a mild questioning tone.

"Hey, no problem," replied Willard.

"Synnova dropped off a light quilt she made for Mom this morning and left a note on it saying she thought Ruth would like it when sitting out on the porch at River's Edge," said Reuben. "I'll take that in to Mom and I should probably stop by to visit a few of the other folks I have been ignoring the last couple of weeks."

Their snack finished, the three men ventured out to attack their chores.

When Reuben arrived at The Cottonwoods and went over to River's Edge, he greeted Ruth with the quilt Synnova had made for her.

"Oh, my goodness, will you look at the work that woman put into this," exclaimed Ruth. "It is simply beautiful! I will be the envy of everyone on the porch."

Reuben smiled and acknowledged its craftsmanship and beauty.

"How did the afternoon go, Dear?" queried Ruth in a soft voice.

"It went well," replied Reuben. That young

# Reuben's Journey Begins

Christopher is becoming a durable young man. He was throwing around the hay bales in the barn like they were basketballs. He seems to be at that age where one minute he is a little boy of six and next, a young man of 21. Maybe that is what fifteen is all about."

"He sure looks up to you, Honey," said Ruth with a confident voice. "Louise said the other day that he wants to build your carriage business into a bigger enterprise but hasn't the nerve to ask you about doing that yet."

Reuben laughed, "I like his attitude and those kinds of dreams are the things that gave us the energy and power to do what we did with the farm; and the carriage business, which I guess has really been more of a hobby for us."

As they visited about a number of townspeople, Ruth's eyes began to close often and Reuben could see that she was ready to sleep. He quietly bent over her and kissed her goodnight, then slipped carefully out of the room to go find Socrates who had been visiting residents around the nursing home.

That night, reading in his bed, he fell asleep and he and Ruth had Christmas with their children.

It was 7:00 a.m. on Wednesday morning when the phone rang in the barn. Willard answered the phone and it was Janice.

"Willie, it's Jan. Is Dad in the barn with you?" she asked.

"Just a minute, I think he's in the milk house,"

## Reuben's Journey Begins

he replied.

"No, wait, it's Mom, and I think both of you should come in right away. Her vital signs are steadily weakening and Doctor Carlson feels she may only have a few more hours left."

"I'll get Dad and we'll be right there," replied Willard.

Willard quickly removed the two milking machines, paused the system, ran to get the pickup and drove down to the horse barn where Reuben and Socrates were just coming out. Quickly picking them up, he stopped by his house and ran in to ask Louise to finish milking the last few cows.

"Oh, to heck with the cows, come on with us," said Willard.

Together, the two men, Louise and the dog headed for The Cottonwoods.

"I've been both avoiding and dreading this moment," said Reuben tearfully. "I knew she wasn't going to last much longer. It's hard, Willie, to see Mom go. I feel like my whole world is ending in some ways, yet I know you kids are still here."

Socrates knew something was wrong and laid his head on Reuben's shoulder, occasionally licking the tears from his face.

They arrived at River's Edge just minutes after Janice's call. They rushed into Ruth's room and were greeted by Marilyn Roberts, the hospice nurse, and Terry, David, Janice, Doctor Carlson

## Reuben's Journey Begins

and Reverend Stendahl, who happened to be visiting others when he heard the commotion in the hallway. Reuben just ignored the young pastor and walked over to Ruth and sat down on a chair near the head of the bed. He reached over to hold her hand and Ruth slowly turned her head on her pillow toward Reuben and offered a very weak, but evident, smile.

"I love you, Reuben Anderson," Ruth spoke in a weak but determined voice. "And now I need to take a long rest. Love our babies for me ... David, Janice and Willard. I love you kids. And take care of my grandchildren. And for Pete's sake, take good care of those horses, Reuben. Honey, I'd like you to take me from the church to the cemetery in the white funeral carriage. I know how you have loved restoring that old carriage we bought in Deadwood, South Dakota years ago. Remember to have your friend, Reverend Freiburg from Sioux Falls, help Reverend Stendahl with the service. I have had Janice write down all my wishes for the funeral service. I'd like Synnova to play the piano and sing along with Annette Smith ... they have always sung so beautifully."

Having observed and witnessed the passing of residents many times, Terry stepped forward quietly and asked Ruth if he could offer a prayer. Smiling, Ruth replied,

"Sure, it wouldn't hurt to have a little Baptist influence when I get to heaven, just in case the Lutherans have missed something," Ruth said,

## Reuben's Journey Begins

expressing her wry sense of humor.

"Terry, that would be nice," said Reuben, fighting back his tears as he petted Socrates who had laid his head on the foot of Ruth's bed.

Reverend Stendahl, looking like he had just been preempted by the Anti-Christ, bowed his head in prayer.

"Our Heavenly Father," prayed Terry, "Bless this kind and gentle servant as she joins you and all the angels of heaven. We thank you for the gifts she has given all of us and now, in this hour, we ask you to take her into your arms and bless this wonderful woman who has given so much to everyone. In thy name we pray, Amen."

"That was beautiful, Terry," said Ruth in a soft voice. "I feel so tired and I think the sandman is coming and I need to close my eyes."

Ruth squeezed Reuben's hand and said, "Please take care of our babies and make sure they get their Christmas presents, Honey."

Ruth smiled and closed her eyes. They stayed by her side. Twenty minutes later, her chest lay still, her beating heart silent.

"Dad," Jan said through tears, embracing Reuben and breaking an overpowering silence, "Mom wanted me to give this to you after she left ... We all know your weren't very excited about planning her funeral with her so David, Willard, Synnova and I helped her during the past couple of months. It was important to her. I typed up this letter last week and she approved it with a kiss and

## Reuben's Journey Begins

a smile."

Through blurry, tear-laden eyes, Reuben took the Bible and in it was a letter and her funeral plans.

"Daddy, why don't you wait until you're home and read the letter? Sometimes people like to sit and be alone with a loved one after they have passed. Would you like to be alone with Mom for a while?"

"Yes, I think I would. But will you kids come back in after a while?" he asked, wiping away his tears.

"Of course, just press this call button when you're ready," said Terry as the group who had gathered quietly left the room.

No sooner had the door closed than Reuben could not wait to read the letter. It was like he could instantly reconnect with her. Taking the envelope from the Bible and carefully opening it with his pocket knife, he once again wiped the steady stream of tears from his face and beard with his shirt sleeves, one arm at a time. Taking a deep breath, he read the letter.

*"Dear Reuben,*

*My dearest Renaissance man, how lovely you've made my life's journey. Always kind, always giving, never asking for anything for yourself ... well, unless we count the carriages and horses, but I always saw that as our hobby, except when you would secretly spoil them with new gear*

# Reuben's Journey Begins

*and treats!*

*As you know, I have always loved to write poems about our journey together. Here's one I wrote today.*

**Best Friends, We'll Be Together Again**

*Since the early spring when we were young,
Teasing each other often at school and play,
About dress, hair and missing teeth,
It was a friendship that grew day by day.
As the early days of summer came upon us,
Our friendship continued to grow with marriage,
Dreams of a new life together and children,
Celebrated often in the wedding carriage.*

*The summer brought our children three,
And the fall, our grandchildren five,
The farm always a beehive of activity,
It was wonderful and so alive.
And now winter's time has come for me,
To take a long and needed rest in heaven,
Along with the many saints we knew,
You and I, best friends, will be together again.*

*I think it describes us perfectly, dear Reuben. It's one thing to be married, but to be married and close friends is the best one can hope for and experience in a lifetime.*

*You've never dealt with death very well … whether it was people, livestock or the pets … and*

# Reuben's Journey Begins

*I have always accepted that as your incredible passion for living life to the fullest and cheating death whenever and wherever you could. I remember the time Silver Foot, your quarter horse, broke his leg and you worked with Doc Gerten for three days and nights to save him, and somehow he lived for a while, but his wounds were too great and he died. It was an experience to watch you become angry at death. My wounds are simply too great now and I choose to leave when I still have my senses about me. I am weary. Please understand.*

*The past three years have been hard for both of us. Being apart has not been fun for either of us. This year has been special, when I think of the time we have enjoyed creating the special Christmas presents for the kids. I know they will love and cherish them forever.*

*Come and visit the folks here often as they love to see you, to hear your stories and reminisce about Prairieville and its people. The residents at The Manor, River's Edge, Amanda's Garden and The Annex love seeing Socrates. And volunteering, which you are amazing at, to get things for people, playing table games, doing puzzles and so many other things here means the world to them as they just don't get that many visitors or get out much. That is a sad but a true fact. Your intentional acts of kindness have meant so much to so many.*

*So now, my final wish, I ask this now of you. I*

# Reuben's Journey Begins

*wish for a grand prairie funeral celebration, remembering our best times, and I would so much like for you and Socrates to carry me to the cemetery and place me next to my mom and dad, and next to where you'll join me some day. It will be nice to rest next to them, and someday you, for eternity. I would also like to ask the kids and grandkids to ride in the wedding coach as a symbol of our wonderful marriage. And the beautiful saddle with the rhinestones you made for me when we got married – would you put that on Boots and tether him to the funeral coach? I will be riding him; you just won't see me or my smile, but you will feel my presence. You and I are sons and daughters of this wonderful prairie, Reuben David Anderson, and it has given us a great life. So now, My Prairie Prince, go now and prepare for the celebration.*

*My love to you for eternity,*
*Ruth*

The tears continued for a time and then Reuben turned his thoughts to Ruth's request.

He opened another group of papers that were stapled together, outlining the family service and funeral service.

## *Family Service*

1. *Please hold at the farm on an evening*

*before the funeral.*

2. *Enjoy a spread of coffee, lemonade, apple and pumpkin pies with homemade ice cream.*
3. *Have the children make the ice cream so they feel like they helped prepare for the service.*
4. *Ask the grandchildren boys and nephews to bring their baseball gloves so they can catch my love. I've signed two dozen baseballs for them to toss about and keep as memorabilia.*
5. *Ask the grandchildren girls to bring their dolls so they can hug my spirit. Synnova sewed two dozen doll blankets for them.*
6. *I would like for everyone to talk as much about their dreams as they will talk about me. As a family, we have always treasured talking about our dreams, and I think it would be something positive to add to the service.*
7. *Sing a couple of songs – maybe you and Ted could play your guitars and do "Michael Row The Boat Ashore," "Blowing in The Wind" and "Kumbaya" ... we used to sing those songs all the time around the campfire at Campsite Grove. And, for Pete's sake, don't practice your fingers raw if you haven't played for a while.*
8. *I would love to have Reverend Barney Freiburgh read a couple of scriptures,*

## Reuben's Journey Begins

*Especially my favorite, Romans, Chapter Twelve. You or he can pick the other.*
9. *One of the things I have valued most about all our immediate family, your sisters and mine and their families, has been the volunteerism they have done in our community, especially for seniors. There is a lot of loneliness in this community and the touch of a caring hug, a kind voice and stopping for a short time for a simple visit, is spiritual gold. I'd like for people to talk about ideas they have about volunteering. I'm especially concerned about those in their eighties and nineties; they are all too often those most forgotten, not intentionally, so they need intentional attention. Without fairly specific intentions to do even the 'littlest' volunteer act, very little ever happens. You do it without thinking; others need to think about it. So please encourage our families, friends and others to help these older persons I so loved to spend time with, as do you.*
10. *Finally, please pray that funny little prayer at the end of the service that you always say when we drive the funeral coach from various churches to their respective cemeteries when we are alone. "Dear Lord, naked we come into this world and serve you the best we can. Too bad*

## Reuben's Journey Begins

*we leave the world poorly made up and dressed by the undertaker. But we know that the warm heart that loved you so much is with you now and the cold embalmed heart here is simply a stepping stone in this river of life to help us step across to his/her eternal journey. Amen." I laughed so hard the first time you prayed that for old Ole Olson, I thought I would pee in my pants!*

The tears stopped and he unexpectedly found himself smiling and saying, as he reached over to hold her hand, "It will be my pleasure, Dear Sweet Love, to honor your wishes and give you a prairie funeral the likes of which the prairie hasn't seen for some time. Rest well, my love, and enjoy your journey to heaven." Smiling, a moment of humor passed through him. "PS, Put in a good word for me with the Man upstairs."

And with that, he took a deep breath, released a prolonged sigh and pressed the call button summoning the others back to the room. An hour had passed as Willard, Louise, David, Kathy, Terry and Janice entered the room. They were somewhat surprised to see Reuben smiling.

"We had a good visit, kids, and as was generally the case in life, your mother has given me a 'to do' list for the rest of the week," he said with a relieved spirit. "I wished her well on her journey to heaven and asked her to put in a good

## Reuben's Journey Begins

word for me."

They all smiled and hugged, acknowledging that they had all been part of listening and helping Ruth create the letter. As they walked out to the front lobby, each person spent a few minutes with Reuben, suggesting ways in which they would help prepare for the funeral celebration.

Relieved of chores that evening as Willard and Christopher would see to them, Reuben filled the Meerschaum pipe Ruth had given him for their $50^{th}$ wedding anniversary. He had only smoked it once, the night of their anniversary, and decided to set it aside for another special occasion. Tonight would be that occasion. It was a beautifully carved pipe of a mermaid exhibiting extraordinary detail in her hair, face, beautiful breasts and the finely sculpted scales in her tail. Taking a glass of Robert Mondavi cabernet sauvignon, a treat Ruth and he had enjoyed on special occasions, he went out on the great porch and sat in his rocking chair.

Next to his rocking chair was Ruth's rocking chair and in it lay a present that had been left by someone during the day. He opened it and it was from his sister, Synnova: an afghan for Reuben that Ruth had requested her to crochet, with two oddly shaped smoke-ring hearts overlapping, and a note. "Dear Brother, Ruth asked Louise to place this in her rocking chair on the day of her passing, and wanted you to lay it on your bed as a keepsake from her. When you are alone on the great porch, put it in her rocking chair and

## Reuben's Journey Begins

reminisce about the life you had together. She used to love watching you blow smoke rings as you puffed on your pipe and cigars. I hope I did the smoke rings justice. It was her wish that the afghan will bring you company when lonely, joy when sad, and will dry the tears that wet your beard when you cry. Love, Synnova"

The evening dew turned once again to rain. Reuben spent the entire chore time sitting and smoking his pipe on the porch with the afghan draped over Ruth's rocking chair, attempting a few smoke rings that would join together. As the evening sent forth a slight chill, he put the afghan in his lap. As he blew another double smoke ring, it floated toward heaven and his tears washed his beard. 'What an incredible person,' he thought. 'To have had this beautiful afghan made, knowing her time was near, and then making such arrangements to keep me company here on the great porch. Simply amazing.' He blew another double smoke ring and watched it chase the other.

The time passed quickly and soon Willard, Christopher and Catherine all came walking across the yard and up to the great porch. The grandkids had not had their time with Grandpa Reuben yet, and now came the hugs and tears from two wonderful kids.

Across from Willard's house came Louise with an armful of fixings for supper. And up the driveway came three more cars, almost as if someone had planned it. It was David, Kathy and Tammy; Terry,

Reuben's Journey Begins

Janice and the twins, Megan and Mary; and behind them, Glenn Orville and Synnova Thomas. He was overwhelmed with a sense of love and the bounty of the prairie bringing forth an incredible gift of support.

The evening passed quickly as everyone told stories and joined in great moments of laughter, remembering those humorous moments and life lessons with Ruth, all a mix of tears, joy, sadness and caring glances for Reuben. And Reuben, too, returning the same to his children and grandchildren whom he knew would dearly miss their mother and grandmother.

As everyone prepared to leave, Synnova said she would spend the next few days at the farm so she could help Reuben begin to organize things, receive phone calls and prepare meals. Glenn Orville needed to return to Comfortville where he and other volunteers of the Salvation Army would still be helping the hundreds of people who had lost their homes and businesses in the tornado during the summer.

As he drifted off to sleep that night, Reuben and Ruth went to a barn-raising dance and celebration at the Engle's farm. She told him she was pregnant with David.

As Reuben awoke on Thursday morning, he lie quietly and sadly in bed and began to imagine preparations for Ruth's grand prairie funeral. Little did he realize at the time that Ruth's assignments were not so much for herself but to help him to move from a place of prolonged grief and sadness to a place of creativity and celebration. It was working like magic.

He now imagined all to come.

He imagined the visitation and open casket at the farm where he would move all the furniture out of the living room and line the great porch with additional chairs for visiting family and friends. He imagined his study set up with two eight foot tables adorned with photographs of Ruth's life. He imagined purchasing bakery goods and having a feast of food for the three days of mourning, and visiting when people came to pay their respects. He imagined how peaceful it would be in the evenings for these three days, to have Ruth with him one last time at the farm and at their home.

He remembered a walk they had taken years earlier along Red Rock Creek when she talked about how she loved the American flag, the Minnesota flag and the Prairieville community flag that she and other women had created years earlier during Prairieville's 50$^{th}$ Anniversary. He imagined lining the route from Bethany Lutheran to the cemetery with these flags that would symbolize her love for her country, her state and her community. He thought about calling Orville Neuhardt, Commander of the Legion Post, and asking him if he would arrange for flags to be displayed on Main Street, and a few along the road on the way to the cemetery – especially the Prairieville community flag. He imagined asking the Red Rock Creek Riders to join the funeral procession and to provide saddled horses for as many people as possible to ride, and if the weather was nice, for the rest to walk the one mile route to the cemetery, just as they had done at prairie funerals before the automobile arrived. He imagined the older family and friends riding in some of the other carriages that he owned, as well as using Charlie Taggert's carriage collection. He imagined the funeral coach, the wedding coaches, Duke and Duchess and Boots, all decked out in their best bridles and riggings for the celebration. He imagined Ted reading the scripture lessons.

    He imagined a service filled with music, a combination of a small brass band characteristic of earlier prairie funerals, as well as organ and piano music. He imagined singing, poetry, Country Western and folk music so dearly loved by Ruth. He imagined their friend, Reverend Barney Freiburg, preaching a great sermon and Reverend Stendahl tied up and gagged with duct tape in the basement of the church ... but knew that was just wishful thinking and at the moment, probably an irreverent thought. He imagined his sister, Synnova, and friend, Annette Smith, singing solos and leading the congregational singing. He imagined their friend, Rusty Olson, reading two of Ruth's favorite poems. He imagined the six pallbearers who would carry the coffin from the church to the funeral carriage where Duke and Duchess, along with Boots, would greet her for the

## Reuben's Journey Begins

procession.

He imagined a graveside service that would begin with the small brass band, guitars and flute, the instrument Ruth had played in the school band years earlier, as the pallbearers carried the closed casket from the funeral coach to the grave. He imagined a final poem and a Bible verse to be read by her dear friends Angie Perkins, Nancy Bauer and Karen Johnson. He imagined Reverend Freiburg closing with the Lord's Prayer and the lowering of the casket, and then the filling in of the grave. He imagined placing a vase and a bouquet of prairie flowers on the grave where it would remain for three days and nights before it was groomed and the headstone put in place.

He imagined returning to the church where there would be a traditional prairie potluck event. He imagined thanking everyone for their support and help.

He imagined doing the Family Service on Sunday evening, as there would be several hours of preparation on Monday morning, preparing all the carriages and horses.

And as the day turned to evening, he imagined finishing the Split Rock Lighthouse puzzle with Ruth.

By now, Socrates had jumped up into the bed and was lying quietly next to Reuben as he stroked his back. There was a commotion out in the kitchen and Socrates bounded out of bed to check out the action.

# Reuben's Journey Begins

"Socrates, you grand German shepherd," shouted a familiar voice. "Where is that lazy master of yours?" teased Reuben's best friend of all, Ted Parker, from Billings, Montana.

Reuben leapt out of bed, grabbed his robe and strode quickly to the kitchen.

"Ted, how in the world did you get here so fast?" exclaimed Reuben with joy and appreciation in his voice.

"Magically, my friend, on the wings of Northwest Airlines," said Ted as they hugged. "Janice called me late Tuesday and said Ruth was failing. I had told her last year that if things changed in her health, to call me so I could be here with you when she passed away. I caught a plane first thing yesterday, flew to Minneapolis and drove down to Lumber Mill last night to stay with my good friend, Tovar Torkelson. He's in the car and would like to come in and pay his respects."

"By all means, please, go out and get him and I'll get dressed," said Reuben as he scurried off to the bedroom.

In the meantime, Ted brought his friend Tovar into the house. Tovar had always been a close friend on Ruth's side of the family and he brought a beautiful bouquet of dried flowers; they had always been a favorite of Ruth's. And in a small box was a gold-plated prairie rose corsage that Ruth's mother had given Tovar's sister years ago as a wedding present. His sister had asked him to bring it to Reuben, to see if he would like Ruth to

## Reuben's Journey Begins

wear it on her blouse or dress. Reuben was very appreciative of the gift and thought it was a beautiful idea.

"We don't want to be in the way and it looks like you've got things under control in the house with Synnova and Louise looking after things," said Ted. "We'll gladly join you for breakfast and then if you have a few things we could help with to get ready for the visitation here at the farm, Tovar and I will be glad to help."

As Synnova began to set the kitchen table for the three men, a knock at the door brought in Rusty Olson and Bob Burton. Reuben, Ted, Rusty and Bob had all been best friends in high school, and the four of them had made up most of their nine-man football team.

"We came out to see what we could help you with, Reuben, as we thought you would probably do the visitation here at the farm rather than the church. We told Stendahl not to get carried away with any plans or arrangements as we know from Janice that Ruth had already planned most things, and that he is not your most favorite minister," said Rusty as they all laughed.

"You know, guys, I had a funny thought this morning while I was lying in bed, imagining the funeral preparations and the funeral service. I imagined Reverend Barney, our friend from Sioux Falls, conducting the service and Stendahl tied up and gagged with duct tape in the church basement," Reuben said, laughing.

## Reuben's Journey Begins

As the men howled with laughter, it was immediately pierced by Synnova's reprimand.

"Reuben David Anderson, how dare you talk about a man of God that way at a time like this," scolded Synnova. And then she smiled and said, "If you are going to tie him up and duct tape his mouth, the least you could do is have him upstairs in his office and not down in the musty basement."

The men all laughed so hard at this that even Reuben guffawed at Synnova's rare moment of irreverent humor!

"What in the world are you guys laughing about this early in the morning?" came a voice from the great porch.

As the screen door opened, a six-foot-three man appeared in his Stillwater County Sheriff's shirt and greeted each man at the table with a huge hug of appreciation as they shared their sympathies with him.

"Thought I would come early, Dad, and see if I could help Willard with chores for the next few days, and anything else."

For the remainder of breakfast, Reuben told his friends and his son, David, what he had imagined for preparations, the visitation, the funeral service, the procession to the cemetery, the graveside service and the final grooming of the grave. They all sat and listened, riveted by the ideas and the possibilities of contributing their support to Reuben over the next four days. Synnova was so proud of her brother as she listened to his 'imaginings' and

## Reuben's Journey Begins

knew that he had carefully read and reread Ruth's letter expressing her wishes. She, too, had sat with Ruth and the kids as Ruth talked about her funeral. Synnova appreciated some of the creative tweaks Reuben had added to Ruth's wishes. She knew it would be a grand prairie funeral and celebration.

With breakfast finished and David off to see Willard, who was probably just finishing up milking, and Tovar offering to join him, Rusty and Bob returned to town, telling Reuben they were available whenever needed. Ted went with Reuben to Windy Marsh where Vince Thorson, the local undertaker and funeral director, would be preparing Ruth's body and casket for the visitation. When they arrived, they discovered that Ruth had already picked out a casket and Vince told Reuben the long story of how Ruth had called him almost a year ago, looked at the caskets and picked out a beautiful greenish copper lid with a walnut wood surround.

"She said the wood reminded her of the walnut furniture you and your dad made for your study from the large walnut trees you cut down in the horse pasture. She wanted to pay for it so you wouldn't be troubled with it, but I insisted on giving it to her free, Reuben. She did so much for me when my mom passed away at the nursing home. I was a basket case and Ruth helped me more than you will ever know. And both of you were so kind to give her a ride in your funeral carriage to

## Reuben's Journey Begins

the cemetery. And two years later, when my wife died of cancer, she was there once again for me, as were you. It is the least I can do to say thank you to one of the finest people I have ever known and to you as a dear friend."

Reuben stood there in sheer disbelief, almost embarrassed, but then Ted reminded him, "Reuben, it is so 'Ruth' to have done something like this."

"Janice brought in her clothes and the dress she had requested to wear," continued Vince. "It is the Western wear she wore during your 50$^{th}$ anniversary when you drove her around the county in your wedding carriage. She had mentioned to Janice that she wanted to have Boots tethered to the funeral carriage with her rhinestone cowgirl hat tied to the saddle horn of the rhinestone saddle. Here is the hat. I had it hand cleaned and brushed for you."

It was all suddenly too much again. Reuben broke down and Vince quickly got him a glass of water and asked if he was okay. Reuben nodded affirmatively and thanked Vince for everything he had done. He then told Vince about his plans for the funeral and Vince said he would bring Ruth out to the farm later that evening, so everything would be ready for the visitation beginning Friday morning.

"Reuben, if there is anything else I can do, please let me know," said Vince. "Janice typed up this biography that is a small twelve-page booklet

## Reuben's Journey Begins

and I'm having copies made up over at the Prairieville Times. Hans Shandler said they would be ready this evening about 8:00, and I'll pick them up and bring them out to the farm. Oh, and one last thing, The Ladies Aid president, Della Olson, called and asked if you would like her to take responsibility for putting up the altar vestments and preparing for the lunch after the funeral. They want to display Ruth's work that she so passionately helped with when serving on the Altar Guild."

"Vince," replied Reuben, "I'm so thankful for everything, and I must admit that it is all overwhelming and just starting to sink in that Ruth prepared so much, and I did so little. I'm not sure how to respond, except to say thank you for your kindness. And, please, let Della know that whatever she does will be fine. I suspect she and Ruth met about this, too."

There was a light chuckle from the three men. Reuben half-laughed as Vince shook his hand and then hugged in friendship and grief, acknowledging that one of Ruth's greatest gifts to the family, friends and her work as a nurse was to always plan ahead.

Lunch was on the table when Ted and Reuben returned to the farm. The house was filled with family and friends, everyone wanting to help. The grandchildren ran to hug Reuben as he entered the house and Synnova, Louise, Kathy and Janice were all directing the kids and some adults to the

## Reuben's Journey Begins

front porch to eat, and others to gather around the kitchen table which had now been increased fourfold with additional leaves inserted and twelve people gathered around.

Suddenly, there was a faint knock at the door and a voice, "May I come in, please?"

It was Reverend Stendahl.

"Please come in, Reverend Stendahl," said Synnova and Janice, as Synnova eyeballed Reuben with her, 'you'd better be nice to him or I'll …' look.

The room grew quiet as everyone in the room knew that Reuben was not the chairman of his fan club.

"Reuben, could I have a word with you in private?" asked the young minister in a voice that wondered why he was being excluded from the planning of the funeral and visiting with everyone.

"Of course, Pastor," said Reuben in a voice that definitely was about to speak his mind to this young man who seemed upset that he wasn't being put in charge of all the planning and conducting of the service. "Let's go into my study."

Once in the study, Reuben closed the huge, nine-foot carved oak doors with inlaid walnut designs of the universe displaying all the planets circling the sun. And below the inlay was the inscription in gold leaf lettering, "Through these doors explore the Universe and all God has created." It was a favorite expression of his father, Caleb.

## Reuben's Journey Begins

Reuben sat down behind his desk and invited the pastor to sit in the chair alongside and to the left of the huge desk. It was the first time Reverend Stendahl had been to Reuben's house, let alone a study fit for a president. He was obviously impressed and surprised by the study's beautiful woodwork and the library shelves that surrounded him, especially one of the walls filled mostly with books on theology and world religions, a collection begun by Reuben's grandfather in the 1800s, continued by his father and enhanced with rare book gifts from friends and other family members. His father, Caleb, had very much wanted to attend the seminary and become a minister but the duties of the farm and family preempted that dream.

"My wife has told me about your extraordinarily beautiful home and farm. I think we've visited most of the parishioners, generally being invited out after Sunday services. We haven't had the privilege of breaking bread with you yet in your home, Reuben," said Stendahl in a slightly airy, arrogant voice. "Wow, you are apparently a well-read man," continued the young pastor, surprise in his voice as he read a few titles, settling on one book in particular. "Emil Brunner's *Eternal Hope* was a favorite of mine in the seminary and I quoted him in my Master's thesis. Was there some particular aspect of his work that you liked, Reuben?" almost sounding as if he might catch Reuben off guard.

## Reuben's Journey Begins

"Yes, as a matter of fact, there was," replied Reuben. "I mostly enjoyed his metaphor about oxygen related to hope. I believe it went something like 'what oxygen is for the lungs, such is hope for the meaning of human life … as the fate of the human organism is dependent upon the supply of oxygen, so the fate of humanity is dependent upon the supply of hope.'"

Stendahl sat unexpectedly surprised by the very articulate and amazingly accurate quoting of a book that had not probably been read in some time, given the layer of dust on the shelf.

"We should have some theological discussions sometime, Reuben," said the young minister in a somewhat pompous voice, suggesting he could teach Reuben more about Brunner. "For now, I must express my concern regarding the manner in which you are seemingly trying to take over all the arrangements for Ruth's funeral. Reuben, I am the shepherd of the flock at Bethany Lutheran and as one of my sheep, I have a responsibility to tend to your needs. And one more thing, I heard you are planning a prairie funeral, whatever that is, with horses and carriages. I would prefer that you not bring all those horses around the church and use the old carriages which I hear occasionally break down. I fear things could break down, be disruptive to this sacred service, and get messy and smelly, let alone dangerous, if people were to slip on the feces. You know, we have modern vehicles that will work nicely," concluded Stendahl

## Reuben's Journey Begins

in a slightly cynical tone.

Reuben sat in sheer disbelief, wondering if he should throw the little brat of a pastor bodily out of the house or just slap the arrogant little bastard's face and let him walk out under his own power. He was momentarily speechless. And then the thought occurred to him that his sister Synnova would be on his case if he did either. Reuben looked away for a moment to gain his composure, took a deep breath and suddenly felt Ruth's presence and that she was chuckling about what was about to happen. Mustering up a little 'anger' to mask the humor he saw in the moment as he visualized Ruth, he turned and looked directly at Stendahl with a piercing stare.

"My dear young minister," said Reuben calmly, "that metaphor is old and inappropriate for the $20^{th}$ century. I am not a lamb or a sheep. I am not part of any metaphorical flock of yours. And you are not my shepherd. You, my dear friend, are a pain in my ass. You work for our congregation as an employee, so you take your arrogant messianic self-perception and stick it in your back pocket or any place close thereof. Your only role in the funeral will be to greet the good Reverend Barney Freiburg and to say the benediction. That is Ruth's directive. That is my command. Between the 'hello' and the 'goodbye,' you are to sit in the front pew without your vestments, next to your wonderful family, and participate like everyone else. You will not dishonor Ruth's desire to have

## Reuben's Journey Begins

her prairie funeral. If you want to challenge Ruth's and my wishes, I will be glad to call a meeting of the Executive Committee of the Church Council today, and we will see whose wishes they will accommodate. Now, if you don't have any more silly things to say or questions to ask, I will show you the back way out?"

The young minister sat there red-faced, upset and ready to explode. Four years of college at St. Olaf College in Northfield, Minnesota, and four years of seminary at Luther Theological Seminary in St. Paul had not prepared him for this moment. It was a true collision in the space-time continuum. Stendahl's mind was a mess.

"Reuben, I think you are being unreasonable and such talk is not becoming a Christian man," said the pastor in a nervous tone. "I didn't come here to upset you in your hour of grief. I came here to help relieve you of your pain and suffering with the loss of Ruth and to pray with you," his voice beginning to quiver as he saw the fire in Reuben's eyes grow as he glanced at another set of nine foot double french doors that led to the great porch.

"Pastor Stendahl," Reuben said sternly, "The pain I feel, as I succinctly said, is in my ass, and I will feel relieved and suffer no more from it as soon as you leave. You are welcome to leave by these doors, and please don't feel any obligation to tend any others in your flock here or at the funeral. I would rather that you don't stop to visit with any of

## Reuben's Journey Begins

the family, for now. I can't say that you are among our most favorite persons, save my sister, Synnova, who seems to justify your ineptness because of your youth and calling. Your title and call does not impress me. I find you arrogant, unfamiliar with the ways of the prairie farming community, narrow-minded, theologically shallow, far too conservative for my taste, and full of yourself. You might spend some time revisiting a number of the parables, and look at 'Christ the servant,' the diakonia Christus, and ponder embracing His teachings and lifestyle in your life and behavior. Please leave my home now, and I would prefer this visit be treated as a pastoral confidence ... in other words, I will not divulge our conversation to anyone and ask you the same. Man to man, we need to discuss our relationship down the road. For now, I need relief from my pain and suffering, best created as you take your leave. Is that acceptable to you?"

Stendahl sat stunned, not believing a member of his flock, let alone one of the most respected men in Prairieville, would talk to him this way. He was trembling and felt strangely weak as he stood up. And his stuttering speech pattern, which he had mastered years ago returned like it had never gone away as the stress of the moment threw him totally out of control.

"Well, I'm n-n-not sure. I-I-I need to think about this. Th-th- this could set a precedent, and I'm not sure it is prudent for the rest of the flock, excuse

## Reuben's Journey Begins

me, I-I-I mean, the congregation," stuttered and choked Stendahl.

"You decide and let me know with a call tomorrow morning. If not, I will call a special meeting of the Executive Committee of the Church Council. I'll await your call in the morning," responded Reuben in a very unusually demanding and stern voice.

"I'm n-n-not sure you have the authority to do that, Reuben," said Stendahl, growing more nervous by the moment.

"Oh, obviously you've forgotten about the essence of the Priesthood of All Believers that serves as the cornerstone of Lutheranism, my young minister," said Reuben with the fire growing in his eyes, and his heart racing. "I have about twenty books here that will help you out if you need to read them to be reminded."

Reuben was furious. He quietly stood up and pointed to the double doors that he wanted the Reverend to use in leaving. Socrates also stood up and uttered a very low-tone growl. The minister was trembling and, as he turned to leave, the back of his shirt was soaked with perspiration. He left quietly and Reuben, featuring a rare and somewhat sinister grin, began returning to the kitchen. Looking up, he said silently, 'Well sweetheart, that was kind of fun. What a little brat that kid is. I was probably a little rough on him, but my feelings about him have been building up for months. It's one of those Norwegian things, you

## Reuben's Journey Begins

know.' Socrates knew Reuben was mad and wondered if he should finish off the minister with a solid bite in his backside as Stendahl almost ran to his car.

"Sit, Socrates. You can have him for lunch another day," Reuben said, smiling, and in a tone that mentally set a future time to finish this conversation ... but not now. The two returned to the kitchen.

"Where's Pastor Stendahl, Reuben?" asked Synnova.

"Oh, he had to get back to the church to take care of some things regarding the funeral," replied Reuben. "And I suspect he still had some work to do on his sermon for Sunday."

"Well, that was nice of him to stop by and offer to help. I'm glad you spent some quality time visiting with him. I'll bet he really appreciated it, and that you are now getting to know him better on a personal basis. Maybe you two can become friends," mused Synnova as she continued washing dishes, knowing full well by Reuben's affect that he had probably been pretty tough the pastor. She continued to hand the washed dishes to Janice to dry.

Reuben, hoping Synnova hadn't figured it out, bit his tongue and, putting his hand on Ted's shoulder, suggested that they go for a walk out to the carriage barn and begin to plan what carriages would be used in the funeral procession. When they got to the barn, Ted knew something had

## Reuben's Journey Begins

really upset Reuben.

"Okay, pal, let's hear it," probed Ted. "I know you like a book and if I didn't know better, I'd say you just told the young minister off. Your neck always gets red when you are mad and it was purple when you came out of your meeting with Stendahl. I also heard him peel out of the drive way as if he were being chased by the devil himself."

"Yes, I did, however, I gave my word not to discuss it with anyone, if he did likewise," said Reuben. "I guess it is best left alone until he decides if he is going to cooperate tomorrow or not."

"Okay, Reuben," echoed Ted, smiling, "I'll not pry for now. I know that resolute look, and you have always been a good keeper of your word and secrets."

"Thanks, Ted," said Reuben with an appreciative sigh of relief, wanting to move on to plans for the funeral.

The afternoon was filled with the initial preparations of getting the carriages ready. Ted and Reuben were soon joined by Willard, David, Christopher and Catherine as they began wiping the dust from the outside and inside of the carriages. As the time passed and Reuben got Stendahl off his mind, there came a sense of anticipation and celebration in preparing for Monday's funeral.

As the evening drew near, Reuben went back

## Reuben's Journey Begins

to the house to see how things were progressing in the living room.  Rusty and Bob had returned to help Janice prepare the living room for receiving the casket around 8:00 p.m.  She and Vince had talked about the arrangements and he'd said he would bring a special guest book for visitors to sign on Friday, Saturday and Sunday.  As he walked into the living room and saw that it was bare of furniture, except for two wing chairs next to the fireplace, the reality of the visitation and funeral hit him hard and he sat down quickly in one of the chairs.

"Are you okay, Daddy?" asked Janice.

"I'm fine," said Reuben with a bit of resignation in his voice, "It's just that the reality of the situation hit me all of a sudden and I wasn't expecting that to happen quite yet.  This room has always been so full of life and a special gathering place for our family for years, and now it is empty, save these two chairs.  I guess it feels cold like death in here, and it has always felt warm and comfortable, and been a special place of retreat."

"I know just how you feel," said Rusty in a consoling voice.  "Let's light a fire in the fireplace and warm it up just a bit.  When my wife died, we had our visitation at our home because the funeral home was being remodeled.  I was used to the television being on, or people sitting around talking, and I always went to that room to find company or to spend time with Edith.  Moving out the furniture somehow became symbolic of her

## Reuben's Journey Begins

dying. It bothered me for days after the funeral, too, even when the furniture was put back."

Bob and Rusty finished helping Janice with a few tasks and bade everyone goodbye. Synnova fixed a plate of sandwiches, salads and desserts and excused herself to return to Windy Marsh to cook dinner for Glenn Orville. Janice suggested that all the kids go over to Willard's house where Louise was making macaroni and cheese for the kids' dinner and had rented some movies for them to watch. She suggested to her dad that he have the evening alone with Ruth. She would stay to help set things up when Vince arrived.

8:00 p.m. Reuben sat on the porch, nervous and unsure of the next hour. As Vince pulled into the long driveway with the hearse, two cars followed him. It was Ted, Tovar, Bob, Rusty, David and Willard; the pallbearers. With the emotional impact of Ruth returning home, he started to cry, and Janice comforted him as the vehicles drove up close to the front porch and parked on the lawn.

"Dad, let's go in the kitchen and let the men bring Mom up the steps and arrange the casket and flowers in the living room," said Janice in an encouraging voice.

Reuben agreed and went into the kitchen where he, Socrates and Janice sat quietly by the table and were quietly joined by Cougar and Mitsy. Janice poured a glass of wine for both of them and they sat, quietly sipping their wine, as they waited

# Reuben's Journey Begins

for everyone to set things up in the living room. About twenty minutes later, Vince and Ted came out to the kitchen and said that everything was ready.

"Reuben, I think it would be good for Ted to spend the night with you and be here if you need anything," suggested Vince in a kind voice. "I've seen a lot of different reactions to spouses seeing their loved one in a casket for the first time, over the years, especially in their homes, and it can be a very difficult moment. As a friend, it's only caring advice I give you."

"I think that is great advice," echoed Janice. "Daddy, Ted's been your best friend all your life and I would feel better, too, if you would agree."

"Of course I'll agree," smiled Reuben, "and I want to thank all of you for bringing my sweetheart home this one last time. It will be good to be with her, and knowing Ted is nearby is a good thing," responded Reuben in an appreciative voice.

Everyone left and Ted excused himself, saying he would be out on the porch if Reuben needed him. Taking a deep breath, Reuben walked into the living room and there was Ruth, the casket open and surrounded by beautiful flowers. The fire in the fireplace lit Ruth's face with a warm and soft light. Shadows made by the bouquets of flowers danced around the room. Reuben's eyes filled with tears and the room blurred as he stood there, motionless, wanting to run and hug her. But he knew from working with other deceased persons,

## Reuben's Journey Begins

especially those who were laid in the funeral coach without a casket, that she would be cold and stiff. He walked quietly over to the casket, kissed her cheek which had been warmed by the fire, knelt on the railing footstool that had been placed in front it, and prayed. He returned to one of the two wing chairs across the living room, stared at the fire with glancing looks to Ruth, and passed through history. At midnight, Ted gently touched his shoulder and suggested he get some sleep.

That night, Reuben didn't dream. He lay in bed, awake, reliving parts of their life together for a couple of hours, then got up, made two root beer floats and drank them both. Returning to the living room with only the fading embers popping in the fireplace, he stoked the fire with a large supply of firewood, returned to the chair he had been sitting in earlier, and dozed off.

Friday morning arrived with the chorus of birds and Stanley announcing the dawn of this special day. Socrates lay next to him and was wide awake; staring up at Reuben as if he had been standing guard to make sure he was okay. The screen door and kitchen door both creaked open about 6:30 a.m. and Synnova eventually entered the living room to find Reuben staring at the remaining embers from the evening's fire. Socrates sat up next to the chair in which Reuben had spent the night, stretched and nuzzled his master.

"Good morning, Brother," said Synnova in a soft

# Reuben's Journey Begins

voice, breaking Reuben's trance. "She looks beautiful. How about a cup of coffee and let's spend a little time in the kitchen. You might appreciate a small break before visitation starts at four o'clock this afternoon. In fact, why don't you go in your bedroom and take a short nap. There's really nothing important you have to take care of this morning. We have more people volunteering than I can manage."

"Maybe you're right, Sis," replied Reuben, gladly complying with her suggestion. He was tired. As he went into the bedroom to lie down, a shock raced through his body. 'Stendahl, I wonder what he has decided.' Picking up the phone, he called the young minister.

"Stendahls," answered Sarah.

"Is your father there?" asked Reuben politely.

"Yes, one moment please. May I tell him who is calling? He is praying in his study," replied Sarah.

"It's Reuben Anderson, Sarah," said Reuben, glad to talk with a kind and civil Stendahl. "How are you, Sarah?"

"I'm fine, Mr. Anderson. Mom says we can come out to your farm again. Could I ride one of the horses someday?" asked Sarah.

"Sarah, you can ride a horse any time you want. Next time your mom comes out to paint, you and I will go for a ride along Red Rock Creek," responded Reuben.

"Sarah, who are you talking to?" came a short and curt voice in the background as Reverend

~ 140 ~

## Reuben's Journey Begins

Stendahl opened his study door and walked into the kitchen.

"It's Mr. Anderson, Daddy, where Mom and I go to paint pictures," said Sarah nervously, sure she had just done something wrong. "Mr. Anderson said I could ride his horse sometime."

"There will be no horse riding unless I say it is okay. Now go downstairs to your playroom and busy yourself, Child," scolded Stendahl.

"Good morning, Reuben, this is Reverend Stendahl," answered the pastor.

Having heard the exchange between Stendahl and his daughter, Reuben's blood began to boil again, wondering how a man could be so rude to such a beautiful child.

"Stendahl," said Reuben in a firm and unrelenting voice, "What have you decided?"

"I have prayed about the situation for hours, Reuben, and this one time I will make an exception to what I think is an inappropriate protocol for such a situation. I feel you have undermined my authority and calling to this congregation. Having said that, I have only discussed this with my wife and apparently she feels your wishes should be honored. I must admit that I'm also troubled by my wife's position on this, too. She tends to be more liberal regarding the theology, proper customs and protocols of the Lutheran Church. Perhaps we can meet sometime later, after things have settled down for you, and discuss my views, which I believe are very much more scripture-based and

## Reuben's Journey Begins

quite different from yours."

Reuben had a second wind now and was tempted to launch into another discussion, but quickly remembered that Ruth was in the other room and felt somehow it would be irreverent to discuss the matter any further. Although he somehow thought that if Ruth were looking down on this episode, she would also find it quite entertaining, seeing her gentle prairie prince actually showing some high octane emotion regarding the minister.

"Thank you, Stendahl," Reuben replied. "I appreciate knowing your decision and it will help us get through the next few days with less stress. You have helped relieve my pain and stress."

There was a moment of silence on the telephone and then, "God bless you, Reuben, and I will look forward to hosting Reverend Freiburg as you requested. Goodbye for now and, if there is anything further I can do for you, please let me know. Please extend my blessings to your family."

As Reuben hung up the phone, he had a weak moment and thought maybe he had been too rough on the young minister. And then he remembered how arrogant Stendahl had been during his visit yesterday, and the recent rather rude exchange with his daughter, and immediately dismissed the thought. For now, there was peace at Bethany Lutheran. He would plot his next move with the pastor in the weeks ahead. Reuben wondered about the oddity of Stendahl and Helen

## Reuben's Journey Begins

getting married and then their beautiful little girl who seemed to always be under the minister's hammer of discipline. Reuben lie down on his bed and fell fast asleep.

He rode his horse, Silver Foot, along Red Rock Creek to the top of Lover's Lane where he surprised a couple of young lovers sitting in their car kissing, totally unaware of the world around them.

Synnova went in to wake Reuben around noon and invited him out to the kitchen where Janice, Louise and Bob's wife, Gert, were preparing the food and desserts that Reuben had ordered from the bakery for those coming to visit. As he walked from the bedroom and entered the hallway, he stopped first in the living room to say hello to Donny Johnson, who was paying his respects to Ruth. Janice was talking with him at the side of the casket.

"Reuben," said Donny in a soft and sad voice, "We'll miss her." The two stood at the side of the casket with arms on each other's shoulders. "I remember when I had my car accident when I was racing hobby stock and was hospitalized off and on for months. Ruth was always there looking after my broken bones. She was the one person who came every day, sometimes several times a day, to check on me, whether working her shift or just stopping by on her time off. She was an incredible neighbor and friend, Reuben. She will continue to be the angel in heaven that she was on earth."

## Reuben's Journey Begins

Reuben visited for a while with Donny and Janice and then went into his study to fetch a pipe and walked out on the porch to smoke for a while. He was soon joined by David, Willard and Ted, who had just finished repairing one of the wheel hubs on the wedding carriage that had been damaged earlier in the summer during Arlyce Johnson's wedding. Willard had driven the carriage with Dancer, who was spooked by a rabbit and swerved, accidentally hitting a deep rut on the side of the lane as he veered too far off the path, damaging the inner workings of the wheel hub.

"Reuben, why don't you come with us out to the carriage barn and let's look them all over to make sure everything has been done to your satisfaction, ready for Monday," suggested Ted. "We've repaired the double seat wedding carriage, replaced the tongue on the livery stable carriage and fixed the hinges on the right-hand back door of the funeral coach."

"Sounds like a good idea," replied Reuben. "I've been meaning to get to those things lately, but with Ruth and all, I just didn't get them fixed. Thank you, guys, for helping."

With that said, the group of men walked out to the carriage barn and got lost in the world of stories surrounding the carriages. The time passed quickly as Reuben reminisced, and Willard and David told about their first times driving the carriages.

About 3:00, Janice came out to the carriage

## Reuben's Journey Begins

barn and suggested that everyone get ready for the visitation. Reuben went in and put on his suit with a new bow tie that Synnova had made for him last Christmas. He had a large collection of bow ties, some given to him by his dad, others store bought, but most had been made by his sister.

All dressed up in his blue pin-striped suit and shoes polished, he was ready to begin a ritual he had attended a thousand times before, but not for a member of his immediate family. It felt strange that in the next room lay his wife of 52 years, where he would spend the next four hours greeting family and friends.

Soon Ted, David and Kathy, Willard and Louise, Synnova and Glenn Orville, Terry and Janice, along with all the grandchildren, gathered in the kitchen with a group of ladies from Bethany Lutheran's Martha Circle, who would serve the visitors.

"I want to thank all of you for coming out today, to help. You have all been good friends and I know the kids here appreciate your help. Please make yourselves to home. You ladies from the Martha Circle probably know the house and farm better than I do. Why, with the Fall Festival coming up again in November, you'll have done double duty this year."

With that said, Reuben greeted each one of the nine ladies from the Martha Circle and then responded to a call from Ted out on the porch.

"Reuben, come out here, you're not going to

## Reuben's Journey Begins

believe this," called Ted. "Look at the cars turning into the driveway. There must be 25 cars behind Rusty Olson's pickup."

As Reuben stood there and watched the parade of vehicles coming up the long driveway, he instinctively knew what Rusty had done. He was sure that Rusty had invited some of their closest friends to gather at the Town Café, have coffee and then go together out to the farm. Christopher and Catherine had run out to greet the first cars and directed them to begin parking on the spacious lawn between the house and the barn. Both of the children had golf carts they used from time to time to bring camping supplies out to the Campsite Grove when special groups were using it. As people began parking almost eighty yards away from the house, they offered them rides up to the great porch where family members greeted them and invited them in with instructions to stop for coffee and dessert after visiting with Reuben.

After Rusty, the first person to arrive and enter the living room was six-foot, six-inch Chris Hollendorf, the former Executive Director of The Cottonwoods who now served as a Regional Director of Operations in Richmond, Virginia for another group of senior living communities.

"Reuben," said Chris, embracing Reuben with a big bear hug, "I was so sorry to hear about Ruth. Janice and Terry called me Friday and I caught a plane from Reagan International Saturday. I wanted to come to her funeral and reconnect with

## Reuben's Journey Begins

you. Our family will always be beholden to you and Ruth for the manner in which she cared for our daughter when she was in the car accident. Ruth watched over her day and night, even during her time off work, and weekends. A better friend, no one could have." As others continued to enter and greet Reuben, this type of story seemed to repeat itself consistently with each person he spoke with.

As Reuben and Chris visited, a steady stream of visitors came to the house and Synnova, Glenn Orville, and Ted continued to greet and direct them. The constant stream of cars continued up until 8:00 that evening. Christopher and Catherine remained busy directing cars and giving rides on the golf carts up to the house. David, Jan and Willard also remained by the fireplace, greeting everyone and receiving their sympathies, condolences and well-wishes. Over two hundred people visited on Friday evening.

Exhausted, everyone having gone home and Ted having turned in for the evening, Reuben kissed Ruth on the cheek and made his root beer float, finished it, dropped into one of the living room chairs, fell fast asleep, and planted corn and beans in the north forty.

Saturday came and went in the blink of an eye. Reuben left the house early and walked down to the barn to visit with David, Ted and Willard who were getting the dairy barn ready for milking. As he walked over to the Dutch door looking out to the barnyard and the pasture beyond, Barney flew in right over Reuben's head and lit on his favorite rafter.

Reuben smiled, saying, "Well, I'll bet you've been feeding those chicks of yours, Young Man."

The regal barn owl looked at him as if to say, 'I have, Sir, and now I must rest for the day.'

Reuben visited with the guys for a short while and then told them that Terry had asked him to come in to The Cottonwoods where some of the residents who couldn't travel out to the farm wanted to pay their respects to Reuben. Reuben had agreed, and planned to go in around 8:30 a.m. for a couple of hours.

The visitation at the farm began at 11:00 and would go until 4:00 p.m.

Throughout the visitation, the football-sized yard between the barn and house was once again a sea of cars of well-wishers coming out to pay their last respects. On the great porch that surrounded the house, the Altar Guild, with the help of the Martha Circle from Bethany Lutheran, had set up chairs and tables and served coffee, sandwiches and desserts throughout the day. Soon, the visitation was over and all was quiet again.

As the table was being set for supper, Synnova wondered to herself why only Helen and Sarah Stendahl had come to the visitation, and not Pastor Stendahl. She sensed things had not gone well between the men and it bothered her somewhat.

"Reuben, was Pastor Stendahl with Helen and

## Reuben's Journey Begins

Sarah today?" came an inquisitive tone of voice from Synnova.

"Ahhh, gosh, I don't remember seeing him," replied Reuben in a slightly sheepish voice. "I suppose he was busy making sure all the arrangements are being made at the church." Anxious to change the subject, Reuben quickly asked, "By the way, did Mildred and Grace find you today?"

"Yes, they are planning to come to the family service tomorrow night and wondered if they could bring any dessert for afterwards," replied Synnova, now distracted. "I told them not to worry as we have enough desserts around here to last us for weeks. They asked if they could help with the service with a reading or something. I told them to talk to you sometime before the service."

The kitchen was full with Reuben's children's families, Glenn Orville and Synnova, and Ted. The evening supper was a feast. Reuben was exhausted and excused himself to go into the living room and be with Ruth for a time. Everyone left him alone until the silence was broken by Synnova and Glenn Orville as they went in to wish him good evening before returning to Windy Marsh.

Sunday, too, came and went quickly with visitation from 1:00 to 3:00 p.m. The day had begun with a prayer service in the kitchen at the farm. Reuben wanted to spend the day at the farm and not go in to church as he still had no desire to encounter the minister. Another 80 people

## Reuben's Journey Begins

attended the afternoon visitation and he continued to hear stories of appreciation honoring Ruth's work as a nurse and an extraordinary community volunteer.

About 3:45, as the last car turned out of the driveway onto the highway leading back to Prairieville, Reuben had a spontaneous idea. All day, he had been thinking about the campfire pit at Campsite Grove and the comments in Ruth's letter. Campsite Grove was where he had proposed to Ruth, and what a special place that had become for them over the years. On every anniversary, they would hitch up the small wedding carriage to one of the horses and go out there to have a glass of wine and reminisce. Campsite Grove had always provided the perfect 'getaway' place for them. 'Why not have the family service out there, instead of the living room?' he thought to himself.

He quickly shared the idea with Janice and she loved it. "I'll call Pastor Freiburg, Daddy ... he and Beatrice are staying at Donny's," said Janice with a sense of excitement and adventure. "Why don't you get Duke, Duchess and Boots ready?"

Reuben turned to Janice with a surprised look on his face, asking, "How did you know that was what I was thinking, that is, to take Mom with us?"

Janice smiled, turning back to him as she walked into the study to call Pastor Freiburg, "Daddy, how many years have I been around you?"

## Reuben's Journey Begins

Reuben smiled in amazement and felt an enormous sense of pride that his daughter had figured out in a split second what he was thinking of doing for the family service at 7:00. He would take Ruth in the funeral coach, Boots tethered to the coach, and build a bonfire in the pit he had rebuilt several days before he proposed to her 53 years earlier. There they would hold the family service this Sunday evening.

About 5:00, Reuben brought the hand-cranked ice cream maker, ice, cream, sugar, salt and vanilla flavoring out to the great porch where Christopher, Catherine, Mary, Megan and several other young children were ready to begin making the ice cream.

It was about 6:15 when Reuben's sisters and their families began to arrive – Ruth's sisters Grace, Mildred and Martha and their families – and a few close friends. Christopher and Catherine were busy telling everyone the plans for the family service while David, Willard and Ted were busy getting the funeral coach and the Belgian team parked outside the house where the pallbearers were ready to bring Ruth out to the coach for the ride to Campsite Grove.

All in all, there were about forty-five people who had gathered for the family service. As the pallbearers brought the casket out of the house onto the great porch and down the five stair steps, Reuben greeted them as he opened the double glass doors at the rear of the funeral coach. Two

## Reuben's Journey Begins

by two, the pallbearers peeled back to the rear as they carefully slid the casket into the coach. Reuben then tied Ruth's hat to the saddle horn on Boots' saddle and mounted the carriage, along with Socrates, to drive out to Campsite Grove. Behind him came the families and friends in their automobiles and pickup trucks.

The sun was beginning to drop lower in the western sky on this September evening, illuminating the fall colors. As he came nearer to Campsite Grove, driving along Red Rock Creek, the aroma of the campfire built with birch, hickory and oak logs rode along on the evening breeze. Ted had gone out ahead of everyone thirty minutes earlier and started the fire, and the fire danced once again like the Russian ballet dancer.

As they arrived, Reuben parked the funeral coach upwind from the fire, knowing that he didn't want to get the glass sides dirty before tomorrow's funeral. The log benches which he and his father had built some 25 years earlier would serve as great seats for everyone, and the altar area that had been built out of three large flat boulders would serve as the resting place for the casket during the service.

As Christopher and Catherine directed everyone to park along a fence line just west of the campfire to help avoid any accidents, the pallbearers placed the casket on the three boulders. Vince then placed the pall, the quilt Synnova had made for Reuben, over the closed

## Reuben's Journey Begins

casket. Reverend Freiburgh gathered his notes for the service. His wife, Beatrice readied her guitar, flanked by Synnova and Annette Smith, who would lead in the singing. David, Jan and Willard compared their notes for comments they would make. Ruth's sister, Grace, brought Ruth's Bible in which she had written a letter for her to read at the family service. All in all, for being a last minute change in place, the setting looked as if things had been planned for weeks. Vince then opened the casket and the service began.

As Reuben looked around, he thought, 'How perfect this moment seems.' The weather was perfect and the campfire flames danced their ballet. The service went exactly as it was planned by Ruth, Reuben and their family. The centerpiece of the family service was a time of reflection with Reuben telling them that Ruth wanted them to talk about the dreams they were still imagining in their lives, and also reminded them about volunteering and Ruth's request that they talk about that, too. For the next hour, many members of the family shared dreams and stories of volunteering, as Ruth's granddaughters listened closely, hugging their dolls which were wrapped in the new blankets made by their grandmother.

The service ended as Reuben shyly prayed The Funny Little Prayer.

Back on the great porch, they all enjoyed the homemade ice cream, pie and cake. In the glow of the yard light, the grandsons played catch with

# Reuben's Journey Begins

their new baseballs which had been signed by Ruth.

At about 10:00 p.m., everyone left for home feeling a special sense of joy that they shared with Reuben and Ruth.

And Monday, too, was just as Reuben and Ruth had imagined: the grand prairie funeral with the carriages, the service, the caravan to the cemetery with the Rough Riders mounted on over 35 horses, the funeral coach driven by Reuben, flags gracing the route to the cemetery, Socrates at his side and Boots tethered just as Ruth wished.

The prairie received its daughter.

As everyone went their own way that evening, Janice decided to spend the night with her dad. As they sat at the kitchen table putting the final pieces of the Split Rock Lighthouse puzzle in their places, they enjoyed two magnificent root beer floats. Just as they were about to clean up the dishes, there was a knock at the door. It was Catherine with a small painting of a horse. "Hi Grandpa, I made a painting of Boots with Grandma's saddle and her hat. I thought you would like this for your den in the horse barn." It was almost too much for Reuben to take in and one of those rare times he was simply lost for words as he hugged her and tears wet their cheeks.

"I will proudly hang this in my den, Sweetheart," said Reuben with soulful deep breath.

Bidding Catherine good night, the puzzle complete, Reuben got out his gluing kit so that he could glue it, frame it and hang it.

And that night, he and Ruth drove along the North Shore of Lake Superior and watched a storm walk across the great lake. Later in the dream, Ruth appeared in the waves, the wind and the spray of water as she smiled at him and ascended into the heavens.

*Catherine's Painting of Boots*

# Chapter Five

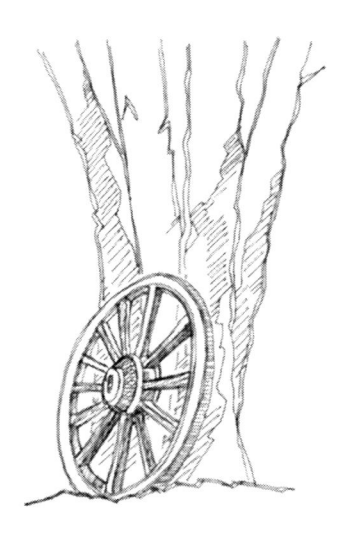

## The Thanksgiving Club

## September, October and November, 1990

On the Tuesday following Ruth's funeral, Reuben cleaned and prepared to cover the two wedding carriages and the funeral coach. It was something he and Ruth had done often together during the years of their marriage. Reuben would wipe down the exterior, clean the wheels, bridles and dress harnesses, while Ruth would take special care to clean the interior glass sidewalls and polish the brass casket slides, rails and lamps.

On this day, he patiently and methodically cleaned the coach and covered it until the next

## Reuben's Journey Begins

funeral for which he and his horses would once again bring the casket from one of Prairieville's, or another nearby town's churches, to a chosen cemetery. Reuben worked closely with several of the area funeral homes, never soliciting business but always willing to rig up the horses and drive the carriage for those who requested this prairie ritual. There was not a set fee; just a request for a donation which went into Reuben's fund for the Muscular Dystrophy Association and Jerry's kids.

As he finished covering the coach, he looked around at his prized collection of wagons, sleighs, two stagecoaches and a variety of carriages. For Reuben, it was using them that gave him pleasure and added a special dimension to an event, as their presence recalled a past now generally left to the journals of history. The two wedding carriages were in constant demand and he loved weddings and wedding anniversaries! He would put on his coachman dress and top hat and carry the bride and groom from the wedding to their reception. If the reception was at the church, he would often take them for a twenty minute carriage ride while wedding-goers gathered for their arrival at the reception.

His horse-drawn Pharmacy & Produce Wagon, used by his father's best friend, George Graham, had delivered medicines, eggs, milk, butter and other produce throughout Prairieville from 1880 through 1925. It sat in George's son's garage for years and in 1960, Reuben traded some hay, a

## Reuben's Journey Begins

side of beef and an old pickup truck for the Pharmacy & Produce Wagon. It was painted green with large white lettering. Its brass-covered wheel hubs and red leather 'dog seat' were often topics of great stories. All in all, he had 24 carriages and sleighs that filled the carriage barn.

Reuben shut off the lights and closed the door of the carriage barn and walked over to see the horses and spend some time in his den. He loved his den in the horse barn, for it was his sanctuary, and in it he explored the world, people, farming and all sorts of wonderful subjects relating to his horses and carriage collection. The walls were covered with photos of people in his carriages and sleighs, all with handwritten good wishes to him and Ruth. On one wall were the drawings of generators and electrical systems created by his father, Caleb. On another wall there were trophies he and his dad had won in draft horse competitions and carriage parades throughout the Midwest.

As he looked at the photos today, it was different. He could no longer recall a memory and use it as a topic of conversation with Ruth. Or, could he? He had often taken a photo from this prized collection along to visit her in the hospital or the nursing home and they would recall the memory, providing them with hours of reminiscing. He rehung two of the last photos that he had brought on a visit just two months earlier; one, a photo of a wedding couple and the other, a photo from last year's Fall Festival.

## Reuben's Journey Begins

    Tears welled up in his eyes as he recalled their last conversation about Annette & Chuck Smith's wedding, and how they so loved a one-hour ride down Lover's Lane and along Red Rock Creek. Ruth adored these two young people who were very active volunteers at The Cottonwoods.  On their wedding day, Ruth had ridden Dancer in an effort to help him become familiar with the route so that when his day came to pull a carriage, he would be familiar with the environment.

    The weeks following the funeral were quiet for Reuben as he withdrew for a while from his schedule of visiting folks at The Cottonwoods.

    September leaves began to change from their summer greens to their October palette of rich browns, reds, yellows and oranges.  The maple trees in his grove just west of the house, where he harvested maple syrup in the spring, were already turning crimson red and bright yellow.  As the October winds began to dry the field corn and ready it for harvest, Reuben and Willard began to prepare the corn picker, corncribs, tractors and end cuts around the fields.  Cutting silage was the first of the late summer harvesting, and soybeans and corn followed shortly thereafter.  By the fourth week in October this year, the corn was almost ready to pick and the yields were looking great.  The next three weeks found Willard, Christopher, Reuben and a couple of hired hands picking corn, chopping the remaining corn stocks and plowing the fields.  The harvest season was now complete,

## Reuben's Journey Begins

just in time for the countryside to receive its first snow.

Saturday, November 17$^{th}$ was a cold, snowy and blustery day, bringing the first snow of the season, and a substantial snowfall at that. On this day, Reuben just wanted to read and be alone. He added some dry cobs and kindling to the silver and black metal wood stove in his den. As the room was warming up, he brewed the strong coffee that he always enjoyed while reading. He reached for one of his favorite pipes and a book he had brought out to his den, and began to reread a chapter in Sanaya Roman's book, *Spiritual Growth*, that had special meaning for him. He read:

*"There is a higher purpose to your life, a special contribution you came to make. Part of your reason for coming to earth is to evolve yourself as well as to serve humanity in some way. We will call the process of evolving yourself your 'life purpose,' and the service you came to offer humanity your 'life's work.' They are intertwined, because as you serve others you will naturally evolve yourself. As you evolve and radiate more light, you automatically serve others. Everything you do to evolve yourself and carry out your life's work is an act of aligning with the Higher Will and your Higher Self.*

*You have a special role to play, something that you are uniquely fitted for. Your life's work will*

## Reuben's Journey Begins

*take on various forms at different times. The form may change from month to month and year to year, so keep in touch with your purpose and vision as it expands and grows. You can discover your life's work through examining the skills you love to use, the things you love to do, and the areas you are naturally drawn to. Whatever you love to do will also serve others in some way, for it is the nature of the universe that when you use your highest skills you automatically contribute to others.*

*Your dreams about your ideal life are showing you your potential and higher path. Don't discard your dreams and fantasies as merely wishful thinking. Honor them as messages from the deepest part of your being about your life's work and what you came here to do."* [1]

He got up and poured another cup of coffee and sat down in his easy chair, an overstuffed brown velveteen chair his father had given him for his study in the house, but which, Reuben had moved it out to his den in the horse barn. While the velveteen fabric was threadbare in areas, it was remarkably comfortable.

This passage from Sanaya Roman's book resonated so favorably with him. Since their marriage when he was twenty years old, Reuben had always thought about his purpose in life and his life's work as being a provider for his family and a caretaker of the earth in his farming. Yet, there

## Reuben's Journey Begins

was always something inside of him that seemed to push him to see a greater purpose in his life's work, by serving others. It made him uncomfortable that he couldn't really put his finger on defining it as specifically as he would like.

He often felt the carriage, sleigh and wagon rides were a form of community service. And sometimes, when special groups couldn't afford the fees, he did them for free. And the little volunteer things he did; he just saw that as being like his dad, lending a helping hand when and wherever needed. He intuited that there was more here. But what? How could he put his finger on it?

Reuben took his pen and underlined the paragraph that had him thinking.

*<u>You have a special role to play, something that you are uniquely fitted for. Your life's work will take on various forms at different times. The form may change from month to month and year to year, so keep in touch with your purpose and vision as it expands and grows. You can discover your life's work through examining the skills you love to use, the things you love to do, and the areas you are naturally drawn to. Whatever you love to do will also serve others in some way, for it is the nature of the universe that when you use your highest skills you automatically contribute to others.</u>* [2]

He focused in on the sentence, *"You can discover your life's work through examining the*

## Reuben's Journey Begins

*skills you love to use, the things you love to do, and the areas you are naturally drawn to."* He thought, 'I'm 72 years old. I'm still a farmer, but I am slowing down. And how much longer can I keep up with the horses, carriage, wagon and sleigh rides? I have the knowledge and skills in these areas, but my body's strength and agility is starting to wane. Dad kept going well into his nineties … Can I? And somehow, having just lost Ruth, my energy level for doing chores feels a little different. So, what am I naturally drawn to?'

He felt a restlessness he had never felt before. He felt that a change, a significant change, was about to take place in his life. Was he about to die or do something significantly new? His spirit and mind were restless.

Reuben got up to put more wood in the stove and stoked the fire. He freshened up his coffee and sat back down to ponder the things he loved doing and areas that he felt drawn to. He thought, 'I love to read. I love to spend time with family and friends. I love visiting with people at The Cottonwoods and around Prairieville who can't get out as often. I guess I'm especially drawn to them, and Ruth talked about them in her letter; the individuals in their eighties and nineties. I know it was important to her to spend time with them. Was that a message from her and The Universe? Is my life's work evolving in that direction? I love giving sleigh, carriage and wagon rides but hitching up the horses is getting a little harder. As a hobby, I'm drawn to maintaining my carriage barn collection. I like having people out to the farm, participating in celebrations around the region and working on projects with various community groups. I always feel a deep sense of satisfaction and joy when we complete a project and celebrate its accomplishment. But I feel like I need to do more. Is there something with more meaning, like Ruth, who cared for babies, the sick and the elderly who are shut-ins? She made a difference for many people every day.'

He reached over to the bookshelf next to his chair and pulled down a copy of a book written by Father Henri Nouwen. He had remembered a beautifully written section that used the wooden-spoked wagon wheel as a metaphor. Being the collector of many of these wheels, it held special meaning for him. He read from *Aging: The Fulfillment of Life* by Henri J. M. Nouwen & Walter J. Gaffney:

*"This is a book about aging. It is a book for all of us, since we all age and so fulfill the cycle of our lives. This is what the large wagon wheel reclining against the old birch in the white snow teaches us by its simple beauty. No one of its spokes is more important than the others, but together they make the circle full and reveal the hub as the core of its strength. The more we look at it, the more we come to realize that we have only one life cycle to live, and that living it is the source of our greatest*

## Reuben's Journey Begins

*joy.*

*The restful accomplishment of the old wheel tells us the story of life. Entering into the world we are what we are given, and for many years thereafter parents and grandparents, brothers and sisters, friends and lovers keep giving to us -- some more, some less, some hesitantly, some generously. When we can finally stand on our own feet, speak our own words, and express our own unique self in work and love, we realize how much is given to us. But while reaching the height of our cycle, and saying with a great sense of confidence, "I really am," we sense that to fulfill our life we now are called to become parents and grandparents, brothers and sisters, teachers, friends, and lovers ourselves, and to give to others, so that, when we leave this world, we can be what we have given.*

*The wagon wheel reminds us that the pains of growing old are worthwhile. The wheel turns from ground to ground, but not without moving forward. Although we have only one life cycle to live, although it is only a small part of human history which we will cover, to do this gracefully and carefully is our greatest vocation. Indeed we go from dust to dust, we move up to go down, we grow to die, but the first dust does not have to be the same as the second, the going down can become the moving on, and death can be made into our final gift.*

*Aging is the turning of the wheel, the gradual fulfillment of the life cycle in which receiving matures in giving and living makes dying worthwhile. Aging does not need to be hidden or denied, but can be understood, affirmed, and experienced as a process of growth by which the mystery of life is slowly revealed to us.*

*It is this sense of hope that we want to strengthen. When aging can be experienced as a growing by giving, not only of mind and heart, but of life itself, then it can become a movement towards the hour when we can say with the author of the Second Letter to Timothy: As for me, my life is already being poured away as a libation, and the time has come for me to be gone. I have fought the good fight to the end. I have run the race to the finish; I have kept the faith. (2 Timothy 4:6-7)*

*But still -- without the presence of old people we might forget that we are aging. The elderly are our prophets, they remind us that what we see so clearly in them is a process in which we all share. Therefore, words about aging may quite well start with words about the elderly. Their lives are full of warnings but also of hopes.*

*Much has been written about the elderly, about their physical, mental, spiritual problems, about their need for a good house, good work, and a good friend. Much has been said about the sad situation in which many old people find themselves, and much has been done to try to change this. There is, however, one real danger with this emphasis on the sufferings of the elderly. We might start thinking that becoming old is the same as becoming a problem, that aging is a sad human fate that nobody can escape and should be avoided at all cost, that growing towards the end of the life cycle is a morbid reality that should only be acknowledged when the signs can no longer be denied. Then all our concerns for the elderly become like alms giving with a guilty conscience, like friendly gestures to the prisoners of our war against aging.*

*It is not difficult to see that for many people in our world, becoming old is filled with fear and pain. Millions of the elderly are left alone, and the end of their cycle becomes a source of bitterness and despair. There are many reasons for this situation, and we will try to examine them carefully. But underneath all the explanations we can offer, there is the temptation to make aging into the problem of the elderly and to deny our basic human solidarity in this most human process.*

*Maybe we have been trying hard to silence the voices of those who remind us of our own destiny and have become our sharpest critics by their very presence. Thus our first and most important task is to help the elderly become our teachers again and to restore the broken connections among the generations.*

*We want to speak, therefore, first of all, about the elderly as our teachers, as the ones who tell us about the dangers as well as the possibilities in becoming old. They will be able to show us that aging is not only a way to darkness but also a way to light. Secondly, we want to speak about aging and care in order to show not just how we can take care of elderly people, but more, how we can allow the elderly to cure us of our separatist tendencies and bring us into a closer and more intimate contact with our own aging.*

*We believe that aging is the most common human experience which overarches the human community as a rainbow of promises. It is an experience so profoundly human that it breaks through the artificial boundaries between childhood and adulthood, and between adulthood and old age. It is so filled with promises that it can lead us to discover more and more of life's treasures. We believe that aging is not a reason for despair but a basis for hope that those who are old, as well as those who care, will find each other in the common experience of aging, out of which healing and new life can come forth."* [3]

This thought tied closely to the Emil Bruner quote he had shared with Reverend Stendahl, regarding hope.

He wanted to talk to Ruth about these things, and so he did. As Reuben talked out loud about Father Nouwen's work, Socrates, lying on a braided rug by the wood stove, opened his eyes briefly as if to see if someone had entered the room.

Reuben smiled and said, "It's okay, Buddy, just talking to my Ruth. She's in heaven. It helps me

## Reuben's Journey Begins

to talk things over with her and you."

It was late afternoon on November 18$^{th}$, the Sunday before Thanksgiving, when Willard came over to talk to his dad about selling the cattle. With winter coming on and with the unattractive milk prices and increase in fee and veterinarian costs, Willard felt strongly that they should discontinue the dairy part of the farm. Though Reuben couldn't imagine farming without the dairy cattle, Willard's arguments made sense. He sadly agreed, recalling Synnova's words as to how things would be different on the farm with Ruth gone.

They called the Hollander Brothers who had a large dairy operation and Steve Hollander expressed an interest in buying the entire herd. With a modern milking parlor and two hired hands, adding 40 to 50 prime milking cows and fourteen calves would be a piece of cake for them. As for the extra twelve head of feeding cattle, Nick Ottson from West Creek had called Reuben to see if he could buy them, but wait to pick them up around the second week of December. In a matter of a week, Reuben had made arrangements for all the cattle to be transferred to their new homes, with the exception of Christopher's 4H calves.

Thanksgiving week began with a call from Janice, asking if she could come out on Wednesday and begin preparing for Thanksgiving dinner. They talked, too, about the Fall Festival which would be on Wednesday. It would be a busy day. While he wasn't really quite ready to

# Reuben's Journey Begins

have a house full of people again without Ruth, he knew very well what an important fundraiser it was for the hospital auxiliary.

"Sounds good, Honey, but I might need your help to fill in for your mother," said Reuben.

"Of course I will, Dad. We'll all pitch in. I know it's going to be difficult for all of us to celebrate Thanksgiving without Mom," said Janice. "I remind myself that her spirit will always be with us, and I think about the years she was working, how she normally left our dinner early to bring Thanksgiving treats to her residents. We might pretend she's at work doing what she loved to do in serving others and that will make it a little easier for both of us."

Janice's thoughts reminded Reuben what a great help the family would be for him this week, and he was thankful.

The Thanksgiving holiday in Prairieville had begun, for nearly a century, on the day before Thanksgiving. Schools closed at 11:30 and most kids were home within the hour. It was a tradition that had begun in part in the early 1900s when people would take half a day to travel to relatives for Thanksgiving. Then in the late '40s, following World War II, it became a day when people would do special fundraising the day before Thanksgiving for the local hospital. Eventually this became the Prairieville Hospital Auxiliary Fall Festival, held at the Andersons' farm; a day during which the Andersons and other volunteers raised money for The Prairieville Hospital. The Festival was now in

## Reuben's Journey Begins

its 44$^{th}$ year.

It was a great celebration, a gathering of friends, and a bake sale that was second to none. There were pies, breads, jams, jellies, cheeses, fresh beef jerky, cookies, cakes and many other wonderful homemade delights. These products were the fruits of the fall harvest around Prairieville, from gardens and fields, orchards and vineyards. Every year, the carriage barn was converted to a pavilion of fundraising and filled with the wonderful aromas of fresh hot apple cider, coffee, hot chocolate and every type of pie known to southwestern Minnesota. All the sleighs and carriages were neatly parked in the alfalfa field just to the east of the house. It was four hours of work just moving them out and another four hours of work moving them back into the carriage barn. Even though the preparations were demanding, Reuben had always loved being part of this very special celebration.

In addition to the bake sale, funds were raised from the hayrides and sleigh rides and, of course, from any donations folks wanted to give.

Wednesday came, and Reuben's spirit was quietly sad with the knowledge that Ruth would not be around to share the stories with her in a visit to the hospital or the nursing home. As people began to arrive, however, he found himself giving the same warm greetings and great service that came so naturally to him.

David had come home a day early to help pitch

## Reuben's Journey Begins

in, along with Willard, to make it a wonderful day for all. To accommodate the many extra rides, the Ladermans had brought over four extra Belgians. Karen and Dallas Laderman drove the large hay wagon for the Baptist Youth League; Reuben and Willard each drove sleighs, some adapted with wheels where there was little snow, with Dancer and Duchess pulling; David drove the double hay wagon pulled by Duke and Dolly with the new rubber tires, making it a smoother ride along Red Rock Creek.

It was 1:30 when the bus from The Cottonwoods pulled into the yard with twenty of the residents who had come out for wagon and sleigh rides. The skies on this day were threatening more snow to accommodate the festival's sleigh rides, adding to a good base that had been improved by last Saturday's early snow.

Among those who arrived on the bus from The Cottonwoods was Elsie Natterson, 96 years of age, and her niece, Karen Johnson. Elsie was not expected to make it through the winter because of her congestive heart disease. Also with her were Reuben's son-in-law, Terry, and one of the nurses from The Cottonwoods, Diane Hunter. Elsie had been planning this day for an entire year. She had been Reuben's first grade teacher and his Sunday School teacher, and she had always loved the hayrides and sleigh rides at the Andersons' farm. Every year, she had brought her first graders out to the Fall Festival and taught them how to make

## Reuben's Journey Begins

homemade ice cream. She wanted more than anything to go on one more ride before she 'crossed over to the other side,' and Reuben was happy to fulfill that dream on this day. He chose his Belgian colt, Boots, so named because of the white feathers (hair) above each one of his hooves, to pull the four-person Missouri River Sleigh he had purchased from Tony Knopik and Jeani Borchert in Bismarck, North Dakota.

It took them about thirty minutes to get everything ready and then, finally, with Elsie sitting next to Reuben, all wrapped up in quilts and sweaters, they moved ahead on a fresh layer of early afternoon snow which continued to fall in the form of big fluffy flakes. As they rode along the trails, Reuben looked over often at Elsie, hoping she was managing the ride comfortably. If smiles and facially-expressed memories could tell a story, she wrote a book during the thirty minute sleigh ride through the rolling countryside, much of it along Red Rock Creek. Numerous times, she asked Rueben if he remembered when this or that had happened, and named a student or event that had taken place during one of the hay or sleigh rides in years past. The sleigh ride was soothing, the conversation rich with history, and then soon they were back at the farmyard where they had begun.

As Karen and Reuben helped Elsie from the sleigh, she said, "Reuben, there was a moment when I wanted us to just climb into the sky and find

## Reuben's Journey Begins

the entry to heaven. I've lived a good life and now I'm just sort of waiting to go to the next part of my journey. Thank you, lovely man, for always being a dear friend. And it would please me so much if you, your children and Socrates would escort me from Bethany to the Lutheran Cemetery when I take the last step in this earthly journey."

Tears formed in Reuben's eyes and as he bent over to kiss her, he said, "Elsie, I owe you so much. You taught me to read, and I've traveled the world in literature. I will forever be grateful to you. My dearest friend, I would consider it one of the greatest honors of my life to carry you to your resting place."

Socrates barked with a resounding vote of approval and there were smiles and some laughter from those who were gathered around. Elsie and Reuben kissed.

Later that night he would be back in the first grade.

It was almost midnight before the carriage barn and horse barn had been returned to their normal orders. Willard, David and Reuben were just finishing grooming the horses and putting fresh bedding in their stalls. Over at the carriage barn, Christopher and his cousins were finishing cleaning the wagons, carriages and sleighs that had been used during the day. Outside, large snowflakes continued drifting down on the rolling prairie, creating a fresh white blanket of snow. It wasn't long before everyone had finished their

## Reuben's Journey Begins

chores and began gathering around the kitchen table. Reuben and David hosted those family members still awake with the traditional root beer floats. Janice, Kathy and Louise sat finishing a puzzle that had been scooted over to one corner of the big pedestal oak table which comfortably seated ten people.

Thanksgiving Day arrived quickly for most who had sat up until almost 2:00 in the morning, talking and reminiscing. Breakfast was David's meal to host. He was a lover of a traditional, big farm breakfast complete with eggs, thick-sliced bacon, venison sausage, ham, breakfast steaks, pancakes, homemade bread and cottage fries the size of silver dollars, as well as any other interesting leftovers in the refrigerator. In addition to the Andersons, there were always old schoolmates of David's, Janice's and Willard's who came out between 6:00 and 9:00 a.m. to eat, reconnect, relive old times and tell of new adventures in their lives.

At breakfast this morning, Jerome Robertson, a close friend of everyone's, told a story about Ruth.

"I was in the seventh grade and had a temperature spike to 107 degrees and no doctor was around. Ruth put me in a cool bath with some ice cubes. I remember freezing and looking up to see tears in her eyes as she told me to hang on and believe in getting well. I did believe, with all my heart, that I would get better. There was a point when I clearly remember seeing a golden

## Reuben's Journey Begins

light around Ruth, and her words were so confident and reassuring that I lived through what others said later could only be attributed to a miracle. And then, of course, they put me on antibiotics. That bout with pneumonia was the sickest I've ever been in my life. So, for me, Ruth Anderson was and is an angel. I'm here today to say, 'Thank you, Ruth, for giving me a second chance at life,' and to thank her for being such a kind, caring and giving person." As Jerome finished talking, it felt as though Ruth was there in the room with them.

Late morning and early afternoon passed as everyone busied themselves with preparations for a full Thanksgiving dinner. On the farm, the noon meal was often referred to as dinner, and the evening meal as supper, but Thanksgiving Dinner was always late, occurring toward mid-afternoon. At 2:30, as they sat down to eat dinner, Reuben placed Ruth's Bible on the plate next to him. Tied to the front side of the back of her chair was a wreath of dried weeds, wheat and flowers with a white sash bearing her nursing achievement pins.

In a solemn voice he said, "It's hard for me say the traditional Thanksgiving prayer I have prayed so many times, partly because Ruth was always a central part of it. This year, I would like each of you to pray your own Thanksgiving Day prayer, giving thanks for the things for which you are most grateful. Let us pray." There was silence for almost two minutes, which seemed like an hour to the kids. And then Reuben spoke, "In God's

## Reuben's Journey Begins

name, Amen."

As people finished the meal with pumpkin pie and ice cream, Janice looked over at Reuben. "Dad, what did Rusty Olson want today when he called?" asked Janice.

"Oh, he said I should stop in tonight after 6:00 to meet some people. I'm not sure if I'll feel up to it," replied Reuben with some tiredness in his voice, and a reluctance toward social events after the busyness of the last two days.

"You know, Dad," said Willard, "I've heard that Rusty has some kind of meeting up there with widows and widowers on Thanksgiving, but no one I know seems to talk much about it. It's something he started about twelve years ago, I think, after his wife, Ann, died. You don't hear much talk about it, but Donny Johnson was telling me that his Uncle Charles has gone for the past few years and seems to really enjoy it."

"Oh, I don't know, Willard, if I feel up to it. I will think about it," Reuben replied with a yawn.

Dinner over, most of the men retired to the living room where the Detroit Lions were playing the Denver Broncos. Reuben watched the game for a while and then quietly slipped away to his bedroom where he wrapped up in a big afghan his sister, Synnova, had crocheted for him.

As he fell fast asleep, he walked along Red Rock Creek with Ruth and they talked about the kids.

It wasn't long before the grandfather clock in

## Reuben's Journey Begins

the living room began striking the half hour chime after 5:00 and Reuben felt a gentle hand rubbing his back.

"Daddy, it's five-thirty and Rusty Olson just called again and asked if you would come in to the Town Café for coffee and pie," said Janice softly.

Reuben rolled over and embraced Janice with a big hug and kiss. "Just talked to your mom," he said, smiling.

Janice looked at him lovingly and he told her about his dream.

"Okay, I don't know that I really feel like it," Reuben said then, responding to her reason for awakening him. "I'm not sure I want to sit around with a bunch of old widows and widowers, either," he added jokingly.

He had no sooner finished his sentence than his Reubenesque curiosity got the best of him and he started getting ready to go to town. Freshening up, putting on his suit but no tie and donning his traditional Minnesota Twins dress baseball cap, Reuben left for town.

When he arrived at the Town Café, the place was a beehive of activity. A small sign on the door simply said, "The Thanksgiving Club, A Private Gathering – Will Reopen for Business at 6:00 a.m. Tomorrow." Reuben felt very unsure about going inside but Rusty had been a close friend ever since grade school. He justified being here because of their friendship.

In the Club Room, a room for community group

## Reuben's Journey Begins

meetings, there was a mix of men and women gathering for the evening. As Reuben surveyed the room, he realized that he knew most of the people who were there. They were from Prairieville and many of the surrounding communities. He was momentarily struck by the perception that he had never thought to think of the people who had lost their spouses in the collective. But here they were as a group. Amazing. As he continued to survey the room, he realized that he had driven some of their spouses from the churches to the cemeteries. Others were constant customers of fresh eggs from his farm. People had already begun to sit down at various tables; there were eight tables, each seating about six, seven or eight people.

    Rusty welcomed Reuben and asked him to take a seat next to Ethel Johnson, whose husband had passed away several years ago after being killed in a farm accident. Ethel hugged Reuben and thanked him for being so gracious at her husband's funeral. Next to Ethel was Eva Jacobson, whose husband died of a sudden heart attack about four years ago while pitching bales of hay. To his left was Dana Bronson who lost his wife to breast cancer two years ago; he was also an old schoolmate of Reuben's. Next to Dana was Hilda Ingvalson whose husband had passed away from a sudden heart attack while building a new barn. And next to Hilda was Henry Torkelson whose wife, Ruth, had died from lung cancer. It all

## Reuben's Journey Begins

hit him like a bale of hay falling off the wagon. Wow, he had never stopped to put all this together. It was somewhat overwhelming and awesome at the same time.

Suddenly, the clanging of a spoon on a water glass rang out through the room. Rusty began with a greeting.

"Welcome, members and guests of The Thanksgiving Club. For the benefit of our guests this evening, my long-time friend, Reuben Anderson, whose dear wife and our good friend, Ruth, passed away in September; my dear neighbor, Nancy Herford, whose husband Richard was killed in a trucking accident in Iowa; and Maria Hofstad who lost her husband to cancer; I say, welcome to our humble gathering, and now I would like to share a little history about our group."

"Twelve years ago," Rusty continued, "after my wife, Ann, passed away a month before Thanksgiving, I was devastated. My friends, Reuben and Ruth, carried Ann in their funeral coach from Bethany Lutheran to the cemetery out by Edith Dahlstrom's farm. The weeks that followed were very tough for me. I cried, I withdrew and I wasn't sure what I wanted to do anymore except to have her back. I spent weeks looking in the rearview mirror of my life, hoping the past would once again become the present. She was my wife and my very best friend."

Rusty choked up and continued, "As you know, we always have a large turnout on Thanksgiving

## Reuben's Journey Begins

Day here at the Town Café. And on Thanksgiving night twelve years ago, after a very busy day at the cafe, my good friend Corrine Osland, now Corrine Osland Olson, the woman who had been my Ann's best friend, helped me clean up. We closed the Café, washed the dishes, cleaned the place up and then sat down in sheer exhaustion to have a cup of coffee and some pumpkin pie and ice cream. She had lost her husband that same year and we ended up talking for hours about how our daily lives and life's journeys had changed. We talked about how our relationships with others in town seemed to change a little bit with some, and a lot with others, after our spouses passed away. We also came to affirm the importance of allowing our grief to continue for whatever time needed, and we realized that the world around us continued to turn and that life goes on in spite of our losses. And though our grief was important to us, those around us seemed to forget that we needed time to process that grief. While folks were very respectful and offered supportive wishes for a month or so after our spouse's deaths, soon there was no mention of our spouses anymore except at a few special events or church services. There was an emptiness that we didn't know quite how to address."

"There was no master plan in creating The Thanksgiving Club," he went on, "it just happened as I told you. And what better day of the year than Thanksgiving to remember what a special role our

## Reuben's Journey Begins

previous spouses played in our lives and how their spirit continues to live in us. This is an evening to reminisce, tell stories, learn from each other and know that grieving the loss of a loved one takes its own path for each of us and matures in its own time. The only dues you have to pay for our club is the expression of friendship, one to another. The only guideline is that we should be careful in sharing the conversations of this evening with others who may not have experienced the loss of a spouse."

Rusty smiled and turned to Corrine Osland Olson, who had since remarried to Duane Olson. Duane had requested to draw for the night's topic.

During the third year of The Thanksgiving Club, Corrine and Rusty had sat looking at each other, along with some other friends, and found themselves a little stumped as to how to start the evening's storytelling.

Corrine had said, "Why don't we make a list of different topics and draw one out of a hat?"

Everyone agreed, and they had made a list:

1. The Times We Laughed the Hardest
2. The Times We Worried the Most
3. The Times We Enjoyed the Most
4. The Things We Miss the Most with Our Spouse Gone
5. The Best & Worst Things About Grieving
6. The Toughest Thing About Being

# Reuben's Journey Begins

Single Again
7. Dealing with the Feelings & Public Comments About Dating & Remarriage
8. How Long Should We Grieve?
9. Learning to Be Alone Again

On this night, Duane drew out number seven, "Dealing with the Feelings & Public Comments About Dating & Remarriage." As Duane read it out loud, there were shy gasps of "Oh, my" and quiet laughter from those who had dated and remarried, and others who seemed quite surprised. A thought flashed through Reuben's mind. He mused, 'Well, this will be interesting, but I'd never remarry. There isn't anyone in this town like Ruth, and besides, the kids would kill me if I ever looked at another woman!'

The evening's conversations were quite remarkable. Duane and Corrine decided to go first.

"Well," Corrine began, "when Nathan was killed in the car accident, I was just devastated. And his insurance business was our livelihood and I was worried sick about how I would be alone with the three kids for the rest of my life, trying to make ends meet. He had a reasonably good insurance policy, but it wouldn't provide for us for more than a few years. He had never wanted me to work and now I had to find a job to support my family. And I never even thought I would once again be thinking about dating, much less getting married."

## Reuben's Journey Begins

"It was about a year after Nathan died," she continued, "that I ran into Duane at the post office one day and he had just lost his wife, Ellen, to cancer. I remember being polite and feeling sorry for him, always thinking he was such a kind man, and I wished him the best. About a year later, we were both serving dinner at the church pancake fundraiser and ended up doing dishes together. My kids had taken my car to go study with friends and I asked Duane if he would drop me off at home. Neither of us thought much about it and he did drive me home, carried my dish and food boxes into the house and went home. The next day, I had phone calls from three people asking me how long had we been secretly dating. I was flabbergasted! Before long, it was all over town."

Everyone in the room began smiling, giggling, laughing respectfully and enjoying the tale.

"About a week later, Duane called me and suggested we go to a movie and dinner. 'After all,' he said, 'we've apparently been dating secretly for some time now. At least, that is the buzz about town.' I laughed and accepted his invitation, jokingly saying it was probably time to come out of the closet."

"That evening and the next two weeks were almost too much for me," Corrine continued. "I couldn't believe it when I got home that first night and my kids were all waiting up, worried and appalled that I hadn't discussed my date with them first. They couldn't believe that I would stay out

## Reuben's Journey Begins

until 1:00 a.m.! They asked me what on earth we could have been doing for the last three hours when they had called everywhere looking for me. And then I found myself using their lines, like, 'We were just talking about everything' and 'No, we were not making out!'"

Everyone in the room roared with laughter.

"It was really a different time for us," said Duane. "My kids were in sports and Corrine's kids were in music. I'm not sure any of them approved of us dating. They would communicate their displeasure in some subtle ways most of the time, and every now and then, they would be very bold about their disapproval. I found myself thinking many times that it would be much easier just to forget the whole thing ... but something had happened. I had fallen in love with Corrine."

"Love can really complicate things," Duane continued. "I went through a period of time feeling guilty about dating again. Worse yet, I found myself asking how could I seem to love two different women equally. Maybe I was a Mormon in a former life."

Everyone chuckled.

"I certainly don't mean any disrespect in saying that," he continued, "but I remember reading about those who had married several wives. There were times I would get so excited about having a new life with Corrine and then suddenly feel like something was wrong with feeling that way. Then I'd become very introspective and quiet. Corrine

## Reuben's Journey Begins

would sense me pulling away. And then we'd have those tough conversations about maybe not taking things beyond a good friendship. That would last about two hours after I would go home and crawl into an empty bed. We'd be on the phone talking like teenagers for the next twenty minutes. It was a time in my life I called 'Zig Zag.' One day I would feel okay about things, and then spend the next day or week feeling guilty. Seriously, the greatest internal struggle I had was taking personal time again to develop a relationship with Corrine, and oftentimes having to choose being with her rather than with my children for a school or community event. Finding a balance in allocating my time between us, her children and my children was tough. It still is, and I don't know that there is an easy answer other than simply making the best of each day in light of the changes that impacted all of our lives."

There was an overwhelming response in the form of heads nodding in agreement and supportive smiles from all corners of the room. Reuben sat captivated by the story.

Corrine then finished their story by saying, "In one sense, the people who you truly value in the community had no problem with us dating and remarrying. There were others who thought we should not marry because of the children and there are days when it is tough blending two families, the traditions and values, the relatives, a diverse schedule of activities and interests, and the list

## Reuben's Journey Begins

goes on. Yet, at the core of our lives is a rich friendship and love that I value and need. I've asked our children to give us some space in much the same way we have given them the needed space in their relationships. For the most part they have done this, but it is hard for them sometimes when we express our love in physical embraces and kisses. A couple of times they have found us embraced in bed, walking in without knocking, and they've been shocked. We understand this and try not to overdo it, but at the same time, we're not going to hide our affection for each other. All of this is not done in disrespect for our former spouses, but in love for each other. Well, that's part of our story. Thank you all for your support and kindness, and Rusty, thank you for continuing the tradition of The Thanksgiving Club. Although I am in my twelfth year attending this gathering, it has meant a great deal to both of us."

With that comment came a round of clapping and agreement, with everyone echoing, "thank you" to Rusty.

The evening continued with several more stories from others and Reuben found himself totally intrigued by the stories that all revealed new beginnings for those who had lost their spouses, then later dated, and some who had remarried. Others had not remarried but, instead, became involved in various organizations. It seemed way too early for him to think of such things, and yet there was a message here that he needed to hear:

# Reuben's Journey Begins

'When one door closes, another often opens.' He just wasn't sure what the new door would be. 'Was it a new partner and marriage; was it the volunteering that Ruth had written about in her letter?'

As the evening concluded, Reuben found himself surrounded by a very warm spirit as people told him how glad they were that he had come to the gathering. They stood around continuing to talk for another thirty minutes, at which time Rusty said it was time to turn out the lights so he could get home and get some sleep before opening at 6:00 a.m. in the morning, which meant getting up at 4:30 a.m. to ready the restaurant for another day of business.

As Reuben drove home in a soft and gentle snowfall, his throat began to hurt once more as he missed Ruth very much. He wondered how Ruth would feel about his going to the gathering this evening, and then somehow he knew it was okay. Dating and marriage; no, that was not for him. He had his horses, carriages, sleighs, Socrates, children, grandchildren and a farm with all sorts of interesting places and critters. There certainly wasn't any time to fit another person into all of this. At age 72, he had a full plate. Yet, he was glad he had gone tonight because he saw the importance others placed on taking time to grieve, reminisce and share stories, and how it was important to continue to embrace the world around themselves as others soon forgot about their loss. More importantly, The Thanksgiving Club was a place where he could publicly continue to talk about Ruth and his love for her. That thought gave him a special spark to think about during the days ahead, and Christmas was just around the corner. He was glad to hear that others, although they resumed a somewhat normal daily schedule, had mourned the loss of their loved one for a considerable time. He didn't have to 'get over it' in a couple of months; he could take years, if he so chose.

That night, he and Ruth went on their first date.

The Friday, Saturday and Sunday following Thanksgiving were booked solid with sleigh rides, given the fresh snowfalls. Reuben couldn't remember many Novembers when there had been such a great base of snow this early for sleigh rides. He enjoyed giving these rides. As Christmas week approached, more requests than ever came in from people returning to Prairieville for the Christmas holidays.

Sunday evening, Reuben went out to his den in the horse barn where he sat down and reflected on the past month. As he did, he reread Sanaya Roman's words again, *"You can discover your life's work through examining the skills you love to use, the things you love to do, and the areas you are naturally drawn to."*

He thought about The Thanksgiving Club and how he was now part of a group he had never imagined being a part of three months ago. And

## Reuben's Journey Begins

now his life's work seemed to be changing, from farmer to something else ... but what? And while very little had changed in his life, everything had changed! 'At 72, what skills do I have?' he asked silently. 'And how do I love to use them? What things do I really love to do? And what areas am I naturally drawn to?' Everything seemed to be a question without many clear answers. And then he thought of Elsie Natterstad and her sleigh ride, and Father Nouwan's words ...

*"Entering into the world we are what we are given, and for many years thereafter parents and grandparents, brothers and sisters, friends and lovers keep giving to us -- some more, some less, some hesitantly, some generously. When we can finally stand on our own feet, speak our own words, and express our own unique self in work and love, we realize how much is given to us. But while reaching the height of our cycle, and saying with a great sense of confidence, 'I really am,' we sense that to fulfill our life we now are called to become parents and grandparents, brothers and sisters, teachers, friends, and lovers ourselves, and to give to others, so that, when we leave this world, we can be what we have given."* [1]

Reuben mused about this silently. 'So I can be what I have given? What have I given to others? I've been a farmer. I've been nice to people. Given a lot of hayrides and sleigh rides, but I've

## Reuben's Journey Begins

gotten paid for most of them, yet donated the money to Jerry Lewis. I've helped out with running errands for residents at the nursing home. I've helped a friend or neighbor here or there. '…What would my legacy be if I died tomorrow?' he wondered. 'Here lies Reuben, having given some of the people here their last carriage ride and now he's here, too. Who'll drive them here now?' He chuckled and continued to ponder.

Elsie and Ruth had great legacies. As a first grade teacher, Elsie set many children on a course of love for education, school, learning and growing. Ruth, as a nurse, helped hundreds of people through some of the most difficult times in their lives. My goodness, it was one of the largest funerals Bethany Lutheran had ever seen. People came from all over the five-state area. Not only did she help deliver hundreds of babies but she cared for people of all ages, and always with a smile and a good word, even for those who were not very nice to her. She left this world being what she had given to others: love, kindness, hope and caring. He knew this to be true because people expressed their thoughts in words the day of the funeral and in over five hundred sympathy cards that took him a week to read.

The day was drawing to a close. Reuben gathered up his pipe and a couple of books and called Socrates to join him as he closed up his office den and the horse barn and walked to the house. The snow continued to fall gently and the

## Reuben's Journey Begins

tracks in the snow told a story of two friends calling it a day.

That night in his dreams, Reuben and Socrates continued their walk through the woods, the east pasture and along Red Rock Creek and Reuben wondered about life, his evolving purpose and life's work that was also changing. At age 72, he pondered a new beginning as he thought about the image of the wooden-spoked wagon wheel leaning against the birch tree, and the circle of life.

# Chapter Six

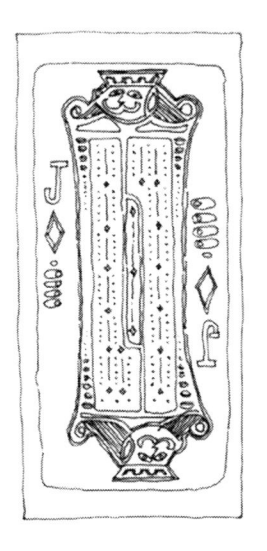

## The Cribbage Game

## December, 1990

It was just a few days before Christmas. Terry, a devoted runner and marathoner, had gotten up early for his morning run. A light snowfall made for a beautiful winter's morning run, though slippery at times. He would generally run on gravel roads east of town to minimize slipping on icy pavement during the winter months. His typical five-to-seven mile training run would take him past the Peterson farm, then the Dahlstroms' place, past the Lutheran cemetery, the Bronson farm and, finally,

# Reuben's Journey Begins

to Lake Augusta where he would turn around and head back to town. On this morning, Terry had seen Reuben at the cemetery at 6:30 a.m. While it seemed out of place at first, about two miles into his run he remembered that today, Thursday, December 20$^{th}$, would have been Ruth's 72$^{nd}$ birthday. As he ran, he also realized that for as long as he could remember, it was the one day each year that Reuben would get up a little extra early and always have a present along with fresh squeezed orange juice, coffee, an English muffin and homemade strawberry jam waiting for Ruth at the breakfast table. Knowing Reuben as he did, he knew that what at first seemed odd because of the early time to be at the cemetery was really very natural for him, to be with Ruth, given the day and events of the past few months. They were having an early morning moment together on Ruth's special day.

Back at home an hour later, Terry and Janice Ryan were getting ready for work. An idea that Terry had been pondering for a few days needed to be explored.

"Honey," raising his voice loud enough to be heard above Janice's shower, "I saw your dad at the cemetery this morning during my run. I didn't stop to talk to him as he seemed very focused on visiting your mother's grave and I could faintly hear him talking to her. At first I was concerned but later I remembered what day this is. It was still too dark to get a real good look, but the light pole near

## Reuben's Journey Begins

the entry of the cemetery clearly illuminated his and Socrates' silhouettes, and I don't think they noticed me," Terry said.

"I'm not surprised," replied Janice, stepping out of the shower. "It's been a difficult morning for me, too, being Mom's birthday today. You know, he has really focused on being quite alone and grieving in a healthy way. We talked about it a couple of weeks ago and I'm so glad he is dealing with this in a thoughtful manner. I think the Thanksgiving Club really helped him put things in perspective. He talked about things he has read concerning grieving in many different cultures. He told me how he has needed some time away from family and friends to process his grief."

Terry and Janice continued their discussion as they readied their twins, Mary and Megan, for school. It was the last week of school before Christmas vacation which began on Friday.

"You know, Honey, I've been thinking about that and I agree that people in our society often don't take enough time to stay with their grief long enough. God knows, we don't at The Cottonwoods. We care about and love these residents, yet, the day they die we're already calling the next person on the waiting list who is waiting to move into the apartment or fill the bed in health care. That part of our work really frustrates me, as we rush to fill the empty space. It's like death is a minor inconvenience but not a big deal. Some days, I feel terrible about how we handle

## Reuben's Journey Begins

death; gone today, forgotten tomorrow. Even though I know I have a responsibility to help the next person waiting in line to move into the community, it's still hard to deal with some days," said Terry. "On the other hand, I also think part of the grieving process is choosing a time to let go and begin moving on with one's life. I sometimes see some people getting stuck in grief too long and I don't think that is healthy, either. There needs to be a balance in grief just as other aspects of our lives need balance. I'm really glad Rusty Olson invited your dad to his Thanksgiving Club," Terry continued.

Janice was wondering where Terry was going with this morning homily. "Well, it's only been a few months for Dad. Do you think he is stuck in grief?" Janice asked.

"Oh, no," Terry responded. "I just overheard a couple of residents at The Annex talking about Reuben. He used to stop by all the time and visit with people before and after visiting your mom. Since your mom's death, he has been understandably absent, but still missed very much by staff and residents. Anyway, what would you think of me calling Reuben today to see if he might like to help with a couple of volunteer things at The Cottonwoods? He has always enjoyed visiting with other people when he came to see your mom. My gosh, he was one of our most regular visitors every day your mom was with us during the past few years. And he was always doing little things for various people and running errands. He really didn't think of it as being a volunteer; he just thought about them as small favors when, in fact, they meant so much to people. His little favors were big favors for many."

Janice thought for a moment as she buttoned her blouse and said, "I like the idea, Honey. He can always say no if he needs more time alone. Or, he might say yes and it would be a good transition for him, back to a more social environment," Janice sighed as if she had already put in a day's work.

"Dear, you sound just like a social worker," chuckled Terry. Janice laughed.

"Any ideas on what we should ask him to do, or should we just have him show up and put him to work?" asked Janice.

Terry thought for a minute as he combed his hair and said, "Well, I'm thinking Peter White might be a perfect beginning. As you know, he is relatively new in town and wants to find someone to play cribbage with him. Bunny Ford played cribbage with him almost every day during September and October when he first arrived for rehab, but then he has been pretty sick lately and Peter's having a hard time finding a new crib partner. I've sort of dropped the ball on finding someone else the last couple of months, with everything going on," Terry sighed in personal disappointment.

Janice rushed about the house getting coats

## Reuben's Journey Begins

and boots for the twins, thinking about the idea for a few minutes. "I like the idea, Mr. Ryan," she responded finally, in a playful voice. "Dad has always loved playing cribbage. It just so happens I spoke to Peter yesterday during our telephone conference with his son, Thomas, who lives in Des Moines. Thomas told me that another crib partner would be so good for his dad's mental state right now. I love the idea. Let's check it out when we get to work," Janice finished as she grabbed her purse, the twins and a pile of paperwork on the way out the kitchen door.

Terry raised his voice as she went into the garage. "Now don't forget, I'll be an hour late today. I have to go to the Chamber's 'Morning Welcome' for the new gift shop opening up next to Bakke's Fairway Foods. Gus and Agnes said their niece, Kari, has a sure thing going and I promised to cut the ribbon this morning at their grand opening at 8:00 a.m. Prairieland Kaffee is bringing the coffee and tea; Arfsteen's Implement is giving away their coffee cups; The Cottonwoods is bringing fresh baked rolls and The Prairieville Times is furnishing those great customized napkins. Love you, girls!" Terry said, raising his voice a little more.

A chorus of voices, "Love you, too," rang back from Janice and the twins.

She opened the garage door, fastened the girls' seatbelts and drove off with tears running down her cheeks. Losing a mother had been painful for her and it was hard to be the strong one in the family.  More importantly, they had been best friends.  As she looked in the rearview mirror and saw the talkative twins comparing their doll's dresses on their first porcelain dolls from Grandma Ruth, they were in some way the continuing presence of her mother.

It was almost 10:00 a.m. when Terry arrived back at work where Janice was just finishing up with a new care plan for Lorraine Ingvalson.  Care plans outlined the type of care services a resident received at certain times each day.  At The Cottonwoods, a care plan was generally developed by the resident's physician, the Director of Nursing, often called the D.O.N., and the social worker along with other selected staff, depending on the resident's situation.  Terry would often sit in on the planning session, too.  Once the care plan was created, it was periodically reviewed by the staff and family members to ensure the best possible care.  Lorraine needed to move over to assisted living in The Annex, from independent living at The Manor, because she was now on oxygen full-time and needed more frequent medication reminders.  Janice had wanted to spend time with her and Sherry, Lorraine's daughter, to encourage them to consider making this move as soon as possible.  It was never an easy job to move someone from one level of care to another, or from one venue to another at The Cottonwoods.

Janice's  days  were  always  filled with a heavy

# Reuben's Journey Begins

schedule of meetings with residents and family members. As she walked around The Cottonwoods, she would stop by to talk with as many residents as possible at The Manor, The Annex, Amanda's Garden and River's Edge. On occasion, she would visit with residents moving over from The Manor with situations similar to Lorraine Ingvalson. Earlier that morning, she had also followed up on the conversation with Terry and stopped by to see Peter White who was adjusting very well to his new home at The Annex. He was soon to begin his fourth month with them, although he had become somewhat reclusive during the past month as a result of Bunny Ford's absence from their cribbage games. His son and daughter were concerned about the situation, as were Terry and Janice.

    Today, she wanted to double check with him about finding someone to play cribbage with him. She stopped by for a short visit. As she left his apartment and walked down the hall, she reflected on his reaction. He was so overjoyed with the possibility that he could be playing cribbage again on a regular basis that Janice was now a little nervous about the possibility of Reuben saying no … Who would she call tomorrow? After all, both he and she were dealing with a tough emotional situation today. Yet deep down, she felt this situation between Peter and her dad was meant to be. Feeling this, she simply let go of her concerns and forged ahead into the day.

## Reuben's Journey Begins

Walking from her office to the library to meet with another family, she saw Terry coming in the front door.

"Hey, Mr. Administrator, kind of a long welcome party this morning for such a small shop," Janice said, teasingly.

"Oh, I know. I got talking to several of our friends whose parents are here and the time escaped me," Terry replied. "Did you talk to Peter about your dad possibly being interested in playing cribbage with him?"

"Oh, yes, and he is so excited he can hardly stand it. His first question was, 'Do you think this man would come over today?' I told him that we have to call him first and carefully added that his wife passed away just a couple of months ago. At first I didn't tell him it was my dad, but somehow he picked up on something in my voice that indicated I was close to this person. He then threw me for a loop and asked if it was my dad. I'm always amazed at what he knows or figures out about other people. So I confessed and told him the whole story," Janice responded. "They have never met, as Peter came into The Cottonwoods just as Mom had come back from the hospital."

"Hmm, what does your social worker training say about that kind of response?" Terry asked, teasingly.

With that comment, a paper airplane she had fashioned out of a sheet of paper containing a resident complaint about the overcooked green

## Reuben's Journey Begins

beans at dinner last night at The Manor hit the center of Terry's tie.

"Bull's-eye! Let's call Dad as soon as I finish meeting with the Brady's," Janice said. "And be sure to address that complaint."

Meeting with the Brady family was tough. Marge, Jim's mother now in her early seventies, and Bill, Jim's brother, were just getting ready to work with Janice on having hospice come in to sit with Jim. Jim, also a marathoner and a very close friend of Terry's, was dying from cancer. At 42 years of age, it was tough for everyone to deal with Jim's situation. He was a teacher and a coach at the high school, and loved by everyone. Bill, Jim's brother, was having the hardest time with the decision to bring hospice into The Cottonwoods, as it was somehow a sign of resignation that his impending fate would happen sooner rather than later. Marge, a former Navy nurse, was much calmer during the meeting, but also very subdued. Bill 'lost it' during the counseling session and Janice had to comfort him several times as he continually asked, "Why?" The care planning session lasted almost two hours and Janice was exhausted. She hugged them goodbye and assured them that they would do everything humanly possible to care for Jim and work with hospice during his final days.

Walking into Terry's office and plopping down in a chair, Terry knew it was a good time to change the topic of discussion and probably talk about her

## Reuben's Journey Begins

dad.

"Who should ask him?" Terry queried as he sat approving invoices for payment, quickly glancing over the top of his reading glasses.

"Why don't you, Mr. Administrator ... I'm just not up to it right now. Besides, I'm just a lowly social worker and have very little authority here or at home," Janice said, breaking out into a tired laugh.

"In your dreams," Terry replied.

They both chuckled as Terry dialed the phone and pressed 'speaker.' It was almost 11:30 and Reuben was just getting ready to go out to check on Dolly who had chipped a hoof during a sleigh ride the day before. With his coat on and ready to go out to the horse barn, he picked up the cordless phone, a feature quite new to the farm and one he appreciated.

"Hello," Reuben answered.

"Reuben, it's your favorite son-in-law," Terry teased, "What's for dinner tonight?"

"I don't know, you'll have to ask your wife," Reuben laughed. "My cupboards and refrigerator are bare. Even Socrates, Mitsy and Cougar are complaining. What's up?"

"Janice has a favor to ask of you," Terry said, smiling. Janice immediately fired a paper ball at him. "No, seriously, we have a relatively new resident at The Cottonwoods who is anxious to play a game of cribbage with someone. He and Bunny Ford were playing together but Bunny has been sick lately and we haven't found anyone here

## Reuben's Journey Begins

who is available today, or who can get away occasionally, to play crib with him. Would you mind coming in for lunch with your favorite daughter and son-in-law?" Terry asked.

"You guys," laughed Reuben, "... good thing she is my only daughter and you're my only son-in-law, because I might be on the spot answering such a question. Sure, I'll come in as soon as I check on Dolly. You know, she broke a piece out of one of her hooves during the sleigh ride yesterday for the Prairieville Baptist Youth League. Those Baptists always seem to be bad luck for me!"

Terry laughed, "Well, I guess I now know where I stand. Hopefully, my bad luck for you hasn't been that bad."

"Oh, you know I'm just kidding. We Lutherans are always looking for an opportunity to stick it to a Baptist or a Catholic! See you for lunch, and you *are* my favorite son-in-law, even though you're the *only* one and a Baptist to boot," Reuben said, chuckling as he clicked off the phone.

A light snow was still falling as he walked out to the horse barn. As the soft flakes landed on his face and beard, he felt as if Ruth was still touching him as she was during their visit at the cemetery earlier. Reuben loved these types of snowfalls. Everything looked so fresh and clean as the snow wrapped the earth in a blanket of white peace.

As he opened the door to the horse barn, Socrates raced in ahead and immediately went

## Reuben's Journey Begins

over to Dolly's stall where he barked softly, getting her attention. Reuben was always amused by the close relationship the two animals had developed. During sleigh rides and other pulling events, Socrates was either sitting next to him or trotting alongside Dolly. Reuben walked into Dolly's stall and began with some firm neck and back pats and then slowly but methodically lifted her left hind hoof.

"Boy, Dolly, we're going to need Doc Gerten to look at this. I'm going to put some McNess's Krestol on it, but we're going to have to patch and file this before you pull again. I'll stop by Doc's place today and see if he can come out and fix you up."

Reuben continued talking to the horses and gave them each a little fresh hay and then called Socrates to get into the truck. In less than fifteen minutes, Reuben and Socrates were walking into The Cottonwoods.

Socrates took off down the hall to Mrs. Schultz's room where he often spent much of his time when they were at The Cottonwoods. Mrs. Schultz was in the River's Edge wing where she had lived for the past four years. She had been Ruth's first roommate at the nursing home when Ruth first fell and injured her back. After being released from the hospital, she spent three months in rehab at The Cottonwoods. During that time, she had shared a room with her longtime friend, Eleanor Schultz, who was suffering from

# Reuben's Journey Begins

congestive heart failure and other health issues. Socrates had routinely sat next to Eleanor's bed while she petted him. Reuben, she and Ruth had engaged in long, enjoyable conversations.

"Good morning, Daddy," Janice said, hugging Reuben and holding the hug for a little bit longer than usual.

"Good to see you, Reuben," Terry said as he hugged Reuben.

"It's nice to see both of you, too. Thanks for the lunch invitation. It's been kind of a tough morning with this being Ruth's birthday and all," Reuben said with a deep sigh.

Terry put his arm around Reuben and said, "Why don't we go over to The Manor's private dining room and have a nice meal. Cookie has prepared your favorite scalloped potatoes with ham, string beans, fresh bakery bread and some German chocolate cake for dessert. I know that cake was Ruth's favorite on her birthday and I thought it would be a nice way to pay our respects."

Janice was now tearing up, as was Reuben, and the two dabbed their eyes with shirt sleeves as they walked to the private dining room.

As they entered the Picasso Private Dining Room, Cookie Pearson, Director of Dining Services, greeted Reuben with a big hug and said, "Reuben, it is so good to see you again! We have missed you, Socrates, Cougar and Mitsy. By the way, where are those furry creatures today?"

## Reuben's Journey Begins

"Well, Socrates made a beeline for Eleanor Schultz's room in River's Edge and the cats don't come outside much in the winter," Reuben said, smiling as he added, "The winter chill seems to penetrate deeper in us old cats. But not to worry, I'll bring them in next month for a visit during one of Dee's activity programs."

They all chuckled as Terry politely seated everyone at the table and served them water and coffee.

"How about some hot tomato basil soup, homemade crackers and fresh potato bread to get the meal started?" Cookie asked.

Everyone acknowledged that would be a great beginning to this birthday meal.

"Oh, Cookie, you remember everything. Mom loved your tomato basil soup and fresh bread. Why, if she is looking down on us, she's probably a little miffed that she can't eat with us today," Janice said, fighting back tears.

Reuben and Terry nodded their heads in agreement. With the mood quiet, Terry lifted his water glass and proposed a toast to Ruth in a quiet and reverent voice.

"Ruth, we miss your presence, but know that your spirit of love and caring still abides in each one of our lives. Thank you again for the many gifts you gave to each of us so many times. And please know that we will always look after Reuben and make sure that he doesn't spoil those horses now that you can't keep an eye on his eccentric behavior when it comes to those four-legged oat and hay burners! All our love to you on this special day, your 72$^{nd}$ birthday."

It was almost too much said well for both Reuben and Janice, as tears started streaming down their faces and they clinked their glasses together in approval.

"Thank you, Terry," Reuben said softly.

Janice just looked at Terry and he knew she appreciated the toast; her silent words continued turning into tears.

Lightening the mood, Reuben said, "Ruth, I'm sure you would agree that only a Baptist would sneak in a word like 'abide' in such a toast!"

They all laughed as both Terry and Janice, sitting on each side of Reuben, squeezed his arms.

The conversation turned to talk about the 'goings on' in town as they ate the delicious lunch that Cookie had prepared for them.

Suddenly, Reuben changed the subject and asked, "So, what's this about someone wanting to play me in cribbage today?" He sat up straight and leaned back in his chair. "You know, I'm a little rusty and losing to this stranger could be bad for my reputation. But maybe I'll dazzle him with my cleverness and speed! And just in case he doesn't have a very nice cribbage board, I brought mine and a new deck of cards from Prairieville Seed."

"Well, Dad, the man's name is Peter White and he recently moved into Prairieville to be near his

## Reuben's Journey Begins

daughter who works at the hospital and is new to town. He moved into The Annex just before Labor Day. He had been living alone in Des Moines, Iowa, where his son, Thomas, lives. However, Thomas is a salesman for ConAgra out of Omaha, Nebraska and he travels every week. His dad finally got to a point where he is wheelchair-bound and needed help with his medications and transfers to other chairs and his bed, and help in the bathroom. His daughter, Tammy, moved here Labor Day Weekend and he moved into the Annex the same week.

"Hmm, don't know that I have met either one of them," Reuben mused.

"No, I don't think you have, Daddy. He moved into The Annex when Mom was over in River's Edge. Peter doesn't spend a lot of time out of his room, although he does seem to get around early in the morning and later in the evening – most of the times you're not around. And his daughter works in the ER now at the hospital and is also a respiratory therapist. She works long hours and I don't think she has gotten around to developing a social life yet." Janice looked over at Terry as she continued talking. "Anyway, Daddy, Terry and I thought maybe you and some of your friends in the cribbage club might consider playing with him once in a while."

"Well, if he can see his way to playing with a bunch of Swedes and Norwegians and a couple of old Germans, all who are not the most gracious

# Reuben's Journey Begins

losers, I'm sure we would be delighted to play crib with him," Reuben said, now smiling. "Is he a Norwegian?"

Janice just smiled and shrugged her shoulders, indicating she wasn't exactly sure about his ethnic origins.

"Hmm, from that response, it is probably obvious. Don't tell me he's a Baptist!" Reuben exclaimed, laughing. "It might be good for me to meet some new people," he continued, "and crib always gets you thinking about pegging and testing your quick eyesight to make sure you've counted all your points. I'm forever miscounting and the guys always tease me, but I know it's their way of getting back at me for making fun of most of them during high school for being poor math students. Shoot, all the stuff I was good at like the Pythagoram Theorum, square roots, algebra, etc. ... you don't use any of that in cribbage. You just need to be able to count by twos."

They all laughed again and in the midst of their laughter, in walked Cookie with a beautiful German chocolate cake and two lit candles, a '7' and a '2,' and 'Happy Birthday Ruth' spelled out in scrolling letters written with bright pink frosting. Together, they broke out in song and sang a joyful "Happy Birthday" to Ruth.

And then Reuben said, soulfully, "Here, Honey, let me blow them out for you." They fell quiet as Reuben blew out the candles and then said in a soft voice, "Happy Birthday, Love."

## Reuben's Journey Begins

Terry passed the tissues and deep sighs filled the room as Cookie dished up the cake and heaping scoops of vanilla ice cream.

They finished the birthday party and each excused themselves to go to the restrooms before going down to Peter's apartment.

Moments later, as they met in the Fireside Lounge at the front entry of The Manor, Terry said, "Well, let's go over to The Annex and meet Peter. Oh, my, look who's coming with us," as Socrates came walking toward them. "Hello, Big Fella, were you down to Eleanor's again? And I'll bet you snuck into the kitchen, too, didn't you?"

Socrates barked loudly to acknowledge both questions. Everyone smiled and off they went to Peter White's apartment.

Arriving at Peter's home, Janice knocked and a voice beckoned them to come in.

"Come on in, Janice. You won't mind coming to my chair to give me a kiss, would you? I'm sure Terry won't mind as long as I pay my rent," Peter said, chuckling.

Janice walked over and gave Peter a big hug and kiss.

"And Terry, a hug from you will do as I have never been comfortable kissing men," said Peter. "And from you, Reuben, your hand, please."

As Peter extended his hand to Reuben, Janice and Terry saw the surprise on Reuben's face. It was as if Reuben was frozen in time for a moment and then they watched his shock melt away and

## Reuben's Journey Begins

turn into utter delight. Peter White was not only a black man; he was as black as the night sky. As he smiled, a tangible warmth filled the room. Then Reuben realized that Peter was blind! Reuben's mind was in a whirl, and coursing through his mind were a thousand thoughts, all centering around a lifelong wish to get to know a 'Negro' and in a flash he knew that word was wrong, too – 'African American' was correct. In these few quiet seconds, Reuben realized he was giving himself away as someone who had never really known a black person. He quickly extended his hand.

"Mr. White," Reuben said in a slightly unsure tone of voice, "it is a pleasure to meet you."

"And you, likewise, Reuben," Peter replied. "I hear you are one of the best crib players in these parts."

"Oh, you know how people like to exaggerate," Reuben responded. "I really enjoy the game. It's more interesting to me than checkers and the games are shorter than chess, so it's a perfect compromise for me."

"Hmmm," Peter started, "I was warned about you supposedly shy and modest Norwegians here in Minnesota. They express humility while talking nice and then straightaway outpeg you ten to one."

The room filled with laughter.

"Got time for a game this afternoon, Reuben?" Peter asked. "I'll certainly understand if you have a busy schedule, with Christmas and all. Maybe another day, especially given everything you've

## Reuben's Journey Begins

been through lately, with the passing of your wife. I'm so sorry to hear about Ruth and even more so that I didn't get a chance to meet her," Peter said in his deep baritone voice.

"Oh no, let's play today. I've got all afternoon," Reuben replied immediately.

Peter's face lit the room with a broad smile.

As Terry pulled up a chair for Reuben and put a large TV tray between them for the cribbage board, Peter continued, "I must tell you how much I have appreciated the kindnesses of Terry and Janice. They have treated me like family. I fear that both of my overprotective children have probably become a bother for them."

"Oh, Peter, stop it," smiled Janice, "Thomas and Tammy are great to work with, and you're darn lucky to have two kids who care about you as much as they do. I'd like to have them teach some of our other adult children how to love a parent like they love you."

As Reuben sat down, his eyes darted around the room, surveying books, tapes, a stereo, a television, family photos, awards and recognition certificates and all sorts of mementos from Peter's career as a teacher and musician. Then he looked at Janice and Terry as if to say, 'Should I set up the cribbage board?'

Before anyone could say a word, Reuben stumbled into an uneasy conversation, saying, "Well, I brought my cribbage board and some cards along just in case. But, but how should I,

## Reuben's Journey Begins

well, I mean, should I call out the cards for you? Do I need to – well, I'm fumbling for words now and I apologize, but I'm not figuring this out very fast," stammered Reuben, embarrassed. "I didn't realize you were blind and no one mentioned it."

"Oh don't apologize, my good man," Peter replied. "Being blind doesn't mean I can't see, much less play cribbage. There are lots of ways to see ... most people just get used to seeing with their eyes. I have many ways to see, just as you do. Reuben, you're too kind. Please don't be embarrassed. I've made you feel a little uncomfortable. Let me help for a moment and explain how I do this. When you don't have eyes to see with, you have to see with your hands in this game and then listen carefully to the voice and sounds made by your challenger. You also need some special equipment that works for the blind guy – that's me – and the sight guy, that's you," Peter said, joking and sounding like a teacher and chuckling.

They both laughed. Pulling up a beautifully tooled leather case from beside his chair, he revealed the most beautiful cribbage board Reuben had ever seen in his life. And in a zipper pocket on the front of the leather case was a very unusual-looking deck of cards. Reuben sat in awe as Peter set up the cribbage board, removing the pegs from another small interior silk pocket.

The cards were a beautiful deck, brightly colored and with Braille type next to each of the

## Reuben's Journey Begins

printed numbers, making it possible for both men to read them. And the crib board! It was simply magnificent with its inlaid mother of pearl border, a graphic design of two jacks of diamonds, their cloaks made of beautiful red coral, blue lapis with silver and gold crowns. Why, it was an absolutely beautiful piece of art, amazingly crafted. By every other peg hole were additional Braille embossments.

"Where did you ever get this? It's incredible!" exclaimed Reuben.

Peter laughed and celebrated Reuben's enthusiasm.

"I'm so glad you like it. My son-in-law, Mel, Tammy's husband, made it for me. He's an artist and doesn't make much of a living doing art, but what he does is always creatively magnificent. My daughter, Tammy, is the breadwinner in the family. When I retired from teaching years ago, he made it for me as a retirement gift. A gold watch wouldn't have done me much good!" said Peter chuckling again.

Then Peter and Reuben both laughed and their conversation began to pick up speed as they started dealing the cards and telling their stories.

Janice, who had been watching the play, suddenly broke into the conversation. "I've watched cribbage some but I've never played," she said. "I know the objective is to accumulate points and move the pegs, but can you explain to me, just for a minute, how the game works?" she asked.

## Reuben's Journey Begins

"Well, Janice, you're right about the points and moving the pegs, which we call pegging," said Peter. "Each player makes a choice to each lay down two cards in the crib, the points which the dealer gets later after the pegging is completed and the cards you keep in your hand determine your points for your initial pegging. Someday, when you have an hour, you should come by and I'll play with you – or, you should play with your dad someday. It's like anything else; the best way to really understand the game is to play it."

"I'll do that. You know, as I watched Dad play over the years I wasn't that interested, but lately, I've found that card games can be very relaxing."

Terry piped in, "Yes, Jan and I have found gin rummy to be a great evening pastime, on occasion. If Jan learns cribbage, she can teach me and we can add that to our gaming repertoire."

Peter and Reuben went back to their game, Janice and Terry watching their play. As Reuben and Peter chatted, played cards, counted and pegged, Reuben was totally intrigued. He had always wanted to have a friend who was black. His introduction to black people was the *National Geographic*, *Look* and *Life* magazines and the one missionary he had met years ago at Bethany Lutheran. He appreciated African American culture and music, and had always been impressed by the talented black athletes. Then there were the race riots and civil rights marches of the Sixties, during which he was appalled by the treatment of black Americans and then, of course, he had read all sorts of books about blacks in America. He saw African Americans on television; he saw them when they went to the shopping malls in Sioux Falls, Mankato and Minneapolis; but he had never come to know a black man as a personal friend. It had always been a silent wish and dream.

As Peter dealt another game, Reuben continued to be surprised at the smoothness and perfection with which Peter's deal was completed. As they continued to call out their pegging and move the pegs, the two men became so engrossed in conversation and the game that neither one of them noticed when Terry and Janice quietly left the apartment.

Reuben said, "Terry and Janice didn't say anything about you, other than that you were a crib player looking for a game. I apologize if I might have offended you with my clumsy words during our introduction."

Peter smiled. "No offense taken, and I *am* just another crib player, Reuben. People are always shocked to meet a black man with the name 'White.' It was my father's weird sense of humor when he changed our name in the '20s, just to mess with folks. I've been blind for 62 years. I fell out of a big ol' tree when I was ten years old and fell on my head. I was in a coma for almost three months and when I woke up, I was blind. It was tough going for me, but I had a mother who taught

## Reuben's Journey Begins

me that it was important to simply find other ways to see the world. It is amazing what you see by hearing with your ears, touching with your hands, tasting with your mouth and smelling with your nose. And then there is that wonderful sense of simply feeling the energy around you. In voices, you hear a man's heart and soul by the pitch and melody of his voice. When you touch an object, you form a strange relationship with it by knowing its temperature, texture, hardness or softness in lifting or moving it; you know its size and weight. I'm glad I had sight for ten years because when I taste a chocolate piece of cake I can also see it in my mind's eye. And smell! – what a gift of sight that many people don't use. From the very worst smells to the sweet perfumes of beautiful flowers or the wafting aromas of good food, you gain a great deal of knowledge about the environment you are in at that moment."

As they continued playing, Reuben asked, "What all did you teach, Peter?"

"Well," Peter replied, "I was a music teacher. After I recovered from my injury, I went through a period of depression and my parents were worried about me. Kids at school teased me to death and I just wanted to die. The first few years of being blind were the worst. Then something wonderful happened in my life. My mother played the piano at our church. One evening while she was practicing at home, I had a strange awareness that our piano was not in tune. I knew very little about

## Reuben's Journey Begins

the piano, except I could hear the 'sour' notes. When I mentioned it to her, she acknowledged that she had wanted to get it tuned but hadn't been able to afford it. I shared the story with my music teacher at school after class one day and asked her how to tune a piano. While she laughed at first, she soon became curious about my ability to hear the 'sour notes.'" Peter paused.

"About two weeks later, my mother got a call from Mr. Watson who was the piano tuner in Des Moines," Peter continued. "I didn't know it at the time, but my music teacher had made a deal with my mother. If I would take piano lessons with her after school once a week, she would have Mr. Watson tune our piano. A few days later, Mr. Watson came to our home and tuned the piano. I asked if I could sit near him while he worked. As he began tuning one of the 'sour note' strings, he placed the tuning key in my hand and showed me how he either tightened or loosened a wire. He helped me feel the hammer pads, explaining which needed replacement, and as I touched the heads I could somehow see the indentations! It was really an extraordinary moment in my life. The two hours he was there passed so quickly and I was hooked on piano tuning. In the following months and years while I was in high school, he invited me to join him often as he went to tune pianos and my 'ear' became so finely tuned that he would often asked me if the tension was right!"

"With my interest in tuning the piano," Peter

## Reuben's Journey Begins

went on, "my life at school changed dramatically during my high school years. My teacher, Mrs. Hendrickson, and the piano tuner, Mr. Watson, introduced me to a world of blind musicians. From piano players to guitarists ... it was incredible. I learned about the works of Arizona Dranes, a blind lady who was a great Gospel artist and one of the first to bring Gospel music to public performances. Her influence among early 20$^{th}$ century artists was immense. And then there were people like Blind Lemon Jefferson, a blues singer and guitarist; Blind Willie McTell, Blind Willie Johnson, Sonny Terry and Blind Boy Fuller. I'm so thankful that my mother, Mrs. Hendrickson and Mr. Watson introduced me to a world of people who could become my heroes. It gave me comfort when my friends talked about their heroes in sports, popular music and history ... I could also join the conversations with pride and dignity. I feel sorry for people who have disabilities and haven't searched for or found their heroes."

Reuben sat, captivated, as they had paused in their cribbage game while Peter told his story. "Did you learn to play everything by ear?" asked Reuben with a searching tone in his voice.

Peter replied, "Well, yes and no. My proclivity was to listen to a piece and then try to play it. However, when it came to Mrs. Hendrickson, she demanded that I learn to 'read' music and it was in the ninth grade that she introduced me to the story of Louis Braille who, as you probably know, also

## Reuben's Journey Begins

went blind from an accident in his youth and at the age of ten, he got a scholarship to the Royal Institution for Blind Youth in Paris. He became a very accomplished cellist and organist. Later on, he refined a 'raised dot system' for reading words and music developed originally by a man named Charles Barbier. Barbier's system was made up of twelve dots and based on sort of a phonetic system. Mr. Braille refined the system and developed one with six dots. Over time, the Braille system was further refined, and today I can read books and music just about as fast as most sight readers."

"Wow, what a story, Peter. Was it hard to learn to read Braille music?" asked Reuben.

"Again, yes and no," responded Peter. "I was a little impatient at first and just wanted to play the song if I had heard it played before, and I sort of cheated. But Mrs. Hendrickson would pull me up short and gently threaten to keep me longer at the lesson and miss my chance to be with Mr. Watson. So I acquiesced, though I was somewhat of a reluctant student at first. You actually had to read with one hand and play with the other; then practice it and commit it to memory. As I learned to read Braille music faster, I actually looked forward to refining my technical skills in playing the piano and other instruments."

"Other instruments?" queried Reuben.

Sporting a big smile, Peter replied, "Well, you know, a music teacher in my day had to learn how

## Reuben's Journey Begins

to play most of the band instruments, no matter how badly, in order to teach the youth. I had some special sheet music that was made for both sight and Braille readers." Pausing, Peter turned toward Reuben and it was if he could see his face. "What about Reuben Anderson? Tell me a little bit about your life's journey," he said.

"Well, it sure hasn't been as interesting as yours, Peter," exclaimed Reuben. Reuben went on to tell him about growing up on the farm, his wide variety of interests, his family, and then his personal struggles the past few months, with losing Ruth.

"Reuben, you've known a world I have often wanted to visit and never had the chance. Why, I would love to figure out a way a blind man could strip a cow's teat and shoot the milk into the mouth of a cat five feet away," Peter said, laughing.

"Peter, one day soon we will go over to my friend Steve Hollander's when they're milking cows, and do exactly that!" promised Reuben.

As they began their seventh game, Peter said, "So Reuben, I picked up on your surprise, that I am blind and black. Tell me about that," said Peter.

"Well, Peter," Reuben replied, "I've only ever met one African American. In fact, it is even kind of hard to say 'African American,' because I've grown up in a culture that has, until the '70s or so, referred to black people as Negroes. I have some real heroes who are African American. Some of my favorite baseball players like Earl Battey,

# Reuben's Journey Begins

Jackie Robinson, Mudcat Grant ... and singers like Curtis Charles, Ella Fitzgerald ... well, the list goes on and on. For reasons I don't really understand, I've always wanted to know a black person, excuse me, I mean an African American," said Reuben apologetically.

"Oh, dispense with the pc stuff," laughed Peter. "I hear the sincerity in your voice; no need to apologize."

Suddenly, Peter's words were interrupted by a clock striking five o'clock. For a moment, Reuben couldn't believe his ears.

"Something wrong, Reuben?" asked Peter.

"Oh, oh no, just that I need to get home for chores," answered Reuben. "Even though we don't milk cows anymore, I do have to feed the horses and other critters and pick a few eggs, and I have to stop by and talk to Doc Gerten, the veterinarian, about Dolly."

"Dolly?" Peter asked.

"Oh, I'm sorry; I sometimes think that everyone in town knows Duke, Dolly, Duchess, Dancer and Boots. They are five Belgian draft horses I have at the farm, and together we pull folks on hayrides, sleigh rides and all sorts of other rides using my collection of antique wagons and carriages. Yesterday, the Baptist Youth Group came out to the farm for a Christmas sleigh ride and Dolly broke a piece out of one of her hooves on a stone or something. She came up lame and I need to have Doc repair her hoof."

## Reuben's Journey Begins

"Wow, they sound like incredible animals, Reuben. Perhaps I could see them sometime?" Peter asked, anticipation in his voice.

"Anytime, my friend, anytime," Reuben replied.

"Perhaps the next time the Baptist group comes out, I could join them," said Peter. "Being a good Baptist, I would fit right in and no one would even notice me," he said as they both shared a great laugh.

"Reuben," Peter continued, "I can't thank you enough for your gift of time this afternoon! It has been a sincere pleasure to meet you, and you are a joy. I'm honored that you have spent this afternoon with me."

Reuben was filled with gratitude as he listened to Peter's words. They shook hands and held the handshake for a few moments longer as if to say to each other, 'This has truly been an absolutely wonderful afternoon.'

"Come, Socrates," said Reuben. "Thank Peter for the wonderful afternoon, and now let's get home to the farm."

As Socrates barked, sat up and stretched, Peter and Reuben shook hands again and the two left Peter's apartment and made their way to Terry's office.

Terry was just finishing up some last minute paperwork as Reuben and Socrates poked their heads into his office to thank him for lunch, and for the introduction to Peter. Janice had left earlier to pick up the twins at school.

## Reuben's Journey Begins

"Well, how did the cribbage games go, Reuben?" Terry asked.

"Absolutely great! What a fascinating man Peter is, Terry. You need to get to know him," Reuben exclaimed.

"I thought the two of you might hit it off," replied Terry modestly, knowing Peter's story.

"You should have mentioned that he couldn't see." Reuben said.

"Can't see?" replied Terry. "Reuben, that man has better eyesight than ninety percent of us! It never crossed my mind to tell you he was blind because I guess I don't see it that way, after getting to know him."

"Guess you're right about that," Reuben replied as he bade Terry goodbye for the evening.

That night as he made his root beer float, listened to a CD of Patsy Cline and worked on a brand new puzzle, he closed his eyes and tried to see the shape of the pieces as he held them in his hand.

## Chapter Seven

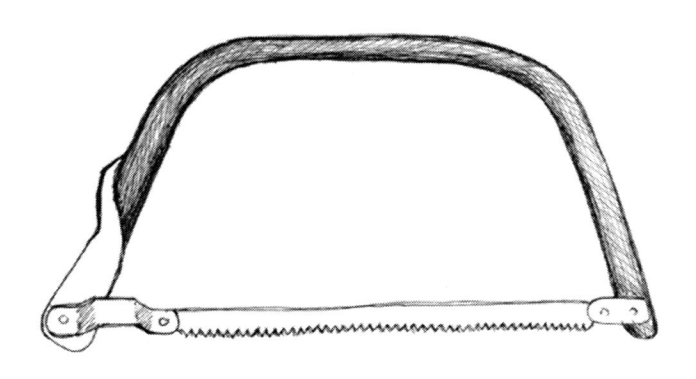

### A Christmas Day Promise

### December, 1990

    On the morning following Ruth's birthday party and his cribbage game with Peter, Reuben awoke about 4:00 a.m. Peeking over at the alarm clock's dimly illuminated phosphorescent letters across the room, he confirmed his best guess; it was 4:04. He stretched his arms and, putting his hands behind his head, scooted up a little on his pillow. Lying on his back, head against the headboard, he revisited yesterday's events. What a day it had been, celebrating Ruth's birthday and meeting Peter White, a most fascinating man. Oh, how he wished Ruth was still alive so he could tell her all about his new acquaintance, Peter White! He had waited a lifetime of wanting to have a friend who

## Reuben's Journey Begins

was an African American. His heart was in a whirl of loneliness for Ruth, and excitement, thinking about his new friend. And then a thought raced through his mind, 'Maybe this is God's way of helping me deal with her physical absence and my loneliness and sadness ... and, just maybe, Ruth is looking down on this, too, and glad to see that I have a new friend.'

Reuben walked into the kitchen and made a fresh pot of coffee, gave Socrates and the two house cats their daily rations of food and was just about to start breakfast. And just as he poured his cup of coffee, he heard footsteps and stomping of feet in the mudroom, obviously kicking the snow off their shoes. It was awfully early for company and Louise and Willard rarely came into the house this early. It was Catherine and Christopher! At 4:30 a.m.! For a moment, Reuben feared something was wrong but as they opened the door to the kitchen, he saw their smiles, and each carried a paper bag and a dish with morning breakfast. Catherine had baked a fresh coffee cake the night before and Christopher had a hot dish with eggs, bacon, hash browns and toast.

"Hi, Grandpa ... We thought we'd bring over breakfast so we could go out into the woods as soon as it is light," said Christopher.

"We have all our Christmas decorations unpacked and we'd like to help you cut down our Christmas trees," added Catherine with exuberance.

## Reuben's Journey Begins

In all of yesterday's excitement, Reuben had forgotten about the Anderson tradition of cutting down a fresh Christmas tree about four or five days before Christmas. His grandfather, Rudolf, had started the tradition many years earlier, feeling that a fresh tree for a week or so before Christmas, and leaving it up for a week after Christmas, was long enough before needles started falling on the floor. He could never understand why people cut down trees a month or more before Christmas and ended up with a tree at Christmas that looked like a plucked chicken. With Christmas only four days away, it was time to harvest the trees.

"Oh, my goodness, kids, what a wonderful surprise," Reuben said in a buoyant voice. "And, to be honest, I almost forgot about cutting down our trees this weekend! Catherine, if you'll set the table and Christopher, if you'll dish up the food, I'll get some fresh milk and orange juice from the fridge and we can dig into this breakfast. What a great treat!" Both children beamed with pride as they set the table and prepared the food.

As they ate breakfast, Catherine began to unwrap several small packages with Christmas decorations she had made in art class at school. "Grandpa, here are some decorations I made for you and Grandma in art class during the second term," said Catherine. "We made them out of dough and then baked them. Then we painted them with acrylic paints and sealed them with a varnish so they won't fade. The horse is supposed

## Reuben's Journey Begins

to be Boots, the barn owl is Barney, the dog is Socrates, the cats are Mitsy and Cougar, the farmer on the tractor is you, and the angel is Grandma."

Reuben's eyes began welling up with tears and all he could do was reach over to Catherine next to him and squeeze her shoulder for a moment.

"I love you, Grandpa, and I miss Grandma. I hope you like the angel best," said Catherine. "It was my favorite, and Mrs. Hanson gave me an 'A' on my project. She liked the angel best, too, especially the little pair of glasses I put on her, just like the ones Grandma used to wear."

"Oh, Honey, I will hang her right at the top of my tree next to my Mother Amanda's angel," said Reuben, silently choking up.

Catherine radiated with a great big smile and hugged Reuben. Almost before he could fully absorb the gifts from Catherine, Christopher reached into a large paper bag in the chair next to him, taking out yet another gift for Reuben.

"Hey, Grandpa, I've got something for you, too," said Christopher. "I had to make a practical tool in shop class this year using leather, metal and wood, and so I made you a Christmas tree saw."

As Christopher pulled the beautifully crafted leather case out of the paper bag, Reuben gazed upon the letters, "Grandpa's Christmas Tree Saw" tooled neatly in the leather of the carrying case. He couldn't believe his eyes. In the leather case was a tree saw about eighteen inches long, with a

## Reuben's Journey Begins

bow top and a beautifully hand carved handle made of walnut. Inlaid in the handle with mother of pearl were the words, "Reuben Anderson." Christopher had made the case, bent and filed the metal bow handle, cut and filed the blade, drilled the holes for the holding bolts, and even had to tool the two bolts that secured the blade. It was truly a work of art.

"Wow," Reuben exclaimed, "Christopher, I had no idea you were such a skilled craftsman! This saw is so beautiful, I may not want to get it dirty!"

"Oh no, Grandpa, you have to use it today," Christopher quickly replied. "Mr. Peterson, my industrial arts teacher, said that our final grade will depend upon how well our tools work when used in real life situations. He specifically said that he would be calling you to ask if we were able to cut down our Christmas trees as well with this saw as your store-bought saws."

Reuben was overwhelmed with his gifts from the kids. "I just don't know what to say, kids," said Reuben. "I can't remember a time when two such important people in my life took the time to make me such absolutely wonderful gifts! I will cherish these gifts forever. Tell you what," he continued, "I'll clean up the dishes and we should have good light about 8:00 this morning, and then we'll hitch up Duke and Dolly and take the old hayrack sleigh and go over to the Campsite Grove where there are lots of fir trees to choose from. In the meantime, Christopher, you can play video games

## Reuben's Journey Begins

in the library, and Catherine, I'm wondering if you would help me wrap a few gifts for your dad, Uncle David and Aunt Janice."

The kids quickly agreed to Reuben's suggestions and, as he walked upstairs to Janice's old bedroom with Catherine, he began to tell her about the Christmas gifts he and Grandma had been working on since the first of the year. She thought the ideas and the gifts were very exciting and she couldn't wait to see them. Catherine loved to wrap gifts, tie ribbons around them and always select the perfect bow. She was a perfectionist when it came to wrapping gifts, which was a trait picked up from her mother, Louise. Once in the bedroom, Reuben organized the various gift wrapping papers, scissors, tape, ribbons and bows so she could delve into the task. In her own right, she was a very gifted young artist who took great pride in each project she undertook, especially wrapping gifts.

Reuben returned to the kitchen where he listened to the morning news on WCCO radio and began cleaning up the morning breakfast dishes. Boone and Erickson were in rare form as they talked about their most surprising Christmas gifts from years past. As he worked, his mind drifted away from the chatter on the radio, back to yesterday's cribbage game and conversation with Peter.

He thought it was remarkable how much this man, who was blind, already knew about the

## Reuben's Journey Begins

people and place where he had only lived for four months. What a truly serendipitous experience it had been to meet him. Perhaps later this morning, after they cut down the trees and stood them up in their holders in the entryways of the homes to settle and let the ice and snow melt off, he could go in to The Cottonwoods and play a couple games of cribbage. Maybe he would stop by the new Cinnamon Bakery and get some chocolate chip cookies for him, too. He had learned yesterday that they were Peter's favorite cookie. The vision of doing both things put a little bounce in his step.

Finishing up the dishes, he filled one of his pipes with fresh tobacco and went out onto the porch to puff on it for a few minutes. He was tempted to smoke in the living room near the fireplace but Ruth had never approved of him smoking his pipes in the house. He dismissed the thought as quickly as he considered it, feeling it would betray a promise he had made to her years earlier not to smoke in the house when she was gone shopping, visiting or at work.

It was a brisk morning and Venus, the morning star, still shone brightly in the sky. He felt proud of his two grandchildren who had taken so much personal time and school time to make him these wonderful gifts. He quietly blew a series of smoke rings, first for him and then for Ruth, and for the kids. Finishing his pipe and setting it down in the ashtray next to his rocker on the great porch,

## Reuben's Journey Begins

Reuben and Socrates walked out to the horse barn where he fed the horses and then walked over to the carriage barn where he hooked up the four-wheeler to the old hayrack sleigh, to pull it over into the horse corral. Opening up the gate and pulling it through, he parked it by the barn and then went into the tack room to select the harnesses and rigging for the sleigh. Oh, how he enjoyed puttering around with this stuff. And today, he would take down the Christmas sleigh bell attachments his father had made years earlier. These were beautiful brass bells hand fired and shaped in the old blacksmith shed next to the horse barn. In the barn, he could hear Duke whinnying a little bit because he knew that was his sleigh to pull; he could see it through the open door.

"Duke, we're going Christmas tree shopping out at the Campsite Grove, Old Boy," laughed Reuben. "Think you and Dolly are up to pulling the hayrack sleigh with me and the kids?" Socrates barked at Duke and, as Reuben opened the gate to his stall, Socrates raced in to nuzzle Duke's nose as the giant horse bent his head down to greet the dog. Just as it was with Dolly, these two animals had a wonderful friendship. Both animals were about seven years old and had grown up together. As a pup and a colt, they had raced around the horse pasture for hours playing, and Reuben, as well as the rest of the family, had never seen anything quite like it before. There had

## Reuben's Journey Begins

once been a goose that befriended a runt piglet on the farm, and they went everywhere together, but that was nothing quite like this. Leading Duke by his halter, Reuben led him out into the dressing area by the tack room and put on the harnesses and other riggings to which he would attach the pull bar of the hayrack sleigh. Next, he brought out Dolly and did likewise.

As they left the horse barn and went into the corral to hitch Duke and Dolly up to the sleigh, Reuben heard the kids running out of the house across the great porch and over to the corral.

"Grandpa, guess what?" yelled Catherine, "Uncle David wants us to wait a few more minutes because he wants to get a tree, too. He just called from town and he'll be here in five minutes."

"No problem," replied Reuben, surprise in his voice, "I didn't know he was coming, but the more the merrier! I think I will hitch up the four-man sleigh to Dancer and Duchess so they can pull you kids and David. With four trees on the hayrack sleigh, there won't be much room for people."

Reuben loved it. He was always looking for an excuse to rig up another horse and sleigh for the task at hand. And just as he finished rigging up the four-man sleigh, David drove into the farmyard and quickly made his way to the horse corral.

"Good morning, everyone," David said in his booming voice. "Socrates, come here, Boy. Good to see you, and you kids, too. Dad, looks like you are ready for business."

## Reuben's Journey Begins

Reuben walked over and hugged his oldest son. "I didn't know you were in town, Son. How's my sheriff?"

"I'm doing great, Dad. Kathy and I thought we would take a few days off work and since Tammy is flying for Northwest Airlines this Christmas weekend, as she had last year off, we thought we'd surprise you with a visit." said David. "Early this morning when we woke up, we thought, 'what the heck, let's go down to the farm and spend a few days.' There's still a bedroom open for us, isn't there? Kathy is going to unpack our suitcases and wrap some presents while we're out getting trees."

Reuben laughed and said, "Of course, your bedroom is always there for you kids. I think it is just great that you and Kathy will be spending the next few days with us. In fact, you can help around the farm with a few chores, to see if you still have the touch." Everyone laughed as they all boarded their respective sleighs, and off they went to Campsite Grove.

It was about a half mile out to the grove. It was a grove of elms, oaks, fir, walnut, blue spruce, Norway pines, cottonwoods and willow trees, and it was beautiful! A long, 45-acre site that meandered along Red Rock Creek as it passed through the northeast corner of the Anderson farm; this place held a lot of Anderson family history! There had been many evenings when the Campsite Grove was filled with campfires, storytelling and the

## Reuben's Journey Begins

roasting of s'mores; it had been the site of family picnics and afternoons of fishing and gatherings of every kind through the generations of Andersons and, of course, it was the special spot where Reuben had proposed to Ruth, and where he had held her family funeral service.

Reuben had fenced in the area so the cattle and horses wouldn't make a mess of it. To keep the grass at a reasonable level, Christopher grazed his sheep in part of the Campsite Grove during the spring and summer. In the fall, they were moved to the east pasture with the cattle, but for those two warm growing seasons, they had the entire grove to themselves.

Duke, Dolly, Duchess and Dancer pulled the sleighs with powerful grace over a bed of freshly fallen snow. The sleigh bells and the brushing sound of the sleigh runners on the ice, the occasional scratching sound of dirt, gravel, small rocks and snow, called up Christmas memories for all of them. David mused on the many sleigh rides he had given to groups and organizations during his high school career, as well as some very enjoyable personal rides with old girlfriends. How sweet those times were. Reuben recalled a more recent memory last year, when he took Ruth on the same ride in the four-man sleigh so she could lie down in the second seat to better manage some of the bumps. Oh, how he missed his best friend and lover!! The kids each silently recalled the first sleigh rides with Grandpa Reuben and how cool it

## Reuben's Journey Begins

was when it was snowing. The farm, fields and woods were always like a winter wonderland this time of year. Both Reuben and Christopher were anxious to see if the Christmas tree saw would pass the test of performing a smooth cut as they cut down the first tree.

Arriving at Campsite Grove, Reuben tied the reins of both horses to a hitching post his father had made many years ago. For Reuben and his dad, the Campsite Grove had been their favorite fishing hole, and it also offered the best swimming pond which was a large backwater pond expanded by high water in the spring and during heavy rainfalls during the year, and fed by two small springs. The pond had been a small gravel pit in earlier times where the county had mined some gravel for area roads. Being spring fed, the water remained clear and was home to some pretty big sunfish, blue gills and crappies that Reuben's longtime friend, Duke Peterson, who was an area game warden, had always stocked with some fingerlings each spring.

As Reuben took his new Christmas tree saw out of the leather case, David said, "Wow, where did you get that, Dad?"

"Christopher made it for me in industrial arts," said Reuben. "Mr. Peterson, his shop teacher, said we should use it this weekend as a test of its performance and then he's going to call me to see how it worked as part of Christopher's final grade. Pretty cool, isn't it?"

# Reuben's Journey Begins

"Wow, looks like something we should hang over the fireplace mantle, Christopher," David acknowledged with a loud baritone approval.

The Andersons walked around the Campsite Grove for about twenty minutes, each finally selecting a tree to be cut down. David just wanted a small tree to put up in his bedroom for Kathy and himself; Christopher and Catherine were looking for a seven foot tree for their living room; Janice and Terry wanted a smaller six foot tree for their home; and Reuben always found a tall nine foot tree for their living room that had ten foot ceilings.

And the saw, it went through the tree trunks like a hot knife through butter. It worked perfectly. It was an A+ gift and class project.

They loaded the trees on the hayrack sleigh and headed for home. As both sleighs pulled into the farmyard, Doc Gerten, the veterinarian, was just coming out of the horse barn where he had attended to Dolly's chipped hoof. The kids took their tree into the entryway of their home and put it in the Christmas tree stand where it would remain for most of the day until the snow and ice had dripped off and it would be ready to decorate later in the afternoon and evening. And while Reuben visited with Doc Gerten, David put Terry and Janice's tree in the red pickup truck and took the other two trees into the house where they would be readied for decorating later that day.

No sooner had everyone gone their own ways that Reuben quickly put away the sleighs, groomed

## Reuben's Journey Begins

the horses and cleaned up to go to The Cottonwoods to play cribbage with Peter White. He checked to see if Terry and Janice's Christmas tree was okay in the pickup, and raced off to town. After dropping the tree off at their home, he went over to Peter's where he spent the afternoon, once again playing cribbage and swapping a dozen good stories.

That evening in all three homes, everyone was busy decorating the trees with keepsake ornaments, paper chains made by the Sunday School class, popcorn strings that Catherine had made the week before, strings of lights, aluminum icicles, and lots of bulbs of all colors and shapes. And for Reuben, as he once again made his evening root beer float and came into the living room where David and Janice had been helping him, he hung the angel Catherine had given him near the top of the tree, just below an older cloth angel his mother had made over forty years ago.

That night, Reuben and Ruth went for a sleigh ride and Reuben told Ruth all about Peter.

Saturday dawned, and it was time for Reuben to finish up his Christmas shopping. His brother-in-law, Glenn Orville, had called early to see if he and Synnova could stop out to the farm and have everyone help wrap the Salvation Army presents for the residents at The Annex and River's Edge. Every year in southern Minnesota, the Salvation Army gave a present to every person living in assisted living residences, nursing homes and also

# Reuben's Journey Begins

other 'shut-ins' throughout the community, especially seniors who still lived in private homes and apartment complexes. Glenn Orville and Synnova had been volunteers for the Salvation Army for as long as Reuben could remember, and he always enjoyed helping them at this time of year. As they finished wrapping the gifts, Janice, David, Louise, Willard, Catherine, Christopher, Glenn Orville and Synnova hand wrote a card to each resident and taped it to the gift. This year, between The Cottonwoods and the private homes, they would deliver over 150 gifts in Prairieville.

When they arrived at The Cottonwoods, Reuben stopped by the administrative offices to talk with Terry, Janice and Nancy about any special requests from residents for Christmas. The list contained about fifteen special requests, all of which Reuben found would be easy to accommodate.

"Eleanor Schultz would like you to stop down and visit. She has a special request but wants to talk to you in person about it," said Janice.

"No problem," replied Reuben, "I'll do that right now while David, Kathy, Louise, Willard, Glenn Orville and Synnova are bringing the Salvation Army gifts around to the residents and visiting with them."

He found Eleanor busy wrapping gifts for some of her friends and she was glad to see Reuben. As they visited, she asked Reuben if he would stop by her daughter Jeanie's home to help look

## Reuben's Journey Begins

through some boxes of old photos in order to find a photo of her brother, Bruno Johnson, and his buddies that was taken in Germany at the end of World War II. Bruno had been talking about his experiences during the war with Eleanor and her friends earlier in the fall and Bruno had said he wished he knew where some of his old friends were; if they were still alive and what were they doing. The idea occurred to Eleanor that if they could find the photo and frame it, it would make a great Christmas gift for her brother, Bruno.

That afternoon, Reuben called Jeanie and they found the photo. Reuben took it into the Fast and Furious Framing Shop run by George Putney, a local artist and art gallery owner who also had this picture framing business. George said he would do his best to have it ready by late Monday morning. As Reuben left the shop, he was hopeful it would be ready. But George was not always that fast, and often got furious if you bugged him about getting your framing done on time. In one sense, the name of the business seemed quite appropriate.

For the balance of the afternoon, Reuben visited a number of stores to buy the special Christmas gifts for the residents at The Cottonwoods. And for his friend, Peter, he bought two new CD's featuring the music of Mozart and Bach. With an hour left before dinner, he stopped by Peter's for two quick games of cribbage.

The next morning, the Sunday School

## Reuben's Journey Begins

Christmas Pageant at Bethany Lutheran began a 10:00 a.m. and was once again led by the Sunday School carolers and finished up with the Senior Choir. Pastor Stendahl was unusually brief in his sermon but was nevertheless banging away on the pulpit, pleading for tithes as the year ended. Reuben wanted to throw his shoe at him as he dropped his annual Christmas check for $15,000 onto the plate. He wanted to write a note and tell him that it would have been another $5,000 if the pastor had stopped complaining about the church treasury and focused on some good exegetical preparation, at least presenting the appearance of being a good theologian.

Sunday afternoon had been promised to Catherine, Louise and Janice as they gathered in Reuben's kitchen after lunch and made Christmas cookies. For years, it had been Reuben's and Ruth's tradition to bake Christmas cookies the day before Christmas Eve and then deliver them on Christmas Eve Day to the Prairieville Hospital, The Cottonwoods and the Prairieville Rest Home, a smaller skilled nursing facility owned and operated by the Baptist Fellowship.

It was about 6:30 a.m. on Christmas Eve Day and Reuben was just finishing a fresh cup of coffee and putting a little fresh tobacco in his favorite Christmas pipe, a calabash pipe reminiscent of Sherlock Holmes' calabash, a curved gourd pipe with a meerschaum bowl, when he heard a car coming up the driveway. As he stepped out onto

## Reuben's Journey Begins

the great porch in the brisk 24-degree weather, the car was already turning into the farmyard. It was his sister, Synnova, and his brother-in-law, Glenn Orville. He was expecting them, as they were to begin distributing the Christmas gifts to the shut-ins around town at 9:00 a.m. and they had preparation work left to do before then.

"Good morning," greeted Reuben. "Merry Christmas!"

"Merry Christmas," came a refrain from Glenn Orville and Synnova, as well as Julius and Ruth Borchert, as they were getting out of the back seat of the car. Julius and Ruth were friends from Bethany Lutheran and lived in nearby Jefferson. Ruth served as the church secretary at Bethany Lutheran and Julius was a salesman for Prairieville Lodges, a mobile home manufacturer in Windy Marsh. Together, the four of them volunteered hundreds of hours of time every year to community causes.

"Come on in, folks, and let's rustle up some breakfast," said Reuben. "Ruth, how about making your wonderful waffles and I'll fry up the bacon, scrambled eggs and cottage fries while we recruit Glenn Orville and Julius to juice the oranges and grapefruit. Synnova, you get to pour some coffee and set the table."

As they busied themselves with preparing a traditional farm breakfast, they visited about the day ahead and talked about their Christmas plans. Reuben told them about the picture of Bruno

## Reuben's Journey Begins

Johnson and his five friends that was taken at the end of World War II, which he needed to pick up sometime late morning.

"Well, George will either have been fast and it will be done, or he will get furious with you if you press him, Reuben," Julius said, laughing. "I've left things there for months, waiting, in the past. If he wasn't such a perfectionist, I would just have them done in Windy Marsh, but the framing shop there has been hit and miss with their quality for years. So I've become very tolerant in waiting for George to get the work done."

"I hear you have had a good year in sales, Julius," said Reuben.

"It has been, Reuben," replied Julius. "On our way out this morning, I was telling Ruth, Glenn Orville and Synnova that 40% of my sales were to farm families who wanted to move their older parents back to the farm to live with them. Most of them have small homes and not enough room to add a retired parent, so I came up with a marketing campaign called 'Parent Suites on Your Farm in One Day.' I sold 35 manufactured homes in the four-county area just to this market. The seniors who wanted to stay on the farm, yet not be in the way of their children and grandchildren, found it to be a perfect solution. By the way, Willard and I are looking at expanding his home with an add-on porch and a greenhouse."

"Julius, I swear, you are one of most creative marketers I have ever met," exclaimed Reuben.

# Reuben's Journey Begins

Breakfast over and the others now wrapping gifts, Reuben called George at 8:30 a.m. and, sure enough, he hadn't finished the framing but would get right on it and have it ready at 11:45. In the meantime, he thought he would help Glenn Orville, Synnova, Julius and Ruth, along with Catherine and Christopher, to tote the gifts. The morning passed quickly and they got all of the gifts delivered.

About 11:30 a.m., Reuben headed for The Fast and Furious Framing Shop to pick up the newly framed photo of Bruno and his World War II buddies. George had once again outdone himself. He had artistically drawn the Army Air Force logo in blue and red ink in the upper left corner of the photo. The frame was beautiful. It was a red, white and blue frame. Although the 8x10 black and white photo had yellowed some with age, George had also tinted the sky blue and the faces and hands a flesh color. The entire package was quite stunning.

"What a fantastic job, George," exclaimed Reuben. "Eleanor will really appreciate the extra care you took in putting this together. I love the triple red, white and blue frame, and the tinting is beautiful, George."

"Thanks, Reuben," replied George. "My dad was in that war and I guess we forget how important it was to them and how appreciative we should be."

"What do I owe you?" asked Reuben.

# Reuben's Journey Begins

"Nothing," replied George. "Tell Eleanor it's on the house and wish her Merry Christmas from me. She has been one of my best customers over the years and this seems like the right thing to do."

Somewhat surprised – more accurately, shocked - Reuben thanked George and assured him that he would pass the greetings and kindness of his gift along to Eleanor. Reuben went directly to deliver the photograph to Eleanor and she responded with gratitude and tears. As he sat down to visit with her, she talked about Bruno discussing how things have changed at the American Legion and VFW Clubs in Prairieville and Windy Marsh.

"Reuben," began Eleanor, "There was a time when there were great programs and social events at both the American Legion in Prairieville and the VFW in Windy Marsh. In more recent years, they have generally become beer halls and Friday night fish fries with bingo. There are many of the World War II veterans who don't get out much, or if they live in assisted living or a nursing home, they have become a forgotten generation of soldiers except for a few veterans' holidays. So much of Bruno's identity is tied to his service for his country and I wish there was a way to help him know that people still care and appreciate him, and others."

"Eleanor," replied Reuben, "you are right, and I think about it often, too. I don't go to the Legion or VFW very often, mostly because of the chores at the farm, but I do go to their Friday events on occasion when Willard covers chores. Let me think about what you've said, and maybe there is something we can do."

With that, the two hugged and wished each other Merry Christmas and Reuben continued on his way. He briefly stopped by Peter's apartment with his gift and played a quick game of 'Christmas cribbage.'

That night, as was the tradition in many southwestern Minnesota prairie communities, Christmas Eve was the time for opening gifts. And as they had done for years, David, Willard and Janice's families gathered at Reuben's for a turkey and ham Christmas supper and then opened their presents. All of Reuben's children were simply blown away by the gifts Ruth and Reuben had been working on for the past year. David was in awe of the sheriff badge collection; Willard was overwhelmed with the bullets, shells and slugs collection; and Janet teared up as she explored the porcelain doll collection so neatly arranged in the baby buggy. It was a perfect response to Ruth's and Reuben's labor of love.

Sunday the 25$^{th}$. Christmas Day. It felt good to be alone. He'd go out a little later in the morning to feed the horses, as he had given them all extra hay and water the evening before. Today, he was thinking about his old friend, Bruno Johnson, the gift his sister Eleanor had given him, and the story she had shared with Reuben. Reuben was also a veteran but he had not served overseas during

## Reuben's Journey Begins

World War II. Instead, he was stationed in the States and worked with a unit that prepared trucks, jeeps and ambulances to be shipped to various theaters throughout the world. He thought about how important reconnecting with some of his friends from that time was to him, and how it must be doubly important if you served in a combat situation.

As he was to be alone today, he thought maybe he would call Peter to see if he wanted to have lunch together, knowing that Peter's daughter was working the holiday shift at the hospital. They could play some cribbage and then maybe he'd stop by to see Bruno, who was living in The Manor at The Cottonwoods. He was anxious to see how Bruno liked the framed piece Eleanor had given him. Morning chores done, he and Socrates headed into town.

During his visit with Bruno, they talked about the others in the photo. From left to right in the photo were Bill Hanson, Stanley Anderson, Bruno, Bob Smith, Radar Knudson and Andy Almquist. Bruno believed that Bill lived in Florida in a retirement community somewhere around Tampa; Stanley had passed away; the last he heard, Bob lived in Georgia. He was sure that Andy lived in Billings, Montana, because Ted had seen him a couple of years ago at a conference. And he was pretty sure that Radar still lived in Waterville, Minnesota.

"I would dearly love to see some of the guys all

## Reuben's Journey Begins

together again, but it is so hard for me to travel and I haven't written or called any of them for some time," Bruno said with a sense of defeat.

Reuben was suddenly overcome by feelings of concern and warmth, and had a confident sense of knowing just what to do for Bruno.

Before he really realized what he was saying, Reuben blurted out, "Shoot, Bruno, let's get ahold of them and invite them to visit you. Heck, I can put all of you up out at my house. I'll be your host and cook the meals, and we can all sit around the living room and visit, go on some carriage rides, play some cards and who knows what else. I have four empty bedrooms just gathering dust most of the time since the kids are grown and Ruth is gone."

"Reuben, are you serious? You would do that? Help me get ahold of them and let all of us stay with you?" asked Bruno, a combination of surprise, gratefulness and hope in his voice. "That would be the greatest gift ever, and it would fill an empty space in my heart where I have been missing my old buddies. Are you sure you want to, and that you will?"

"I promise," replied Reuben as he gripped Bruno's right hand with both of his hands and stood gently shaking it. "Let's say that it is my Christmas Day promise and a wonderful gift for us to look forward to sharing together with old friends."

That night, Reuben prepared trucks and jeeps

Reuben's Journey Begins

with his Army buddies to ship them overseas.

# Chapter Eight

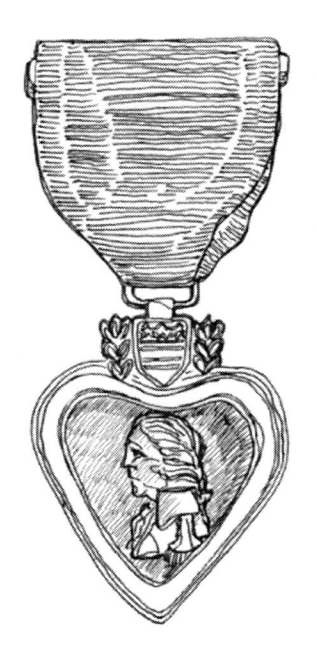

## Veterans' Courage™

## January - July, 1991

As the New Year began, Reuben was visualizing ways to help Bruno plan for his reunion with his Army buddies. He mused over Bruno lamenting about the disconnection with these old pals during recent years, and how he would like to reconnect with them. He could sense that Bruno had a deep spiritual need for a reunion with these men from his past.

# Reuben's Journey Begins

Somewhat to his surprise, Reuben had immediately visualized all of them spending time at the farm, where he would be their host. He saw them having meals together, enjoying their tobacco pipes and cigars on the great porch, taking carriage rides together, sitting around a campfire at Campsite Grove, and days of celebrating friendships that were created at a time when lives depended on watching each other's backs as a matter of survival.

This almost immediate visualization of a solution to a need, want or interest expressed by another person was a phenomenon that seemed to be happening more and more often to Reuben. And in more and more detail. As someone talked about a desire, whether it was a need, a want or an interest, Reuben found himself visualizing a way to personally respond to it, or find others to help him. 'What's this all about?' he thought. As he looked back on things, he knew it had happened many times in the past but he had never really thought about it as being unusual. Lately, however, it seemed to be happening more often and then he wondered, 'Maybe this happens to everyone ... or does it?' And why now, at this age and time in his life, did there seem to be more specificity in these imaginings? He contemplated, 'Is there something here that I need to pay closer attention to when it happens? Could this be about my evolving life's purpose and changing life's work?'

## Reuben's Journey Begins

Along with his desire to help Bruno, the New Year would also usher in more cribbage time with his new friend, Peter White, and volunteering around The Cottonwoods and in the greater Prairieville community, as well as throughout Cottonwood County. And Reuben often joined Glenn Orville and the Hospital Auxiliary Volunteers who did errands and other volunteer work for elderly people still living in their single family and mobile homes as well as apartment complexes. He found that he was spending at least two to four hours a day, three or four days a week doing volunteer work for these folks. And then, he still had the farm chores of tending to the horses and chickens as well as assisting Willard with various crop work and other tasks. Sometimes he felt like he was even busier these days than when he was farming and milking cows full time.

On New Year's Day, he drove in to The Cottonwoods to play cribbage with Peter, having talked with him the previous evening about starting a cribbage club at The Cottonwoods. As he arrived an hour earlier than planned, he decided to stop by Bruno's apartment at The Manor first, and talk about the promise he made to him on Christmas Day to host his Army buddies at the farm. He had been imagining what a great time he could create for the veterans to get together to reminisce and celebrate the camaraderie they shared so deeply in their hearts. Reuben had also spent an hour on the telephone with Bruno the day

## Reuben's Journey Begins

before, talking about the reunion.

As he knocked on the door with his signature seven taps, there was a peppy, "Come in, Reuben" invitation from Bruno as Reuben opened the door and entered.

"Happy New Year, my friend!" Bruno exclaimed. "Man, all I could think about lately is seeing my ol' buddies again. Reuben, you are a great friend. This is going to be the best time, and doing it out at your farm is a terrific idea. I can't wait to go on carriage rides and have some campfires out at Campsite Grove."

"It will be a great time, Bruno," replied Reuben, "The more I thought about it last night after we talked on the telephone, the more I realized that we'd better get started contacting these guys before their late June and early July calendars fill up. What would you think of having them come around the 25$^{th}$ of June and stay through the 4$^{th}$ or 5$^{th}$ of July? There is always a great parade in town and a celebration at the high school honoring veterans on the 4$^{th}$, and we could participate in both. Why don't we sit down with the photo and you can tell me a little bit about the men I don't know."

The photo included Bill Hanson, Stanley Anderson, Bruno Johnson, Bob Smith, Radar Knutson and Andy Almquist.

For the next hour, Reuben sat transfixed as Bruno told a dozen stories about how each man Had contributed to their Army unit in combat.

## Reuben's Journey Begins

Suddenly, Bruno looked at his watch and sighed, "Oh, my, I guess I could go on for days, but you didn't come here to listen to a replay of World War II. I suppose we should start making a list of where these guys are now living and see if we can get in touch with them. It's been a few years since I've communicated with them, other than Christmas and some birthday cards."

Bruno began by talking about each man in order as they appeared in the photo.

"I believe Bill Hanson is still living in Florida, somewhere around Tampa. Stanley Anderson, God rest his soul, was killed in a farming accident, as you know, being your close cousin. Then there is me, a much thinner and more handsome man than I am today ..."

Both men laughed, as Bruno continued, "And next is Bob Smith," Bruno paused, looking up at a shadow box above his kitchen table containing his service decorations and a Purple Heart in the center of it, "our unit's Sergeant, and I think he is living somewhere in Georgia now with his sister. Next is our good friend, Radar Knudson, who still lives on his farm over Waterville way. And, finally, Major General Andy Almquist, who retired some years ago from an impressive career in the Army and moved back to his boyhood town of Miles City, Montana."

"Bruno, this will be great fun. We'll plan for a grand reunion in late June and early July," said Reuben. "We'll definitely take carriage rides, enjoy

# Reuben's Journey Begins

our pipes and cigars, some good beer and wine, cook up some great meals and enjoy lots of conversation, especially a couple of nights around the campfire at Campsite Grove. I'll contact each of them and we'll see what dates are open. Once we get those tasks done, we can begin planning the week."

"Reuben, please let me know what I can do," said Bruno with deep appreciation. "My bad knees and hip make it so darn hard to get around. Worse yet, being deaf in one ear and wearing this damn hearing aid in the other makes it so frustrating for me to talk on the phone. I avoid it most of the time." Bruno paused, sighed, and then got up from his chair and walked across the room.

"Reuben, I have one more favor I'd like to ask of you." Bruno turned to his desk, opened a middle drawer, took out a small leather case and handed it to Reuben.

"I want you to take this money and offer to pay for the airline tickets for Bill, Bob and Andy. And I would like you to ask Glenn Orville to drive over to Waterville to pick up Radar when we have our reunion, and give him a donation for the Salvation Army for his trouble," said Bruno. "I think there is about $4,500 in this envelope for airfares and gas money, and then I want you to put the rest toward beverages and food."

"Bruno, that is very generous of you," began Reuben, "but you don't have to give me money for hosting this reunion at the farm. It will be my treat

## Reuben's Journey Begins

just to be around you and the guys. I never had a chance to serve overseas and your stories will be a gift to me. Besides, it gets a little lonely out at the farm these days and the company will be good for me and Socrates."

"You know, Reuben," began Bruno with a rather father-like voice, "I've heard you say that before, but the work you did in the Army in the States, preparing vehicles for transport overseas to support those of us at the front lines, was just as important as our service. I read a book a few years ago where the author said that if you aren't serving the customer directly, you need to be serving those who are. That was you, my good friend, serving us."

Reuben shrugged his shoulders, nodded in appreciation and bade Bruno goodbye.

As Reuben left Bruno's apartment to go play cribbage with Peter, he thought it would be best to go down to Eleanor's apartment to pick up Socrates, as Peter relished seeing the German shepherd. He felt a warm feeling of joy growing inside him. As he walked, he thought about how just the act of planning the upcoming reunion seemed to be healing Bruno's spirit. And for Bruno to see his buddies again would likely bring some closure to the restless feelings he had felt, wanting to reconnect with them for some time. In their conversation, he had noted a pause in Bruno's voice as he spoke about Bob Smith. Reuben wondered for a moment if there might be more to

## Reuben's Journey Begins

this gathering than just a reunion to reconnect with old friends. He sensed that there was some unfinished business between Bob and Bruno.

The morning passed quickly as he and Peter played several games of cribbage and then Peter's children stopped by to visit on New Year's Day and Reuben and Socrates returned to the farm.

Reuben's proclivity to address tasks as soon as possible led to a busy schedule the next day. He began calling around to get the contact information for the four remaining friends in the photograph.

First he called Esther Hanson, a cousin to Bill, and got Bill's address and phone number. Sure enough, a few phone calls later, he found Bill living at Royal Palms Senior Living Community in Largo, Florida, which had just opened within the past year. Bill said he would be glad to come at the end of June and stay through the 4$^{th}$ of July. Getting Bob Smith's information took a little more effort but, eventually, he got his phone number in Atlanta. After a few phone calls and leaving several messages, the men finally connected and Bob agreed to join them for their reunion in June.

The next day, after helping Willard feed the horses, pick eggs, put the full egg basket in the egg washer and help look after the sheep, the few head of feeding cattle and Christopher's calves, Reuben drove over to Radar Knutson's farm in Waterville, Minnesota. It had been some time since the two men had spent time together. Radar and Reuben had attended grade school and high

## Reuben's Journey Begins

school together and enjoyed many hours of horseback riding as their farms were near each other. They had also shared a common fancy for Ruth, who Reuben later married. Radar never did marry, and often teased Reuben about foiling his plans for marriage, yet Radar seemed to be one of those content Minnesota Norwegian bachelors. After two hours of conversation, a pot of coffee and fresh coffee cake, Reuben had sealed the commitment from Radar to attend.

Back home again, Reuben called Reverend Almquist, Andy's father who was a retired Lutheran minister now living at his lake place north of Prairieville. Andy had retired from the Army and was living in his boyhood town of Miles City, Montana. He had achieved a remarkable career in the service and was both a hometown hero and a c celebrity. A few more phone calls, and Andy expressed his great excitement about returning to Minnesota for the reunion.

Finally, after a long day of making arrangements, the reunion date was now set for everyone to arrive on Tuesday, June 25$^{th}$ and stay through the 4$^{th}$ of July, returning to their respective homes on July 5$^{th}$. That evening, as he made his root beer float, he took out a puzzle of the Iwo Jima Memorial. Cougar, anxious to help move puzzle pieces around, sat as a regal lion watching Reuben organize the edge pieces. Eventually, he completed the border frame and decided to turn in for the evening. And just for kicks, he closed his

## Reuben's Journey Begins

eyes and felt the shapes of various pieces, placing them in small piles of similar shapes. In a way, it seemed to bring him a bit closer to his new friend's world. Peter White and cribbage had become an important bridge in exploring a new agenda for his life.

The next morning, Reuben drove in to The Cottonwoods to join Terry, Janice and a few other staff members for breakfast before delivering a variety of items he had picked up at local stores for some of the residents.

As they all sat down for breakfast, Reuben said, "You know, I've been thinking a lot about Bruno Johnson the past few days as I've been helping him organize a reunion for his World War II Army buddies out at the farm in late June. All this planning has got me thinking about our veterans who live here at The Cottonwoods. I see Bruno as being kind of lonely right now, and he seems to be spending a good deal of time thinking about his life as a veteran. I'm wondering if the same is true for other veterans ... that is, that they would enjoy some program built around their service to our country and whether they might enjoy getting together once in a while."

"I think you are right, Reuben," said Dee Rice, the Activities Director. "Last month we had a program centered on Pearl Harbor Day. Bruno was very engaged in helping plan the program and told some great stories about his experiences in World War II. Before I knew it, the whole room

## Reuben's Journey Begins

was abuzz with stories and reminiscing. I also noted that there were many widows of veterans who attended, and the program seemed to have a meaningful impact on them as they reminisced about their lives with their spouses."

Terry chimed in with his Tennessee tone, "Bruno and other veterans around here do seem to appreciate the programs and celebrations we have honoring them. Their stories are incredible. What a courageous group of men and women the World War II veterans have proven to be."

"You know, Terry, I think you have just given me an idea," said Reuben. "Just as you said the word 'courageous,' I imagined a club devoted to regular monthly gatherings for the veterans. The club could become a special, scheduled time for the veterans, their spouses, friends and family members to reminisce as well as continue to celebrate the contribution they made during that time in history. What about calling the club 'Veterans' Courage?' After all, these men and women who served in the armed services were brave and steadfast individuals."

"Reuben Anderson," exclaimed Dee, "that is a great idea! Developing a club and a schedule for them around which they can plan monthly programs and special gatherings would be great fun. Reuben, would you help me organize the club and the first meeting?"

"I would love to help you, Dee," said Reuben with an enthusiastic smile, glancing over at his

# Reuben's Journey Begins

daughter.

"Veterans' Courage," exclaimed Janice. "I like that. They are courageous individuals. I think it is a great name for our veterans club."

"So be it, then. Veterans' Courage," repeated Terry.

With breakfast over and the others going off to meetings, Reuben spent the next few hours visiting with Eleanor Schultz, Peter White and others at The Cottonwoods as he delivered items he had purchased for them. During this time, the idea of the veterans club was expanding by leaps and bounds in his mind and he couldn't wait to get home and begin writing down some ideas to help get things started. All sorts of images were racing through his mind. Conversations he had had during the past years with veterans living at The Cottonwoods and around Prairieville began to replay themselves in his mind. He reflected on many of the veterans celebrations he had attended, ranging from Memorial Day programs to Pearl Harbor Day.

Back at home that evening, Reuben began to review in his mind the many stories he had shared over the years with his Army buddies and those he heard about from friends and neighbors. In particular, he remembered a conversation he had with Eleanor Schultz who had lost a cousin in the Korean conflict. As he pondered these things, he decided to write a poem that might give some focus to the veterans club.

## Reuben's Journey Begins

He thought he'd go out to his den in the horse barn where he could light a fire in the potbellied stove and smoke his pipe. In fact, he thought a glass of cabernet sauvignon might be the perfect beverage to enjoy while he relaxed and created the poem. Summoning Socrates, he filled his favorite Savanelli pipe with a mild Virginia tobacco, selected a Robert Mondavi cabernet and headed for his den.

As he entered the barn, the horses all greeted him with various whinnies and snorts. Boots pawed at the floor, hoping to get a treat and Reuben, obliging, reached into his pocket and produced an apple he had left in his jacket from earlier in the day. Overhead, there peered another critter watching the unexpected entry: Barney. Reuben looked up at his owl friend and winked as if to say, 'I see you, Barney.' As Reuben greeted them all by name, he hurried into his den, made a fire in the potbellied stove, turned on the student lamp on his desk, opened the wine and poured his glass about a third full, lit his pipe, selected his pen and paper and, as the temperature rose in the den, he began to make notes about key ideas and words that he would use to develop the poem. Over a thirty minute period, he wrote down a series of words and phrases. His mind was awhirl with ideas about how these could be sculpted into a poem that would share an authentic veteran's experience, capture the idea of what courage means to a veteran, and suggest ideas for the

## Reuben's Journey Begins

purpose of the new veterans club.

Reuben completed his first draft of the poem in about an hour, the second draft an hour after that and, four hours from the time he'd sat down in the den, he had finished a final draft with which he was satisfied, for now. He leaned back in his large, burgundy-colored leather desk chair and felt a deep sense of joy. It was the joy that his father had talked about often. He felt that this gift of poetry to the veterans at The Cottonwoods and others in the Prairieville community would help give a focus to a host of gatherings and community enrichment. He also imagined ways the club at The Cottonwoods could interact with the local American Legion, their auxiliary, the VFW and the DAV.

Another hour had passed and Reuben had dozed off for a while and awakened as a slight chill in the air signaled the dwindling fire in the stove. Reuben cleaned out the ashes in his pipe, corked the bottle of remaining wine and carefully folded the poem, inserting it into a somewhat tattered brown envelope for safekeeping. He and Socrates returned to the house where they once again watched television for a couple of hours. Reuben made his root beer float, sharing a bit with Cougar and Mitsy Kittikins, and finally turned in for the evening.

That night, Reuben told Ruth all about Veterans' Courage and the poem he had written.

The next morning, Reuben and Socrates left

# Reuben's Journey Begins

early for The Cottonwoods. He was excited to show his poem to Bruno and get his reaction. As they drove into town, Reuben was overcome once again with a sense of happiness, hopeful that his friend would like his poem. The feeling of joy that filled his whole being was a sense that he was on the right path. Years earlier, he recalled a conversation he had had with his dad about joy.

"Every now and then you will feel a deep sense of joy for something you are about to do or have done for someone," his dad had said. "It isn't a prideful or a boastful joy; it is a deep sense of fulfilling your life's purpose. This 'feeling' of joy is God's way of telling you that you are on your right path in life. You feel it when you are dead tired or when you are passionately energetic. It is a feeling that transcends your moment-to-moment emotions. It is the feeling and knowingness in your spirit."

Oh, how he wished he could talk with his dad about life again, just for an hour, and share his new poem with him. He missed his dad.

As he drove into the parking lot by The Manor at The Cottonwoods, Terry was just getting out of his car.

"Good morning, Reuben and Socrates," said Terry, greeting them. "What brings you here so early? Is everything alright?"

"Hi, Terry. Guess I didn't pay much attention to the time," replied Reuben. "I wrote a poem last night about Veterans' Courage and I wanted to

## Reuben's Journey Begins

share it with Bruno to see if he likes it, and then maybe share it with Dee, you and the others a little bit later at our planning breakfast."

Terry smiled and opened the door for Reuben. "I would love to read the poem, Reuben, and I suspect that Bruno and the others will be excited and appreciative of your work. Why don't you plan to join Dee and me for breakfast in forty-five minutes. I'll check to see if Ted Morrison, Bruno, Bunny Ford and Eugene Herding are still planning to join us and discuss the planning for the veterans club. Dee was excited about your idea and couldn't wait to get things started. By the looks of things and a new poem already, you didn't waste any time starting work on plans for the club, either."

"Breakfast sounds great, and I'll walk down with Bruno after I show him the poem," said Reuben as he departed from Terry and headed straightaway to Bruno's apartment. Knocking with his familiar seven-tap knock on Bruno's door, his excitement began to grow as he waited to enter. It all seemed to be coming together.

"My goodness, Reuben," said Bruno in a surprised voice as he answered the door. "And Socrates, to what do I owe this early morning honor?"

"Good morning, Bruno," said Reuben. "Sorry that I didn't call ahead of time, but I wrote a poem last night to help give some focus to our veterans club. I wanted to see you before our planning

## Reuben's Journey Begins

breakfast. Would you read it and give me your opinion?"

"Why, of course I will," responded Bruno with a smile as he surveyed the excitement in Reuben's face. "Let me get my reading glasses and have a look at your poem. And, by the way, you never have to call first when you come over."

Bruno sat down in his chair, turned on his reading lamp and read the poem. Reuben watched him intently with nervous anticipation. For a few minutes, Bruno said nothing and then he turned to Reuben.

"Reuben Anderson," said Bruno in a soft and somewhat professorial voice, "Although you have disguised yourself as a farmer, I believe you are indeed a prairie shaman. You have this amazing ability to take someone's need or want and create a gift for them. You truly have an ability that I'm not sure you fully understand."

"Oh, now, Bruno," said Reuben, somewhat blushing and looking away at Socrates, winking, "Let's don't start that shaman talk again. So you liked the poem?"

"Like it!" exclaimed Bruno, "It is simply wonderful and captures so much that is important to me, other veterans and their families. Now, don't go avoiding my comments about you as a prairie shaman. You need to remember that I am more than just a retired farmer ... in my day, I was a research scholar and a history and social sciences teacher. I've also traveled the world and

## Reuben's Journey Begins

actually met some shamans. Your spirit and gift is of their ilk."

"Bruno, I don't mean to discount your words. In fact, I've read a good many books about shamanism and, while I do seem to have a pretty active imagination, I've never thought of myself as being like them. Of course, I guess we all see them a bit differently. I'm just a mostly-retired farmer with time on my hands," replied Reuben in a humble but inquisitive tone.

"Reuben," began Bruno, "years ago when I was overseas in the army, I met a shaman in Tibet and, later, when I was visiting our friend Ted Parker in Montana, I met a pipe carrier, Gene Walking Bear. While both men were from very different cultures, they both possessed an ability to understand the needs of another person by some holistic transcendence and to respond with healing practices, whether physical, emotional or spiritual. In much the same way, I have watched you continually grasp the 'wholeness' of a situation involving someone's desires, be it a need, a want or an interest, and respond in the most creative and wonderful ways. And oftentimes, your response brings healing to that person's spirit, mind or body. While you may not always see it this way, people often talk about you as this creative genius; kind and always giving to others, making a real positive difference in their lives. Many times, your response does definitely bring a form of healing to the individual or group. So, my

## Reuben's Journey Begins

dear friend, I have taken it upon myself to refer to you in my mind, and occasionally to others, as a shaman."

"And perhaps the most significant event that coined the phrase, 'the prairie shaman' for me," Bruno continued, "was the time we were cutting alfalfa in the meadow near Campsite Grove and you hit a rabbit's nest, killing the mother. You stopped to hold the dying mother. You were angry with yourself, and it was like you felt her pain. You grieved with her as she somehow knew she would not be able to care for her babies and, in a moment, I swear I saw you connect with her. She closed her eyes and then you picked up all the baby rabbits and brought them over to our place so Donny could help raise and release them. That same day when I went out to the field to see how the hay looked, I saw where you had buried the mother rabbit, putting a small stone altar above the grave which you have still cut around every year since. You have this aura about you that sees and cherishes all of life as a whole and you have always acted accordingly. I believe you are a shaman, a prairie shaman, as you bring healing to so many, in wonderful and creative ways."

Reuben wasn't sure how to respond. Finally, he found the words.

"Bruno, I don't know what to say," he began. "Those are very kind words and words that I'm not sure I am worthy of. I do like helping other people and I guess there have been times when I wonder

## Reuben's Journey Begins

about my overactive imagination, which I have often thought about as being both a curse and a blessing. My imagination used to get me in trouble with my mother and father, as well as my sisters, when I was young. In my later years, it seems to have been more helpful in imagining ways to do things more efficiently around the farm and helping others in the community. You've certainly put a new twist on things for me."

Bruno smiled, "My dear friend, no need to be humble in my home, but then again, that is one of your most endearing qualities. What do you say about going down to breakfast to join some of our friends that Dee has invited to the veterans club planning breakfast? You will be my prairie shaman who is helping us develop a veterans club here and helping me plan a reunion with my Army buddies this summer."

As the two men and the dog walked over to the dining room to join their friends, Reuben felt joyful, silently continuing to visualize a dynamic veterans club.

As they walked into the dining room, there sat Terry, Janice, Dee Rice, Ted Morrison, Bunny Ford and Eugene Herding, all chatting away about driving conditions and the day's weather which had now delivered almost two inches of fresh snow since 5:00 a.m. Reuben realized that he'd been so excited about having Bruno read the poem that he had ignored the snow-covered roads driving into The Cottonwoods.

## Reuben's Journey Begins

"Dad, you might have to spend the day and night here," teased Janice. "The snow is supposed to continue through tomorrow and they're saying we should get up to fifteen inches. Bruno, could he sleep on your couch?"

Everyone laughed and welcomed Bruno, Reuben and Socrates to join them for breakfast. Socrates barked, assumed his tableside position below Reuben's chair, and began to enjoy the bowl full of dog food that Terry had brought in for him.

"You know, Reuben," began Bunny, "I was thinking about asking you to stop down to the Legion Club and see if Bob Graham might talk to some of the young men and women who are home on leave or returning from Saudi Arabia where they were part of Operation Desert Shield. I believe Jeffrey Peterson just came home last week. He was over there for almost five months. It would be nice to hear him tell us about his tour of duty."

"That's a great idea," responded Reuben. "I will stop down there this afternoon and see what I can find out about Jeffrey and others. Bob Graham does a good job staying in touch with all of our local kids who are serving in the armed services. The American Legion in Prairieville, Post 391, continues to provide a great service to our community. The support they give to Boys State and Boys Nation has meant a great deal to many young men from Prairieville."

"That's a great thing he does," echoed Ted

## Reuben's Journey Begins

Morrison. "My wife and her friends at church have been sending over care packages to about twelve young people who are in Saudi Arabia and Kuwait. They make them up and Bob wraps and mails them. I have to believe it is an awful hot and miserable place to serve, and getting letters and gifts from people at home means so much to them."

"It sure does, Ted," replied Eugene. "I remember being in Germany at the end of World War II and I hadn't heard from my family for some time when, suddenly, my sergeant brought me three letters from home. Talk about a rush. I read those letters almost every couple hours for a week. And when we returned to England, where I was stationed for six months finishing up my service, I remember getting several care packages full of the best treats ever. My wife and I have been supporting several groups who continue to do this work now during this conflict. It's sort of a way of giving back to the stream of life, I guess."

"I like that metaphor of giving back to the stream of life, Eugene," responded Reuben. "It's a great way of getting people to think about how current words and actions can have meaning in the future. Sort of like, when they are downstream. I need to remember that idea."

"Reuben," interrupted Bruno, "You need to read your poem as we begin to eat so we can talk about it during breakfast."

"Well," began Reuben, "I wrote a poem last

night that I would like to share with all of you this morning. I thought it might possibly serve as an initial focal point to encourage others to write poems and stories about serving our country in the armed services, and then share them at club meetings. Eugene's words about giving back to the stream of life are a great metaphor that really captures a lot of what I was feeling when I wrote it."

Suddenly, there was clunk at the door and as everyone in the room turned to see what the source of the noise was, in rolled Peter White in his wheelchair, smiling and bidding everyone good morning.

"Might I find some fellow veterans here?" queried Peter. "I heard about this gathering from a fly on the wall, or maybe it was Angie Perkins. Don't remember at the moment, but couldn't resist coming down and sitting in with such a prestigious group of fellow veterans. I do believe I hear a couple female voices gracing this gathering."

There was a chorus of 'welcomes' for Peter. Reuben sat thinking with utter surprise, 'Now how would he have ever served in the armed services, much less be a veteran?'

"I suspect my dear friend, Reuben, is sitting there wondering, 'How in the world would Peter have been in the armed services?'" said Peter in a rhetorical voice, a smile on his face.

"As a matter of fact, Peter," replied Reuben, "that is exactly what I was thinking. You have to

## Reuben's Journey Begins

tell us the story, and you have our full attention."

"As most of you know, I have been a musician and music teacher all my life," began Peter. "During the middle of World War II, the Navy was looking for some volunteers to help develop a number of their bands. I was volunteering at the veteran's hospital in Des Moines, Iowa, with Disabled American Veterans. Several of the men had lost limbs and others had lost their sight in the battle. After rehabbing, they still wanted to serve our country and continue their pursuit of being musicians, playing various instruments. So I put together a small band of handicapped and blind musicians. They all still wanted to serve their country, some feeling as though they had failed, but as musicians, a new door of service opened for them. I taught some of them Braille and others simply learned to play by ear. We practiced often, and I'll be darned if we didn't become quite the musical outfit."

The group was listening in rapt attention as Peter continued. "One afternoon, we were playing at the Luther College in Decorah for a disabled veterans benefit and, after the concert, an Admiral from the United States Pacific Fleet came up to thank us and stayed to have a drink with us afterwards. As he listened to our story, he was so moved that he asked us to come to Washington, D.C. to play at a special event. Two months later, all eighteen of us boarded a bus to Bethesda, Maryland, where we played a concert, and then

## Reuben's Journey Begins

one in D.C. proper. Two days later, we were invited to play another concert at The Pentagon. At the conclusion of that concert, I was officially granted the status of an Honorary Captain in the United States Navy along with all of my band members receiving special commendations from their respective services. It is a source of great pride for me to be considered a veteran. Fourteen of us gathered two years ago at Luther College and played a concert for returning veterans."

As Peter was telling his story, Janice recalled the photographs of Peter with a band where the members were all wearing different service uniforms, and vaguely remembered he was wearing a Navy uniform. Suddenly, everyone at the table started to clap spontaneously and the perfect quiet turned into a 'wow' moment at The Cottonwoods.

"I think this would make a great story and presentation for one of our first veteran club meetings," exclaimed Dee.

"I agree," boomed Bruno's voice. "Wow, Peter, I had no idea. What a great thing you did for those guys who had lost their limbs and sight, but not their love for music and their country. That is simply outstanding, my friend."

"Well, thank you all for the kind words," replied Peter. "It wasn't a very difficult thing to do and it made me feel good to be able to serve my country in some small way. Now, I will refrain from dominating the conversation and will enjoy

## Reuben's Journey Begins

listening to the plans being made for putting together this veterans club I heard about from Angie, the fly on the wall!"

Everyone laughed.

"Reuben wrote the most beautiful poem last night and shared it with me this morning," said Bruno. "I would like to have him read it to all of us. I think it is a great poem that presents an idea for the purpose of our veterans club. Would you read it, Reuben?"

A chorus of 'yes's' filled the private dining room at The Manor. Reuben took out his folded piece of paper and shyly said,

"I suppose I could, but I really didn't think I would be reading this to such a large group. I really just came to read it to Bruno in hopes he would say he liked it and then I could present it to Dee, Terry and Janice as one idea at the planning breakfast."

As Reuben looked around the room at the anticipation in the faces of his friends, he had a moment of feeling nervous and a fleeting thought of, 'Gosh, I hope they like it.' Reuben took a sip of his coffee, cleared his throat and read the poem:

"Veterans' Courage
By Reuben Anderson

Seventeen and surrounded by
Veterans voices from days past;
Proud fathers, mothers, uncles, aunts

## Reuben's Journey Begins

And neighbors who served.
Eighteen, filled with a desire to honor them
And a dream to serve, too;
A courage grows from
The desire to carry on their legacy.
The paper is signed.

Then comes the bus ride to boot camp,
Filled with loud, anxious talking;
Suddenly a surreal world unfolds
As the drill sergeant yells.
Then come long days and short nights;
Dreams of serving and courage dim;
You miss days taken for granted,
Sleeping in and a bed made by mom.

Muscles aching like never before,
Tired and torn;
Self-image that often stood tall and alone
Now suppressed to the whole.
The weeks pass and new uniforms
Are handed out for graduation;
The ceremony and parade,
Cheers and hugs
And voices of days past.

Home for a visit and seeing
Family and old friends, wishing you well;
Mother's joy and smiling faces
Washed with tears of pride and worry.
A plane ride with much quieter voices

## Reuben's Journey Begins

And now a nervous courage;
You land near a combat zone
And your boots are now on the ground.

Advice from everyone now focuses on
The enemy and your survival;
Days later you meet the enemy,
But it is different from boot camp.
They move like real people,
Have a flesh face,
Real arms and legs;
Heart pounding, you aim
And close your eyes the first time.

The days turn to weeks,
The weeks to months, and years follow;
You're wounded,
Your courage becomes a numbing fatigue.
You've witnessed man's inhumanity to man,
And man's humanity to man;
The oppressed liberated praise you,
The dream and courage grow bright again.

Now twenty-six, you return home
To parades and speeches;
Your mind filled with the good,
The bad and the ugly images of war.
You choose to join the voices of
Your youth, proud to have served;
Your courage now faces a new life
Of adjustment for job and family.

## Reuben's Journey Begins

You draw down on your courage,
Honed in the service of your country;
The ability you developed
To do something that frightened you.
The challenges of finding a career
That fits, and a life purpose;
A courage that found
An inner strength in the face of fear
Leads your life's journey.

Now eighty-six, you reminisce
And think about courage again
As you age;
Your aging cocoon with thinning skin,
Aches and pains and
Loss of friends and family.
Your courage now seeks to find
An inner strength in the face of
Grief and fear;
Once again, your veterans' courage
Returns to serve you.

Knowing this courage has
Given you strength,
You now ponder its value for other
Veterans, young and old;
Would gatherings to share
Stories, poems and songs
Help aging veterans maintain their pride
And help young veterans heal?
Perhaps a club called Veterans' Courage

## Reuben's Journey Begins

Is just the right acknowledgement
For those who
Faithfully served their country."

    You could hear a pin drop around the room. Eugene's voice broke the silence with, "Reuben, wow!" and the entire room once again erupted in applause and a chorus of appreciative words. Reuben's heart filled with relief and happiness.
    "What on earth's name is all the noise about in here, folks?" came a familiar voice into the room. It was Angie Perkins, the Assistant Administrator.
    "Oh, my, it is the fly that was on my wall early this morning," joked Peter, and everyone laughed and invited her to join the meeting. "We're just a group of veterans reminiscing about days long gone by, but hoping to resurrect their meaning in some way, Angie," said Peter.
    "Peter, I'd love to be a fly on the wall whenever you veterans meet," continued Angie. "Most of you know that I lost my father a few years ago and his veteran friends and meetings at both the Legion and VFW were so important to him and me. His military funeral was a wonderful event. Reuben and Ruth carried him from the church to the cemetery in their beautiful funeral coach."
    "Angie, we'd love to have you help Dee, Reuben and this great group of people start a Veterans' Courage club here at The Cottonwoods," said Terry. The room filled with nodding heads and words of agreement.

Reuben's Journey Begins

Over the next six months, Veterans' Courage met on the 4$^{th}$ Thursday of each month at 1:30 p.m. for one and a half hours. The first meeting was in February, and it was a great beginning. As each of the veterans, spouses of veterans, friends and family members entered the community room at The Cottonwoods, everyone wrote their name on a slip of paper and put it in one of several armed services baseball hats for a later drawing for the hats. There were U.S. Army, Navy, Marines, Coast Guard, Air Force, Army Air Force, and Vietnam hats for the drawing. Terry opened the meeting by greeting everyone and the room was filled with almost fifty people. The Junior ROTC from Prairieville High School was invited to advance and retire the colors as Peter led everyone by piano and voice in singing, "The Star Spangled Banner," and then Bruno led The Pledge of Allegiance. And just as was suggested earlier in January, Reuben and Bob Graham introduced Jeffrey Peterson, who was again home on leave, as the guest speaker, along with a friend of his, Amy Hartman from Windy Marsh, also home on leave from the Gulf War. They told wonderful stories and expressed their undying appreciation to Ted Morrison, his wife Josie and others at the Prairieville Baptist Church who had sent them care packages during their deployment. Next in the program was a surprise that Reuben and Bunny Ford had planned and that was a very emotional 're-presentation' of the Purple Heart that Bruno

## Reuben's Journey Begins

Johnson had received following World War II. As surprised as Bruno was, Reuben noted hesitancy on Bruno's part to receive the medal. Something wasn't quite right.

As the program concluded with retiring the colors, drawing the names from the hats to hand out to the winners and Peter playing and singing, "America The Beautiful," everyone gathered around Jeffrey and Amy to hear more stories. Off to the side of the room, Reuben stood proudly with Janice hugging his arm and Terry putting his arm around Reuben's shoulder.

"Bruno is right, Reuben," said Terry. "You are indeed the prairie shaman. We are very grateful for the support and creativity you have brought to this group of veterans. Just look at this wonderful event!"

Surprise on his face, Reuben looked at Terry and asked, "So he has been spreading that rumor with you, too?"

They all smiled; Terry and Janice quietly acknowledging with their touch that Reuben had done something very special for this group of residents and members from the greater community.

As the seasons changed from winter to spring, Reuben once again began to plant his seedlings in small paper pots for his garden. This would be the first year he had planned the garden alone. The garden, 25 yards by 50 yards in area, featured a plethora of plants. On the east side of the garden,

## Reuben's Journey Begins

he planted six rows of sweet corn; next were several rows of tomatoes, then rows of potatoes, two rows of beets and three rows of broccoli; added in square patches along the west side of the garden were the vine plants like watermelon, cucumbers, muskmelon, squash, pumpkins and string beans; and at the far end of the garden were two rows of sunflowers that Christopher and Catherine loved harvesting, salting and roasting in the fall. The greenhouse that was added to the edge of the washhouse in 1976, in celebration of the United States 200$^{th}$ Anniversary, had been a dream come true for Ruth, who loved to can just about everything as the fruits and vegetables matured.

One of Reuben's innovations was adding a number of remarkable chimes to the garden to discourage rabbits, raccoons and other critters from invading this lush wonderland of goodies. Socrates had learned to chase rabbits and deer away on a regular basis and had tree'd his fair share of raccoons who always loved the sweet corn. Throughout the garden, Reuben had built and distributed some seven scarecrows, each with a wind chime and windsocks for pants, with arms to frighten away unwanted visitors. For the most part it worked, but there was always a small loss in spite of these creative initiatives.

Soon spring transformed into early summer, and Reuben was busy making all the arrangements for Bruno's reunion at the Anderson

# Reuben's Journey Begins

Farm. On an early Monday morning, Reuben drove into Prairieville to pick Bruno up and bring him out to the farm. Together, they sat down and reviewed the schedule they had been working on for weeks:

<u>Tuesday, June 25<sup>th</sup></u>

- Everyone arrives
  - Bob Smith flies from Atlanta to Minneapolis in the morning and Terry has agreed to pick him up and bring him to the farm.
  - Bill Hanson is also flying into Minneapolis on a flight arriving about the same time as Bob, and Terry will pick him up, too.
  - Andy Almquist from Miles City, Montana, flies into Sioux Falls, South Dakota and Angie Perkins has made plans to pick him up.
  - Glenn Orville will drive over to Waterville and pick up Radar Knutson.
- Everyone will be at the farm by 5:30 p.m. and Reuben will barbecue chicken, salmon and steaks.
- Weather permitting, all will go out to Campsite Grove for the first of several campfires and storytelling evenings, concluding with root beer floats and one of their favorite pastimes enjoyed in the

# Reuben's Journey Begins

service – joke telling.

## Wednesday, June 26<u>th</u>

- ➢ The day begins with an old-fashioned farm breakfast which Janice has volunteered to cook while the men enjoy early morning coffee.
- ➢ Later in the day, weather permitting, Reuben, David (who will be home for a few days to help out with the reunion), Willard and Christopher will take the men on a three-hour carriage ride around the farm and along Red Rock Creek that will include an old-fashioned picnic lunch by the creek.
- ➢ Early afternoon will be a nap time.
- ➢ Around 3:00, all will sit around the table to play poker, which they had done hundreds of times during their tour of duty.
- ➢ The evening will feature a barbecued whole pig which Donny Johnson and Janice will barbecue during the day.
- ➢ That evening, Reuben will pass out cherry wood pipes and some wonderful cigars that Bill Hanson had somehow gotten from a friend who brought them back from Cuba, and on the porch that night, everyone will once again enjoy smoking and drinking coffee, beer and wine

# Reuben's Journey Begins

together as they reminisce.

## Thursday, June 27th

- ➢ Begins as each morning will for the rest of the visit, with a grand old-fashioned breakfast of eggs, steak, bacon, omelettes, cottage fries, fresh squeezed orange and grapefruit juices, fresh sourdough bread and freshly ground and brewed coffee.
- ➢ On this morning after breakfast, everyone will prepare their stories and presentations since they will be the special guests at the Veterans' Courage Club monthly meeting at The Cottonwoods where 200 people are expected to attend.
- ➢ Following the Veterans' Courage Club meeting, the six men will spend the late afternoon at five different cemeteries, placing wreaths on the graves of their fallen comrades.
- ➢ There will be a special reunion dinner with old friends at Bethany Lutheran Church, concluded by a remembrance memorial service for their dear friend and comrade, Stanley Anderson. Somewhat reluctantly, Reuben had agreed to allow Reverend Stendahl to conduct the service.

# Reuben's Journey Begins

## Friday, June 28th

- Following breakfast, Janice will host a gathering of several veterans home on leave from the Gulf War who will join the men for a day at the farm, carriage rides and another evening campfire.

## Saturday, June 29th

- Will be a day where each of the men can plan their own schedule to relax, explore the town and/or make arrangements to visit with people in town or at The Cottonwoods, as each of them will have made connections with other veterans and spouses during the Thursday Veterans' Courage Club meeting.
- A dinner of hotdish and vegetables, with apple pie for dessert
- On the porch that night, they will once again relax and reminisce while enjoying their cigars and pipes and drinking coffee, beer, wine or water.

## Sunday, June 30th

- Will be a special day. Reuben's dear friend, the Reverend Barney Freiburg from Sioux Falls, has written a special worship service as a tribute to all veterans

# Reuben's Journey Begins

past and present. Reuben, David, Willard and Janice will create a special outdoor chapel setting at Campsite Grove. The service will be a combination Protestant and Catholic service, also attended by Father Joe Martin.

- Sunday afternoon will be horseshoes, poker and an all-afternoon snack buffet fit for a king.

## Monday, July 1st

- Leave 4:30 a.m. for a trip by car to the North Shore of Lake Superior where they will enjoy a fishing trip around the Apostle Islands and an overnight stay at the Lighthouse Lodge in Bayfield, Wisconsin.

## Tuesday, July 2nd

- The men will enjoy breakfast at the Lodge and then a leisurely return to the farm late afternoon/early evening.
- A casual late dinner of soup and salads on the porch

## Wednesday, July 3rd

- Another morning of carriage rides

# Reuben's Journey Begins

- A noon picnic at Campsite Lodge, weather permitting
- Another evening of poker, root beer floats, reminiscing and joke telling

## Thursday, July 4<sup>th</sup>

- The high school program and Prairieville parade
- A final evening of storytelling and reminiscing on the great porch with cigars, pipes and a special zinfandel wine Reuben ordered from Oregon

## Friday, July 5<sup>th</sup>

- The out-of-towners return home and Reuben and Bruno enjoy an evening alone at the farm to review the reunion and recount stories.

And so it was; everything planned went as planned through the 3<sup>rd</sup> of July. The weather cooperated as if a higher power was watching over the event with great interest. It was an extraordinary experience for all of the men.

On Wednesday evening, July 3<sup>rd</sup>, Reuben went into his study after they had finished their root beer floats, and the others had gone to their rooms to find Bruno quietly pondering the document in front of him which he was writing.

# Reuben's Journey Begins

"Hi, Bruno," said Reuben. "Your guests have all decided to turn in early tonight. Bob's legs were bothering him from all the walking this past week so I sent him out to the wash house that we converted some years ago into a sauna and spa house. The others have all retired to their bedrooms. What are you working on so intently?"

Bruno raised his eyes from the paper and smiled, saying, "My dear, dear friend, you have done something extraordinary for me these past days. I'm writing a letter to my friend, Bob, and asking for his forgiveness."

"May I inquire why?" asked Reuben in a puzzled, but somewhat unsurprised, voice.

"Well, I've never told anyone about this and it has been the heaviest weight I have had to carry all my life since the war," began Bruno. "Bob and I were in Germany in a foxhole, having just been shelled by a machine gun nest about sixty yards away from us. Bob was our sergeant and squad leader, and he directed me to move around to a point where I could toss a grenade into the machine gun nest and take them out so we could advance the troops behind us into a more strategic position. I froze and disobeyed his directive, only to watch him in disgust, without saying a word, bolt out of the foxhole, take on fire from the machine gun nest and take lead in the shoulder, leg and ankle. He was lying there, bleeding like a stuck hog and crying for help. I suddenly jumped out of the foxhole, ran crazy-like straight at the machine

## Reuben's Journey Begins

gun nest, tossed two grenades, one right after the other, and took it out. I then ran to Bob, carried him into the foxhole and got him to a medic who patched him up and got him to a hospital tent nearby. In the excitement of things, I didn't realize I had also been wounded; just a couple of flesh wounds."

Bruno began to cry and as the tears fell on the paper, causing the ink to splotch, he continued his story.

"Reuben, although I did save Bob's life and for that I received the Purple Heart, I was the one who caused his injuries, as sure as if I had shot him myself. I have never forgiven myself, and Bob has always been silent on the story and never told anyone why he was injured. By rights, he should have received the Purple Heart for his injuries but it somehow fell through the cracks and, afterwards, he never asked for the medal. So here I sit, 46 years later, ready to ask for forgiveness and tell the truth about the story. I feel like such a fraud and it really got bad at the Veterans' Courage Club meeting in February when they recognized me once again for my bravery during the war. Reuben, how does an old man ask for forgiveness?" The tears fell freely.

Reuben closed the tall, nine-foot double doors to his study, pulled a chair up alongside of Bruno, and put his arm around his shoulders.

"Bruno, we all make mistakes during our life's journey," he said. "You were young and just a kid,

# Reuben's Journey Begins

barely out of high school. The idea of you jumping out of that foxhole paralyzed you for a moment, because it was probably the first time in battle you saw your death as possibly imminent and, in that moment, I believe Bob saw the fear and knew in an instant you couldn't perform his command. But you have to know that he knew he would be sending you into a sure death in that state of mind and in the flash of an eye, he took it upon himself to save you, and others, and advance the troops. I suspect he is the type of man who holds no grudge. The fact is, my good friend, that people got wounded in all sort of situations during the war, and you instantly responded to save his life which you did at great risk to your own life. Bruno, that is one of the messages of the Purple Heart."

    For the first time during their conversation, Bruno lifted his head and, through his tear-washed face, looked at Reuben and said, "And all I've put you through just to get to this moment. Reuben, I couldn't even be honest with you about why this reunion was so important to me, and had to cloak it in somewhat of a fraudulent fashion. I thought by bringing our squad together one last time I could find the courage to talk with Bob, but I haven't been able to do it, and now, just one day before everyone is to leave, I sit here with my heart racing, washed in guilt and paralyzed once again as to what to do. Reuben, you couldn't have helped plan a more perfect time and yet I've failed myself again."

## Reuben's Journey Begins

Reuben removed his arm from Bruno, stood up and moved around to the back of his chair and began to massage Bruno's shoulders as an idea flashed through his mind's eye.

"Bruno, I have an idea and an intuition," Reuben began. "I've watched the interaction between you and Bob all week. In Bob, I see a man whose love and appreciation is as authentic as anything I have ever observed. In you, my good friend, I have seen and felt a conflict all week. Bruno, what really has to happen here is for you to forgive yourself and, if asked, I think Bob will be somewhat surprised to hear you ask for his forgiveness, but he will understand. For what became a significant negative moment for you, became a life-giving moment for him, regardless of your momentary paralysis. Yet, you need to ask and not leave the question on paper only for him to read and then expect him to respond verbally. I believe that as you say it out loud, you will begin to forgive yourself and his response will purge this horrible regret from your spirit and body. I suspect it has become a regret that every time you think about it, you have both an emotional and physical reaction to that event, coupled with your guilt about being unworthy of receiving the Purple Heart."

"Gosh, Reuben," began Bruno, "I've never thought of it quite that way. Is that all I should do?"

"Well," replied Reuben, "there is one more thing you should do. I think you should invite Bob into the living room in a little while and offer him your

## Reuben's Journey Begins

Purple Heart, telling him exactly how you feel. I know he will not take it from you and will once again recount the story much as I have imagined. However, I suspect in doing this, you will heal yourself and your relationship with Bob will grow even closer."

"Reuben, would you mind calling someone at The Manor and see if they would go into my room, get my Purple Heart and bring it out to me this evening?" asked Bruno.

"It would be my pleasure," responded Reuben, and he called Janice to make the arrangements.

Thirty minutes later, about the time Bob was returning from the hot tub and spa room, Angie Perkins drove up with the Purple Heart in its presentation case and brought it to Reuben.

"Thank you so much, Angie," said Reuben. "This will mean a great deal to a couple men this evening."

"My pleasure, Reuben," responded Angie, "I hear things have been going extraordinarily well this week."

"They have, Angie," replied Reuben. "And this evening will be the greatest moment of all for Bruno, which I will share with you sometime next week if Bruno gives me permission to do so."

And so it was. Bruno did exactly what Reuben had suggested and toward the end of his opening words, he pulled the new letter out of an envelope that sort of made it official. Bob responded just as Reuben had imagined and the two men, Bob and

## Reuben's Journey Begins

Bruno, talked and reminisced long into the night and early morning.

About 1:30 a.m., as Reuben was ready to turn in, Andy walked by Reuben's study on the way to the kitchen.

"Reuben, are you still up?" asked Andy, surprised to see him.

"Oh, just finishing up some plans for tomorrow, and I spent some time with Bruno tonight," replied Reuben.

"I saw Bob and Bruno in the living room in what appeared to be a somewhat private conversation so I didn't want to bother them. Is everything okay, Reuben?" asked Andy.

For a moment, Reuben pondered whether or not to say anything about what had happened, and then suddenly he felt it would be the right thing to do as he felt Andy's spirit and thoughts were in the right place. He told Andy the entire story. As he finished, he saw that Andy was thinking hard about something.

"I sense you have an idea," said Reuben.

"I do," said Andy. "What a story. And you gave him excellent advice. We need to create an opportunity tomorrow, at the 4$^{th}$ of July program at the high school, to give Bob Smith his Purple Heart. And I think we should let Bruno do it. Here's what I'm thinking. In my suitcase, which has traveled all over the world with me, I keep a small case with various medals, my service decorations and my two Purple Hearts, as well as

## Reuben's Journey Begins

extras to bestow on those who never received them, or who lost them. As for an official commendation, I'll make a phone call in the morning to notify the appropriate people and get Bob's name added to the list of recipients. I can send in the necessary paperwork after the fact. Even though it is a holiday tomorrow, I have people I can reach by phone if they're not in their office. We'll need to talk to Bruno in the morning, and I will call Janice to see if she can create a presentation certificate. Although it will be a temporary one, it will look very authentic."

Reuben smiled and said, "Andy, you are, indeed, a very kind and generous person, and what a creative idea. Bruno will be thrilled and it will put this issue permanently to rest for him. I'll call Janice right now; she's a late-night person, and the 'heads-up' will help her plan the morning with Mary and Megan, as well as take care of her duties at The Cottonwoods before the high school program."

"Sounds good, Reuben," Andy replied. "In the meantime, I'll go upstairs and fetch the Purple Heart and the certificate which I carry in a document portfolio in my suitcase. Perhaps we can fax a copy to her office and it will be there in the morning."

"I'll do it as soon as you bring it down," replied Reuben.

That night, Reuben went to bed about 2:30 a.m. and slept well. He went for a very long walk with

## Reuben's Journey Begins

Ruth and Socrates along Red Rock Creek.

And Bruno ... he finally went to bed and slept well, also, with a heart that no longer carried the heavy weight of his regret.

Morning came early for Reuben and Socrates and it was wonderful to awaken with a gentle kiss from Janice on one cheek and Socrates laying his head on Reuben's other shoulder, as if to say it was simply too early to get up. The house was filled with laughter, the wonderful smell of fresh bacon, eggs and home fries cooking on the stove and the aroma of fresh pipe tobacco wafting into the kitchen from the pipes of Bob and Bruno who were already out on the great porch, smoking with an early morning cup of freshly-ground hot coffee being drunk out of enamelized tin cups reminiscent of the cups from their Army mess kits. Reuben had picked the cups up at Minnesota Antiques a month earlier when he was in the Twin Cities with Janice and Terry.

The 4$^{th}$ of July program began at 10:00 a.m. as it had for many years in Prairieville. The program was a great Independence Day celebration and had become a fundraising day for JROTC at the high school, as well as raising money for needed building repairs at the Legion and VFW clubs. Most of these funds were raised by the afternoon circus created by the clubs. This year, one more club joined the group – Veterans' Courage.

The program began with the JROTC and American Legion Color Guard advancing the

## Reuben's Journey Begins

colors and everyone singing, "The Star Spangled Banner." Reverend Peterson and his daughter Barbara from the Prairieville Baptist Church offered the opening prayer, and then the Bethany Lutheran Choir and the High School Choir led everyone in "America the Beautiful." The guest speaker for the day was John the Barber from Prairieville who talked about community service and how important it was to maintain a culture that valued it.

When John finished, it was Bruno's turn for his standard part of the program. Bruno Johnson began giving a little talk about the value of the armed services that went back to The Revolutionary War. As a former history and sociology teacher, his stories and anecdotes were always entertaining and educational. As he concluded his remarks, he turned to Major General Anders Almquist, who was waiting just offstage, and Andy came on stage and stood next to Bruno. It was impressive, as Andy was in full formal dress, sidearm and all. The crowd stood and applauded him as he walked on, all so very proud of the service he had rendered to his country.

Bruno began speaking again. "At this time, I would like to introduce everyone to a dear friend of mine with whom I served in World War II, Major General Anders Almquist, and many of you have read about him in the Prairieville Times. Andy."

"Thank you, Bruno. I would like to take this opportunity, on behalf of the President of the United States, to make a presentation to Mr.

## Reuben's Journey Begins

Robert Smith who has been visiting your community this past week along with several others of us who served with Bruno Johnson in the European theater during World War II. Mr. Robert Smith, retired Sergeant First Class, would you please come forward."

Bob sat in his chair, in shock, and after an awkward pause he cautiously made his way down the row toward the center aisle of chairs set up on the gymnasium floor and walked up and onto the stage.

"Retired Sergeant First Class Robert Smith, it is an honor for me and Bruno Johnson to present to you, on behalf of the President of the United States and the First Battalion which you so faithfully served for seven years ... for unconditional bravery that put your life at risk with only regard for your command, we proudly present you with The Badge of Military Merit, The Purple Heart." Reciting from memory, Andy continued, "'Let it be known that he who wears the military order of the Purple Heart has given of his blood in the defense of his homeland and shall forever be revered by his fellow countrymen.' Bruno, would you do me the honor of presenting this veteran's sash with the Purple Heart to Retired Sergeant First Class Robert Smith?"

With tears now running down his face and favoring his right leg with a slight limp, Bruno proudly placed the sash with the Purple Heart over Bob's head and right arm as he positioned it for all

## Reuben's Journey Begins

to see.  The men shook hands with General Almquist, saluted each other and then embraced in a joyful and tearful hug.  The audience erupted into loud applause and a standing ovation, cheering for the two men.  For almost two minutes, which seemed like an eternity to Bruno, the applause continued.

Next, Bruno said, "I also have another presentation I would like to make, and that is to my friend, Reuben Anderson, who has been a wonderful host to my Army buddies the past ten days.  Not only has he thought of every possible thing to make it an extraordinary experience, but he has also helped me heal some old wounds and has been a wonderful catalyst in helping create the Veterans' Courage Club at The Cottonwoods.  Reuben, would you come up to the stage, please?"

Reaching over to a table near the podium, Bruno uncovered a beautiful sculpture by Mike Capser of Billings, Montana.  It was a sculpture and a framed award for Reuben's help in creating the veterans club.  The sculpture was of a farmer with his German shepherd dog, standing in a wheat field looking at his crop.  In the framed certificate of appreciation, Reuben's volunteer help was described as a special kind of sensitivity, calling Reuben, "The Prairie Shaman … bringing love, wisdom and healing to the critters and people of the prairie."  The gymnasium, filled with over 500 people, once again broke into loud and uproarious applause which evolved into another

## Reuben's Journey Begins

standing ovation.

Bruno then told the audience why he had dubbed Reuben "The Prairie Shaman," telling the story about the shaman he had met after World War II while traveling overseas in Tibet, and the Native American he met later in Montana. He described a shaman as someone who develops a special 'sensitivity' and 'knowingness' about a person's situation and then helps create a one-to-one solution that brings help, healing and wholeness to the person. He described what Reuben had done in volunteering to help create the veterans club as a wonderful shamanistic act that had brought healing and joy to a group of old friends.

And so it was, the afternoon parade and circus passed quickly and soon it was evening at the farm. Bruno and his friends spent the last night together at the farm as planned, playing poker, enjoying their cigars and finishing with Reuben's root beer float tradition.

Early the next day, they returned as they had come, all except for Bruno, who was to spend this last night recapping the successes and experiences of the reunion with Reuben.

The prairie shaman had made his contribution by bringing together Bruno's old Army buddies and, in the process, discovered that his notion months ago that there was 'more to this' had proven to be right. And the serendipity that followed seemed almost too good to be true. And

## Reuben's Journey Begins

yet, it was true. It was wonderful. For the first time in his life, Reuben quietly imagined and humbly entertained the thought, 'Could I, an old farmer, be some sort of a prairie shaman with a gift God has given me and yet don't truly understand? Hmm, seems like fanciful thinking. Of course, Sanaya Roman said I should pay attention to such things. Lately I have often pondered her words,' ... *"Your dreams about your ideal life are showing you your potential and higher path. Don't discard your dreams and fantasies as merely wishful thinking. Honor them as messages from the deepest part of your being about your life's work and what you came here to do."* [1]

    Reuben continued pondering, feeling a deep and longing sense of searching for answers. 'My dreams and ideal life ... now at age 72, what are they? What could be my potential and higher path? My life's work at this age ... my goodness, what could it possibly be? What have I come here to do?'

# Epilogue

## Of Barns, Shamans and Storytellers

**Of Barns ...**

From the earliest days in America, they were one of the primary centers for agricultural commerce.

They were often built by neighbors and other community members at community barn raisings.

They were all sizes and shapes. They were made of a plethora of different materials from the forest and earth: wood, tin, steel, stone, block, and bricks. They were painted the colors of the rainbow, with most being red, many white, and some yellow.

They housed the hay and straw, both baled and loose. They housed cows for milking and, often, their offspring began their lives in the barn's calf pens. They housed horses, and occasionally sheep, pigs and other livestock would be housed in barns, especially during the harsh Minnesota winters.

It is in these cathedrals of straw beds, feeding and milking that the farmers of the prairie in Minnesota spend their early mornings, late afternoons and

## Reuben's Journey Begins

early evenings, caring for their hers and collecting the milk to support part of their livelihood.

In these repetitive mornings and evenings from the 1930s on, the barn radio entertained and stimulated the farmer's thinking and their conversations with wives, husbands, sons, daughters, neighbors and hired hands.

The barns were the classrooms where daily conversations explored and embraced family, community, religious and political issues and prepared the farmer for dialogue at the school, township meetings, political gatherings, the church, the town cafe and, most importantly, the breakfast, lunch and dinner tables in their homes.

Farmers worked together, not only in barn raising, but also in harvesting crops and solving the many challenges that the prairie offered from season to season.

While most of the prairie farmers of the early part of the 20th century completed varied years in school, they were well schooled in the important topics for conversations and issues that mattered and, more importantly, they developed a healthy portion of heart that often led to community service.

# Reuben's Journey Begins

## Of Shamans ...

They are healers of the body, mind and spirit.

They do not represent a religion, but exist in many religions.

They have developed their gifts of insight and spiritual connections with God, the Universe, the soil and stone of the Earth, Wind, Fire, Water, Animals, Plants and People.

They live in the marshlands, deserts, meadows, mountains, prairies, farms, villages and cities.

They are males and females. They are young and old. They are rich and poor.

They are driven by truth, purpose, caring, preserving traditions and knowledge.

They are those who know intuitively and through experience and, in their knowingness, do what needs to be done.

## Of Storytellers ...

They are amongst the greatest healers of all.

# A TRIBUTE

## To Our Parents Who Expressed Great Love And Kindness To Others, And Volunteered Often

Julie's parents, Ruth Dordal Borchert and Julius Max Borchert were tremendous human beings who knew a great deal about faith, hope and love. Their children and all those around them had the benefit of learning from their example and being comforted by their spirit. They taught a curiosity for learning, a love of family, and an appreciation for life itself that encompassed all humanity. As they very actively volunteered at their church and in their community, they were a beacon for others to follow.

# Reuben's Journey Begins

Gary's parents, Marie Synnova Hofstad Solomonson and Glenn Orville Solomonson were people of the prairie in southwestern Minnesota, both growing up on farms where they worked with their parents in tending their fields, gardens and livestock. They started out in one-room school houses and emulated a Midwestern work ethic that was rooted in always expressing kindness to others. They lived their commitment to their church, schools and community organizations each and every day. In both their career and retirement years, Glenn and Synnova volunteered thousands of hours to the church, the schools, the Storden Senior Center and to the Salvation Army as persons in southwestern Minnesota often called for their help and support during disasters and personal challenges.

# Acknowledgements

**Pat Adams** – A former colleague who read *Reuben's Journey Begins* and kindly shared her insights

**Andrew Bond** – Our oldest son who has provided graphic design and creative input, and has taken the books and The Yellow Barn Society to the Internet

**Bruno Boucher** – Who was an inspiration as he wrote poems and told stories about his veteran experiences and provided support in developing a wonderful veterans program at Regal Palms in Largo, Florida

**Steve & Bob Bucher** – Our friends, a son and father, who read and appreciated Reuben's adventure; Bob took the time to share his own life experiences as they related to The Yellow Barn

**Frances Clanton** – A talented artist whose passion for caregiving and volunteering is only exceeded by her passion for art; Fran created the cover art for the trilogy

**Burt Elmer** – Brilliant architect and artist who has journeyed with me through many senior living communities and who created the chapter illustrations for this trilogy.

# Reuben's Journey Begins

**Kahil Gibran** – His poetry has been a guide in my life

**Sydney Goodman** – A gentle and dynamic spirit who always had a kind word for the work I did

**Caleb & Amanda Hofstad** – My dearest grandparents whom I loved; I will always cherish my memories of them, their values and kindnesses expressed to everyone around them

**Ruth & Reuben Hofstad, and their children David, Willard and Janice** – My aunt, uncle and cousins who provided the inspiration for the leading characters; their kindnesses as I spent time with them at their farm during many summer visits are a bedrock in the memories of my life

**Ellen Jensen** – An incredible 92-year-old volunteer who has given many thousands of hours in Largo, Florida and took time out of her busy schedule to read the trilogy

**Robin Katchuk** – Whose support for me at The Palms of Largo, and throughout the process of writing this book, has been invaluable; Robin wrote the foreword for this book

**Patti Kurowski-Rowray** – Owner of The Mocha Moose on Old Highway 61 just south of Two Harbors, Minnesota, where I spent many hours of North Shore vacation writing the trilogy

# Reuben's Journey Begins

**Father Henri Nouwen** – A spiritual colleague whose writings and personal encouragement inspired me to create The Yellow Barn Trilogy

**Our Five Children: Amy, Alex, Andy, Rob & Will** – Who patiently gave up their family time with us as we worked and edited on many early mornings and evenings

**George Peltier** – A former father-in-law who taught me how to play cribbage and, together, we enjoyed many games of counting and pegging, our pipes and gin – a truly kind and wonderful human being

**Dan Peterka** – A passionate colleague in a nine year journey, collaborating on exceptional environments, programs and services for seniors

**Sanaya Roman** – Whose book, *Spiritual Growth*, has been an inspiration to me for decades, providing rich and original theory regarding life purpose and work

**Holly Russell** – Who took her personal time to help with the layout of the books and design brochures for The Yellow Barn Society

**Bob Smith** – An unforgettable character, stubborn and kind, a cynic yet thoughtful, serious and light-hearted; a great husband to Ruthie, a loving grandfather to Kristy, and a very good friend to me

# Reuben's Journey Begins

**Julie Solomonson** – The best partner at home and work; I will be forever grateful for her counsel and editing talent

**Jerry Walker** – Who has helped me explore the world of seniors in their eighties and nineties, those who become the focus of the third book

**David Wolfe** – Mentor who inspired me in learning how to serve individuals during their mature years

**Diane Wyffels** – A talented human being who patiently read The Yellow Barn Trilogy and helped with initial editing

# NOTES

## Chapter 1

1. "On Children" from THE PROPHET by Kahlil Gibran, copyright 1923 by Kahlil Gibran and renewed 1951 by Administrators C.T.A. of Kahlil Gibran Estate and Mary G. Gibran. Used by permission of Alfred A. Knopf, a division of Random House, Inc., pp. 41-42.

## Chapter 5

1. From SPIRITUAL GROWTH by Sanaya Roman, copyright © 1989. Reprinted with permission of H J Kramer/ New World Library, Novato, CA. www.newworldlibrary.com

2. Ibid.

3. From AGING by Henri J.M. Nouwen and Walter J. Gaffney, copyright © 1974 by Henri J.M. Nouwen and Walter J. Gaffney. Photos copyright © 1974 by Ron P. Van den Bosch. Used by permission of Doubleday, a division of Random House, Inc.

4. Ibid.

## Chapter 8

1. From SPIRITUAL GROWTH by Sanaya Roman, copyright © 1989. Reprinted with permission of H J Kramer/ New World Library, Novato, CA. www.newworldlibrary.com

## The Yellow Barn

A TRILOGY
Written by Gary Solomonson
Edited by Julie Solomonson

BOOK TWO
REUBEN'S NEW DREAM

**Book Two** of the trilogy, *Reuben's New Dream*, begins with Reuben's trip to Montana to visit his old friend, Ted Roberts, and make a new friend, Gene Walking Bear, a member of the Confederated Salish Kootenai Tribes. Reuben discovers things about himself that he had always sensed but never fully understood. During the flight back home from Billings, Montana, he has a moment of serendipity and imagines a new use for the old yellow dairy barn, creating a new dream for his farm and for volunteerism in Cottonwood County.

**The Yellow Barn**

REUBEN ANDERSON & SONS

A TRILOGY
Written by Gary Solomonson
Edited by Julie Solomonson

BOOK THREE
REUBEN CREATES THE YELLOW BARN SOCIETY

As gatherings of volunteers become more frequent, *Reuben Creates The Yellow Barn Society*, a place where volunteers gather to share their stories about intentional acts of kindness by, for, or with 89ers™. These stories in **Book Three** are rich in ideas and examples for volunteering. Reuben introduces a new model for one-to-one volunteering, "The Three Month Gift," and presents his essay with over 200 examples, "Look in the Mirror and Imagine," which is included here in the Addendum.

**Look in the Mirror & Imagine**

## ADDENDUM

In the 3rd book of *The Yellow Barn Trilogy, Reuben Creates The Yellow Barn Society,* Reuben hands out an essay in a community meeting where he lists over 200 specific ways individuals can volunteer one-to-one by, for, or with 89ers. In the essay, he encourages each person to look in their bathroom mirror in the morning and imagine one thing they could do that month as a volunteer. Reuben's essay becomes a great source of inspiration and encouragement.